HOLD ME WHILE I BREAK

Faith, Mental Health, and the Sacred Work of Falling Apart

by

McCarthy Anum-Addo

"This book is not a solution—it's a sanctuary for your story."

COPYRIGHT

Hold Me While I Break

Faith, Mental Health, and the Sacred Work of Falling Apart

Published by Anum-Addo Press
Washington, D.C.
www.mccarthyanumaddo.com

This book is a work of nonfiction and spiritual memoir. While based on personal experiences, certain names and identifying details have been changed to preserve the privacy of individuals. The author is not a licensed mental health professional. The content is intended for reflection and support, not as a substitute for medical advice, diagnosis, or treatment.

Always seek professional help when needed.

Cover Design & Glyph Art: McCarthy Anum-Addo
Interior Layout & Typography: Anum-Addo Creative Studio
Hardcover ISBN: 979-8-9942218-3-9

Paperback ISBN: 979-8-9942218-2-2

Library of Congress Control Number: 2025911261

∞REACH™ and the spiral glyph logo are trademarks of McCarthy Anum-Addo.

Used here under author imprint license to signify works of sacred reflection, psychological resilience, and spiritual renewal.

Printed in the United States of America

First Edition

10 9 8 7 6 5 4 3 2 1

TABLE OF CONTENTS

DEDICATION

For the ones who kept showing up—
even when the breath shook, even when the faith flickered.
You are not broken for needing to be held.
You are proof that staying is its own kind of prayer.

FOREWORD

As a therapist, I often seek ways to bring together the clinical and the spiritual. Reading this book, I found myself moved—not just by its insights, but by the tenderness with which it tells the truth of how when the mind and body come together there is peace, but more importantly, that there is a place for both the sacred and mental health to come into harmony. Whether your faith and mental health journey has called you to question your purpose, has highlighted the need to establish values, and/ or build community and connection, the weary soul can find refuge in this text to keep on. Hold on. And breathe.

I believe we all carry a story of breaking and healing. Some of us name it. Some run from it. Others never learned the language to speak it. The questioning of God's presence in the midst of trials, grief, and anger, all begs for the answer of how do we keep moving forward? Whereas mental health shapes how we may hold our own grief, our fragile hopes, and the flickers of joy that remain. "Hold Me While I Break" offers us a companion through the complexities of faith-based trauma, while uplifting the quiet, spiritual work of restoration. I have had the pleasure and honor of seeing Anum-Addo's journey unfold in real time, witnessing his ability to no longer keep his spiritual practice and mental health journey separate, and also find meaning after experiencing faith-based trauma. He continues to demonstrate courage and a will to live, and has provided a generous offering for those still learning how to break without disappearing.

The spiritual journey, often associated with religion, has been seen for generations as its own entity. One that provides wisdom to understand how the world moves around us, navigating the perils of life, providing instructions for how to fellowship with one another, all while learning how to trust and believe in the unknown. Nevertheless, when you are still at a loss of how to steer these unique issues and feel that your spirit is being challenged by long-suffering and hopelessness, we can see where one's faith can be broken. This book holds space for the weary, the waiting, and the ones still searching for words. It helps make the sacred visible again.

In this work, the author invites us into a journey of reckoning—with self, with faith, and with the kind of healing that begins when we name what was once hidden. It offers clarity and direction. It helps us remember that we are not broken beyond repair, and that healing is a way of returning to meaning and purpose. We can recognize that for true healing of mental and spiritual pain, and affliction, there needs to be an exploration of all the above, not just one in isolation.

This book helps to bridge the gap for those that have ever wanted to explore mental health therapy but were apprehensive, because it went against their spiritual teachings and/or promoted the reliance on something created by man. Likewise, it is a beautiful step forward for those that clung solely to mental health therapy, and still do not feel connected to themselves and/or the communities around them. This work is bold and brave, inviting the reader into the honest spaces of confession, struggle, and possibility. As a therapist, I believe it is important for us to start seeking and accepting that multiple truths exist, and we need only find our own.

There is a deep trust and vulnerability in being "held" in any capacity. It is the ability to release tension and experience the ease of resting. It is the ability to challenge our "what ifs" and reframe them as "even ifs." This book is not an answer—it is an offering. One that helps us remember that even our breaking can be sacred. I am honored to recommend it.

Healing requires both scientific precision and spiritual hospitality. In this work, those worlds meet—not to compete, but to complete one another. Here the therapist's room becomes a sanctuary, and the sanctuary becomes a clinic for the soul.

Cassandra J. Edwards, M.S., LCPC, CCTP I, CIMHP

Washington Nutrition Counseling Group

EPIGRAPH

"The wound is the place where the Light enters you."
— **Rumi**

There are songs the breath remembers before the voice does.
There are prayers the body repeats long after belief has unraveled.
There is a kind of holiness found only in the breaking.

We are not only healed by silence.
We are healed by the permission to speak again—slowly, shaking,
in the tongue of trauma, of tradition, of sacred contradiction.

Blessed are the ones who stitched their faith back together
with the trembling hands of doubt.
Who touched the hem of something
they were told they no longer deserved.

There is no such thing as unbelonging from the Divine.
Even the fractured belong.

va'rell khe-tomai shai'lin ves'torah
(The fracture remembers what the breath dared not name)

If you've come here carrying silence,
you are already speaking.

AUTHOR'S NOTE ON SCOPE AND VOICE

This book is written from both sides of the therapeutic table—patient and listener, seeker and skeptic. I do not write as a clinician, but as someone who has spent years in the patient's chair, learning what it means to stay when everything in me wanted to leave. The language of healing entered my life not through textbooks, but through breathwork, relapse, rupture, and return.

What follows is not a manual or prescription. It is a field journal from the interior—the voice of someone who has been both the observed and the observer. These pages are confessions and prayers, fragments of insight gathered from therapy rooms, sanctuaries, and long nights when belief faltered but breath continued. They are written for those who inhabit the in-between: too spiritual for clinical detachment, too clinical to disappear into faith alone.

I write from the dual seat of patient and pilgrim, translating what I have lived into words that might accompany others. Sometimes the voice here sounds like analysis; sometimes it sounds like liturgy. That shift is deliberate. Healing, like language, is dialectal. It moves between science and spirit, between the measurable and the mysterious.

There are moments when I speak as the one trembling on the couch, and others when I become the one listening from the chair beside it. Neither cancels the other. Both are true. Both belong.

This is the vantage point from which these pages unfold—
not from certainty,
but from witness.
Not from expertise,

but from endurance.

If there is authority here, it is the authority of survival: the slow, unglamorous art of staying.

BRIDGE

Before every story, there is the breath that steadies the hands.
Before every confession, there is the silence that decides it's finally safe to speak.

This book begins there—
in the pause between exhaustion and hope,
between what we carry and what begins, at last, to carry us.

You do not need to be healed to begin.
You do not need to be brave to stay.
You only need to be willing—
to sit inside the ache long enough for the light to find you again.

Somewhere beneath the noise, the body is already whispering its prayer.
It begins not in words, but in breath.
It begins here.

PREFACE – WHAT WE CARRY IN

I entered the room with silence clinging to me like a second skin. Not the silence of reverence, but the silence of someone who no longer knew if speaking would matter. My mouth was full of words I had never dared to say, and my chest ached with the weight of holding them. I sat in a pew and tried to sing, but the sound died before it left my throat. It was easier to stay quiet than to risk being heard and misunderstood.

That was what I carried in.

But I was not alone. I only thought I was.

We enter faith spaces carrying more than scripture and song. Some of us walk in with panic disguised as reverence. Some come with depression masked by a carefully rehearsed smile. Some arrive with grief tucked neatly behind our folded hands, hoping no one will notice the tremor. We sit beside one another, each convinced our pain makes us an outsider, each believing our struggle has no place in the sanctuary. Yet in truth, we are already a congregation of the wounded.

What we carry in is not shame alone, but the silence around shame. We have been told in sermons that anxiety means weak faith, that depression is proof of hidden sin, that medication is a substitute for prayer. We have heard healing described as victory, while our own lives remain fragile, cyclical, unfinished. And so we learned to keep quiet. We learned to pray in whispers no one else could hear. We learned to pretend.

And yet what we carry in is also longing. Longing for a word that does not condemn us. Longing for a prayer that admits exhaustion. Longing for rituals wide enough to bless trembling bodies, racing hearts, minds that do not quiet even when the hymns swell. Longing for community that can hold us when we fall apart, and for a God who does not turn away when our faith is stitched with doubt.

This book begins here, in that tension: between silence and longing, shame and hope. It is not written to solve the mystery of suffering or to offer simple answers. It is written as a witness to what we carry in, and as a companion for those who fear they carry it alone.

Fragments of my story are woven through these pages, but only as doorways. They are not the destination. I have carried depression into sanctuaries, panic into prayer, suicidal thoughts into waiting rooms where pastors and therapists alike struggled for words. But this is not my diary. These pages are not for my catharsis. They are written so that my fragments might become mirrors, where you might see yourself and know you are not alone.

Because your story, too, is here.

If you have ever walked into a faith community and wondered if your panic was visible, this book is for you. If you have ever swallowed medication in secret, hiding the bottle from those who might shame you, this book is for you. If you have ever prayed with doubt loud in your chest, or felt the psalms echo too closely your own despair, this book is for you.

And if you have never struggled in these ways, but you love someone who has, this book is for you as well. Because what we carry in is not only ours to bear alone. Healing, like faith, requires community.

Across traditions, there are threads waiting to be gathered: the Jewish practice of teshuvah, returning again and again; the Islamic practice of dhikr, breathing the name of God into the body; the Buddhist practice of metta, extending compassion to self and others; the Christian psalms, lamenting without shame. These are not foreign rituals—they are survival strategies passed down through generations of the wounded faithful.

Clinical voices join the chorus too. Therapists, chaplains, clinicians have long recognized what our sacred texts often overlook: that healing is not linear, that relapse is not failure, that the body remembers trauma even when the mind longs to forget. Their wisdom, too, belongs at the altar.

This book is an attempt at weaving. Weaving memoir with theology, survivor testimony with clinical research, silence with new liturgies. It does not claim to be definitive. It claims only to be honest.

What we carry in is heavy. But what we carry out can be different. Not lighter, perhaps, but named. Not finished, but blessed. Not silent, but spoken together.

If you read these pages and hear your own story, know that you are part of a larger witness. You are not alone in your trembling, not abandoned in your doubt, not cast out because of your panic or your despair. You are part of a congregation that stretches wider than walls, one where survival itself is a prayer.

So let us begin here, together, at the threshold. Let us admit what we carry in, not to be condemned, but to be held. And let us trust that even in the fragments, even in the silence, even in the ache, there is a holiness that has never left us.

Breath Marker – First Inhale
Inhale: I am still here.
Exhale: I am still becoming.

INTRODUCTION THE LANGUAGE WE DIDN'T HAVE

There was a season when my vocabulary shrank to silence. The words I once trusted—hope, healing, prayer—felt too brittle to hold what pressed in on me. When depression settled heavy in my chest, I searched the psalms for a phrase that matched the fog. I found lament, but no pastor ever told me lament could be prayer. When panic scattered my breath, I looked for a hymn to carry me through. They were full of triumph, while my body shook with terror. I had words, but not the right ones. I could describe doctrine, but not despair.

That was what I lacked: a language that could place faith and mental illness side by side without shame.

But I was not the only one. Across traditions, countless others found themselves at the same loss. The Jewish friend who could chant Torah but could not find a blessing for her anxiety. The Muslim student who knew every surah by heart yet wondered if reciting them could quiet his panic. The Buddhist who practiced silence but could not explain the roar of trauma memories inside that silence. The Christian who could recite creeds but never heard depression named at the altar.

We lacked words. Not just me. All of us.

It was not that faith traditions had no resources. Our scriptures are filled with cries, sighs, silences, breaths, returns. The problem was that we had learned to treat these texts as distant history rather than present medicine. We repeated them without translating them into the language of nervous systems, trauma memories, psychiatric wards, relapse, medication. We kept sacred language and clinical language in separate rooms, as if they could not speak to one another.

Without language, stigma flourished. Depression became sin. Medication became faithlessness. Panic became weakness. Trauma became a secret. Words that should have named survival became words that condemned it. In therapy, people sat unable to describe their faith for fear of ridicule. In sanctuaries, people sat unable to describe their mental illness for fear of shame. Silence became our only shared vocabulary.

This book is written to recover the language we didn't have.

It is not a dictionary of new terms, but a weaving of old ones. Words already given—lament, teshuvah, dhikr, metta—expanded to meet our wounds. Words already studied—relapse, resilience, trauma, regulation—brought into sanctuaries where they can become prayer. The language we lacked was never about invention. It was about permission. Permission to say depression in the pulpit. Permission to panic in the pew. Permission to bless medication at the dinner table. Permission to let clinical and theological words meet and hold one another.

Language is more than expression. It is survival. Psychologists have shown that naming feelings reduces their grip, that speaking shame aloud loosens it.[1] Theologians have long insisted that naming is an act of creation: Adam called creatures into being; prophets named injustice; Jesus called people by name. What are unnamed festers in the dark. What is named can be carried together.

I once sat with a Jewish friend who described *teshuvah*—the return—as the slow recognition that the soul had never truly left. A Muslim chaplain told me that in *dhikr*, the remembrance of God is not performance but pulse: the heart's memory of mercy. I began to realize that across faiths, language may differ, but the longing is the same—to be remembered by the sacred we thought had forgotten us.

So, these pages are not written as a memoir of one voice, nor as a textbook of detached analysis. They are written as a gathering. Each chapter holds fragments of memoir, portraits of survivors, the wisdom of clinicians, the practices of faith traditions, and the poetry of new liturgies. It is an attempt at shared language—something wide enough to name depression without shame, to name relapse without condemnation, to name survival as holy.

The language we didn't have becomes, in these pages, the language we will practice together.

If you come to these words weary, know that they are for you. If you come to them skeptical, know that skepticism has a place here. If you come with faith but no words for your fear, know that these pages were written with you in mind.

We lacked language. We lacked breath. We lacked liturgies wide enough for our wounds.

What follows is not perfect language but living language. Words that tremble, words that bless, words that breathe.

Inhale: the silence is broken.

Exhale: we can speak at last.

Liturgy for the Broken

We come with hands that tremble, with hearts that race, with thoughts that do not quiet.

We come carrying pills in our pockets, tears in our throats, silence in our bodies.

We come not because we are triumphant, but because we are tired.

We are the anxious and the grieving, the depressed and the addicted, the ones who cannot pray in sentences, only in sighs.

We are the ones who stayed alive one more day without knowing why.

We are the ones who show up still, even when showing up feels impossible.

We name what has too long been hidden:

that faith does not erase panic,

that prayer does not cure depression,

that shame has no power to heal us.

We bless what has too long been condemned:

the trembling hand,

the medicated body,

the nervous system that struggles to calm.

We confess not our weakness, but our humanity.

We confess that survival itself is prayer,

that relapse does not end grace,

that our breath is holy even when shallow.

So gather us, O God who holds the broken.

Gather us, Spirit who breathes through panic.
Gather us, Christ who weeps and does not walk away.
Gather us into one body where stigma cannot survive,
where silence becomes song,
where wounds become witness.

We are broken, and still we breathe.
We are broken, and still we return.
We are broken, and still we are beloved.

Inhale: we are still here.
Exhale: we are still held.

Amen.

Echo Fragment

After speaking, we still carried silence.
But silence no longer carried us alone.

So we begin, not with answers, but with breath.

✦ INTERLUDE *WHAT THE PSALMS DON'T SAY*

The psalms never tell you what to do with silence. They don't say how long to wait for peace, or how to breathe when prayer dissolves before it reaches the sky. They end in praise or promise, but they skip the long hours between verses—the hours when faith is a whisper too faint to hear.

I used to think the psalms were proof of belief. Now I think they're proof of endurance. Each one sounds like someone who stayed one breath longer than they thought possible. Every line is a tremor disguised as prayer, a pulse refusing to surrender to stillness.

Between the verses, there are absences. The psalms we never hear. The cries that never became words. The quiet survivors who sat in the temple's shadow, too broken to sing but unwilling to leave. I imagine them rocking in the dust, their breath uneven, their hearts fractured, still choosing to be found. Their silence was not faithlessness—it was fidelity by another name.

A therapist once told me that lament is the nervous system's way of seeking safety again. The trembling is not weakness; it's discharge. The sob is not surrender; it's release. What the psalmist calls crying out, neuroscience calls regulation. Both are correct. Both mean life continues.

Maybe that's the lesson the psalms never write down: you don't need to believe to belong. You don't need to sing to be heard. The body has always been the first psalm—the lungs the temple, the breath the offering.

So, if you can't pray yet, just breathe.

Inhale: the ache.

Exhale: permission to still be here.

And in that pause between the inhale and exhale—where even words fall silent—let the psalm continue without you. It has always known how. It will hold your silence, too, until you're ready to speak again.

PART ONE: THE THRESHOLD

CHAPTER ONE: THE FOURTH ATTEMPT

There are thresholds the body remembers even when the mind tries to forget. Rooms where the air was too still. Waiting chairs lined up against walls that smelled faintly of disinfectants. The heavy quiet of a chapel when you have run out of prayers. The phone that rings in your pocket with a counselor's number you are afraid to answer. Many of us have stood in these places. Many of us have felt that strange pull at the edge of survival: not quite gone, not quite here, caught in the silence between.

It was not only once. For some, it has been four times, or ten, or countless rehearsals of the same thought. The attempt is never only about ending life—it is about trying to end the unbearable dissonance between faith and despair, between what we were told God should be and what our bodies were carrying.

Depression does not wait for Sunday. Panic does not pause for Ramadan. Suicidal thoughts do not skip holy days. And yet when they come, many of us have discovered that the language of our traditions is thin in these moments. We are told to pray harder, to trust more, to fast longer, to meditate deeper. But none of these are enough when the body itself feels like an enemy.

In one room, a survivor clutched their hands together until their knuckles whitened. They whispered every psalm they knew, hoping for a voice to break through the silence. None came. The silence pressed heavier. They wondered if silence itself was proof of abandonment.

In another room, a survivor called a crisis line. The counselor on the other end said, "I'm here." Breathe with me. No scripture, no lecture, no solution—only breath. And in that moment, it felt closer to God than any sermon had in years.

In yet another space, someone sat on the edge of their bed with pill bottles lined up. They remembered the imam's words about mercy, the rabbi's teaching on return, the therapist's promise that despair passes. None of these erased the ache. But what they clung to was the memory of one friend who had once said, you don't have to be alone in this. That memory was enough to make them wait until morning.

Faith communities often do not know what to do with these thresholds. A pastor preaches about joy but cannot name depression. A rabbi reads psalms of lament but does not ask who in the pews is suicidal. A mosque fills with voices for prayer, but panic attacks are met with confusion. A meditation hall praises silence, while silence for a trauma survivor feels like suffocation. Without language, communities respond with avoidance. Survivors hear it clearly: your suffering does not belong here.

But the truth is, these thresholds are as sacred as any altar. The waiting room, the therapist's office, the sterile hospital bed, these are places where survival decisions are made. They are holy ground, even when they feel like exile. The presence of despair does not cancel the sacred; it reveals it.

Clinical research confirms what tradition has always known but often fails to practice: isolation kills, and connection saves. Survivors who feel supported are less likely to attempt again. Communities that can name depression without shame reduce suicide risk. Silence, when it becomes acknowledgment rather than avoidance, steadies the nervous system. In therapy, clinicians call this co-regulation: the way one body's calm can steady another's panic. In faith, we call it being held.

The attempt is not just an individual act; it is communal rupture. Families fracture, congregations grieve, entire communities whisper about what could have been said or done. Yet these ruptures can also become communal awakenings. Some churches begin suicide prevention training. Some synagogues add prayers for mental illness into liturgy. Some mosques create circles for youth to speak openly about despair. Some temples train teachers to distinguish meditation from dissociation. Change begins when the unnamable is finally named.

The body remembers these attempts long after the moment passes. Muscles tense when walking past the hospital. Breath shortens when hymns about joy are sung without space for lament. Panic flares when silence falls too heavy in prayer. But the body also remembers rescue: the friend's voice on the phone, the counselor's steady breathing, the community that stayed even when words ran out. These memories embed themselves as counterweight.

Fragments overheard in these rooms could form their own scripture:

"I didn't want to die, I wanted the pain to end."

"The silence was worse than the despair."

"When she sat beside me and didn't leave, it felt like the first prayer God answered."

"The pills were in my hand, but so was her memory."

These are not verses from sacred texts, yet they are no less holy. They are testimony from the threshold.

The work now is not to hide these attempts but to integrate them into our theology. Suicide must not remain unspoken in sermons, in liturgies, in pastoral care. Depression must not be dismissed as weakness. Panic must not be rebuked as lack of faith. Communities must learn to stand at the threshold with those who cannot hold themselves up.

When traditions remember their own scriptures, they already hold language for this. The psalms cry, How long, O Lord? The prophets collapse under despair. The desert fathers faced depression in their caves. Mystics across religions spoke of nights darker than their own endurance. Trauma survivors today are not anomalies; they are inheritors of a long lineage of holy suffering. What we lack is not precedent but courage to name it aloud.

One evening, a group of survivors gathered in a church basement. Not for worship, not for therapy, but because none of them wanted to be alone. They lit a single candle. They did not share testimonies or offer solutions. They simply said their names, one by one. Each name spoken was a declaration: still here. When the last name was spoken, the silence that followed was not suffocation but shelter. The candle flickered. Their bodies breathed easier.

Fragments of Survival

We did not all pray, but we all breathed.

We did not all believe, but we all stayed.

We did not all speak, but we all listened.

We were still here.

When the night ended, nothing had changed and everything had. Depression still pressed on their chests. Panic still rattled their nerves. Suicidal thoughts did not vanish into light. But now survival had witnesses. Now the attempt was no longer a secret wound. They left carrying each other's names, and that memory itself became medicine.

The fourth attempt did not succeed. Not because despair had ended, but because community interrupted it. And that interruption—fragile, imperfect, temporary—was enough.

For the grace to keep breathing
until peace remembers our name.

I still remember the hum of the fluorescent light after that session—the way it pulsed against the silence like a slow heartbeat. My body kept the tremor even after my mouth had stopped confessing. The counselor asked me if I felt "safe in my body," and I wanted to laugh. How could I feel safe in a body that kept trying to die?

I stared at the clock instead. Each tick felt like an act of defiance, proof that time still recognized me. There was a Styrofoam cup of water on the table, the kind that caves in under pressure. I pressed my thumb into it until it bent but didn't break. That's what healing was, I think—learning to bend without splitting open.

When I walked outside, the air felt wrong against my skin. The world kept happening: buses hissed, someone laughed too loudly across the street, a church bell rang somewhere I couldn't see. I thought about how strange it was to want to die and still notice beauty—the slant of light on a passing car, a child tugging her mother's sleeve. It was unbearable and holy all at once.

That night I didn't pray. I just sat on the edge of my bed, breathing in fragments. My chest felt too small for air, my mind too full for thought. But I kept breathing anyway. Maybe that's faith in its rawest form—the will to inhale when nothing in you wants to stay.

CHAPTER TWO: SANCTUARY

There are places that feel like shelter long before we call them holy. Sometimes they are carved in stone and glass, echoing with chants. Sometimes they are subway cars rumbling under a city, kitchens fragrant with garlic and oil, park benches in the last glow of sunset. Sanctuary is not always an altar. It is whatever space allows the body to breathe when it has forgotten how. My shoulders dropped before I realized I was safe. The air in that quiet room had its own pulse. My jaw loosened. My breath came back in small, uneven waves—as if my body had been waiting for permission to arrive before I did.

Survivors of depression and trauma know this hunger for shelter in ways doctrines often do not. Panic attacks come without warning, and the body scans frantically for safety: a corner to lean against, a steady rhythm to match, a breath that feels less alone. When churches close their doors at night, when mosques echo only with emptiness, when meditation halls stand far away, sanctuary must be found elsewhere. The nervous system improvises. A hand pressed against a train pole, a steady hum in the crowd, the click of beads sliding through fingers—all become sanctuary in miniature.

Communities often forget that what they call sacred is first of all what the body names safe. A cathedral may look holy, but for a survivor shamed in confession, its silence is terror. A mosque may resound with verses, but for a woman excluded from the main prayer hall, its walls echo rejection. A meditation retreat may promise calm, but for a trauma survivor, silence can feel like suffocation. True sanctuary is not guaranteed by architecture; it is measured by whether a trembling body finds rest inside it.

Scriptures, if read carefully, already hint at this truth. The psalms do not describe temples as perfect—they describe them as refuge from enemies, shade in heat, shelter in storm. Jesus sought lonely places, not grand sanctuaries, because stillness itself became his prayer. The Prophet sought a cave before a community. Buddhist texts honor groves, rivers, and the quiet under trees as places where the mind could release its grip. Diasporic ancestors made sanctuary out of fields and forests, singing until the night air itself became church. Sanctuary was never about the grandeur of a building. It was about whether survival could continue one more night.

A trauma therapist once told me, “Sanctuary isn’t a place—it’s a nervous system that no longer expects threat.” I wrote that in my notebook and underlined it twice. Sacred stillness begins in the body.

Clinicians speak of sanctuary in other terms: regulation, safety cues, windows of tolerance. A trauma survivor enters a therapy office and scans for exits, watches for tone of voice, notices whether the chair feels too exposed. The body is asking: Am I safe here? Therapy works not because of technique alone, but because the space itself becomes sanctuary—predictable, boundaries, steady. The nervous system learns to unclench not through words alone, but through presence that proves non-threatening.

In faith traditions, the same principle holds. Sanctuary is not sermon, ritual, or doctrine—it is nervous system permission. Where you can sigh without fear, where you can cry without judgment, where your silence is not interrogated—that is sanctuary.

One survivor found sanctuary not in the church that told them to pray harder, but in the kitchen where their grandmother hummed hymns while chopping onions. The rhythm steadied them. The smell grounded them. Another found it in the call to prayer drifting through open windows at dusk, reminding them that breath could sync to something larger than their panic. Another found it in the chorus of monks chanting at dawn, the low vibrations settling their racing heart. Another in the laughter of cousins around a dinner table, each joke loosening the muscles in their jaw that had clenched all day.

These sanctuaries looked nothing alike, yet each gave the same medicine: safety in the body, enough to keep going.

But the absence of sanctuary wounds deeply. Survivors tell of entering churches where their panic was met with suspicion: Where is your faith? They describe synagogues that made no room for neurodivergence, mosques where gender lines excluded them, temples where silence amplified their trauma. In these moments, faith became not refuge but risk. The nervous system, instead of loosening, braced harder. What should have been holy became hostile.

This is why sanctuary must be reimagined not as fixed architecture but as living practice. It is not the stained glass that heals, but the permission to sit trembling in the back pew without being told to leave. It is not the call to prayer alone, but the hand that guides you into line without judgment. It is not the retreat center itself, but the presence of a teacher who notices when silence overwhelms and allows you to step outside. Sanctuary is not static. It must move with the body's needs.

Communities that understand this become medicine. They place tissues in the pews without shaming tears. They train ushers to notice panic before it spirals. They design meditation retreats with trauma-sensitive practices. They teach clergy to welcome antidepressants as companions to prayer. They let kitchens, subways, backyards, and even hospital waiting rooms become acknowledged as holy. In these ways, sanctuary expands.

Fragments overheard in places like these:

"I sat in the last row and nobody asked why. That saved me."

"The hum of the train was steadier than my thoughts. I clung to it."

"When she handed me food and didn't ask questions, I breathed again."

"Silence didn't feel like absence that night. It felt like shelter."

One evening, a group gathered not in a church or mosque, but in a living room. No pulpit, no icons, no altar—just a table pushed aside and cushions on the floor. They lit candles, shared bread, sang softly, sometimes off-key. One person trembled through the whole night but did not leave. Another sat in silence and was not pressed to speak. At the end, they blew out the candles and washed the dishes. It was ordinary. It was survival. It was sanctuary.

Testimony Fragments

The sanctuary was the kitchen light left on.

It was the song hummed low while I cried.

It was the silence that did not accuse me.

It was the chair no one asked me to leave.

The body remembers where it was allowed to rest. That memory itself becomes a map, a way back when panic rises again. This is the gift of sanctuary—not perfection, not permanence, but the steady possibility of return.

A Buddhist teacher once told me, "Stillness is not the absence of movement; it's the place movement returns to." I heard the same truth one Sunday in a church basement, where a woman with shaking hands began humming a hymn before she could find words. The sound didn't fill the room—it steadied it.

I used to think sacred spaces were built from wood and stained glass. Now I think they're made from breath—the kind that wavers and then steadies, like a body remembering itself.

In the meditation hall, silence was not empty; it was communal. You could feel others breathing beside you, a subtle orchestra of survival.
In the Black church of my childhood, the same current ran through us when someone whispered "Take your time" during testimony. Different languages, same pulse.

Sanctuary is not always peaceful. Sometimes it's a trembling body that refuses to disappear. Sometimes it's the moment you admit you need quiet more than answers. I didn't know it then, but the stillness I feared would one day become the medicine that found me.

CHAPTER THREE: WRESTLING

There are nights when the silence is heavier than the suffering itself. You call out, but nothing answers. You close your eyes, but no vision comes. You repeat prayers, mantras, verses, but each syllable feels like it dissolves before reaching anywhere. The weight is not only that God is silent—it is that silence itself presses against your chest like a second gravity.

This is the wrestling. Not the polished theological kind debated in seminaries, but the raw, embodied dissonance when trauma meets faith. Depression says: you are alone. Anxiety says: you are unsafe. Faith traditions insist: you are never alone, God is near, peace is possible. But the body disagrees. The body trembles, panics, despairs. It feels abandoned. And in that gap, survivors wrestle—not only with God, but with their own communities, their own memories, their own bodies.

The psalms are filled with this struggle. How long, O Lord? Will you forget me forever? These words are not polite laments; they are accusations born of despair. They name divine silence as unbearable. Jacob wrestled with an angel until his hip gave way; the limp itself became testimony that wrestling does not end cleanly. The Prophet endured years without revelation, a silence so profound that companions feared he had been forsaken. Buddhist koans are puzzles that offer no answer, forcing the practitioner to sit in contradiction until something inside breaks open. Each of these stories is less about triumph than survival through dissonance.

Yet communities often skip over this part. Sermons leap from despair to deliverance without pausing in the middle. Silence becomes taboo, unanswered prayer a sign of failure, doubt treated as rebellion. Survivors who already feel crushed by despair now hear that their wrestling itself is sin. They learn to hide it. But what is hidden festers, and what festers deepens despair.

In therapy, the wrestling takes other forms. A survivor tells their clinician, "I keep praying, but nothing changes. The clinician does not rebuke them; instead, they name what is happening: "You are in the place of dissonance. Your body does not feel what your faith proclaims." Naming it removes shame. Wrestling becomes expected, not failure. Clinicians know that healing often requires sitting in contradiction long enough for the nervous system to stabilize.

The body registers wrestling in tremors, shallow breaths, racing heartbeats. Survivors clench their fists in prayer, pace in meditation halls, repeat verses compulsively. These are not marks of weak faith; they are trauma's imprint. The nervous system, desperate for safety, cannot yet align with words of peace. Wrestling is the gap between theology and physiology.

One survivor sat in church week after week, singing hymns about joy with tears streaming down their face. They were told to sing louder, to rejoice despite sorrow. They sang, but the dissonance grew. Joy as performance became its own kind of violence. Another survivor sat on a prayer rug at dawn, whispering verses until their lips went numb. The silence afterward felt like abandonment. Another sat in meditation, breath counted steadily, but panic rose sharper with every inhale. They told themselves they were doing it wrong, not realizing that the body was simply overwhelmed.

These stories are not isolated. They are archetypes of what trauma does to devotion. Wrestling is not the exception—it is the rule when faith collides with suffering.

Traditions, at their best, make space for this. The psalms do not edit out despair. Jesus himself cried out, Why have you forsaken me? The Prophet spoke of the weight of silence before revelation returned. Buddhist teachers warn against forcing calm when the mind is in turmoil. Diasporic ancestors turned lament into survival music, refusing to let silence erase them. These practices remind us: wrestling is not a sign of failure. It is part of the journey.

Yet the survivor in the pew, the mosque, the temple, the circle, still feels alone. Communities rarely narrate this struggle aloud. Therapy rooms do, and this is why survivors sometimes find more sanctuary in a clinician's silence than in a preacher's words. Not because clinicians replace faith, but because they refuse to rush wrestling into resolution.

Theologians might call this theodicy: how a good God can allow suffering. But for survivors, the question is more visceral: Why does God not answer me right now, in this panic, in this ache, in this suicidal thought? Wrestling is not abstract—it is sweaty, desperate, embodied. It is pacing floors at 3 a.m., begging for relief. It is whispering prayers with clenched teeth. It is pressing your face into the carpet, demanding a sign that never comes.

Clinicians might call this cognitive dissonance. Survivors call it despair. Communities should call it holy, but too often they call it sin.

And yet, even in the silence, something happens. The body learns endurance. The limp of Jacob. The tear-stained hymnal. The prayer beads worn smooth. The meditation cushion bearing restless bodies. These are testimonies of wrestling. The survivor is still here. That itself is survival.

Fragments from those who wrestle:

"I said the words, but they dissolved in the air."

"My chest hurt from silence more than from panic."

"When she did not try to fix me, I felt less alone."

"The wrestling is not answered, but it is witnessed."

One evening, a survivor sat in a circle. No one offered solutions. They simply listened. Tears came. Silence followed. And this time, silence was not absence. It was presence in another form. The wrestling did not end. But for that night, the survivor did not wrestle alone. The silence in the room carried a different texture than the silence in their bedroom. It was not the void of unanswered prayer but the quiet of shared survival. Each breath in the circle became a thread, weaving one body to the next. No one solved anything, but presence itself became the intervention.

That is what wrestling needs—not quick answers, not theologies polished smooth, but witnesses who can sit without retreating. Too many survivors have been left alone with their questions, told to pray harder, to fast longer, to wait for a joy that feels like betrayal when the body cannot stop shaking. Alone, the silence corrodes faith. Together, the silence becomes bearable.

The psalmists knew this when they wrote lament not as private diary but as communal song. Their cries were meant to be sung in temple courts, echoed by many voices, not whispered alone in despair. The power of lament is not only that it names pain, but that it insists: others must hear it with me. A lament is not complete without response. The same truth animates Buddhist sangha, where questions that have no answers are still carried together in stillness. And the same truth hums through diasporic spirituals, where grief became call-and-response—one voice breaks under sorrow, another lifts to carry it.

Clinicians put it differently: what cannot be resolved must be regulated. A therapist may not erase silence, but they can keep a survivor's nervous system from being devoured by it. Co-regulation means a trembling body finds steadiness in the presence of another. This is not miracle, but biology—and yet, it feels like grace.

One survivor described it like this: "I used to think wrestling meant I had to fight until I won. Now I think it means I have to endure until someone else sees me still here." Another said: "The silence did not end, but I stopped thinking it was proof of abandonment. It just was." Another: "I wrestled less when she stayed in the room with me. She didn't say a word, but it felt like God finally did."

We are so often taught that faith means certainty, but the stories of our traditions testify otherwise. Jacob limped for the rest of his life. The psalmists never received answers, only breath enough to write another verse. Jesus cried out in abandonment, and still the silence was not lifted. The Prophet endured long years with no revelation, returning again and again to the cave. Saints, sages, ancestors—they all knew wrestling. They carried silence like a wound that did not heal and yet still called it holy.

When survivors today wrestle with despair, they are not outside the story of faith—they are in its center. Their panic belongs beside the psalms. Their suicidal thoughts belong beside the laments. Their silence belongs beside the prophets. If only communities would remember this, fewer would feel exiled by their own traditions.

The wrestling never ends neatly. Some nights the silence crushes again. Some mornings the panic returns stronger. Some prayers dissolve unanswered. But each time a survivor is met with presence instead of rebuke, the wrestling shifts. The limp remains, but it is no longer proof of failure. It is proof of survival.

"She stayed with me until dawn. That was enough."
"The silence was still silence, but it wasn't empty."
"My hip still aches, but I walk differently now."
"I do not call it faith anymore. I call it survival."

These are the fragments that remain after the storm—half-prayers, half-memories, still breathing long after the voices that spoke them have quieted. They are not victory chants or moral lessons; they are the residue of endurance, what the body remembers when words run out.

I have learned that healing is less a crescendo than a repetition. It sounds like people showing up in quiet ways—a hand on a doorknob, a message left unread but still answered, a meal dropped off without note. These are the small liturgies of belonging that keep the living tethered to one another.

And so the chapter does not close with resolution, but with endurance. Wrestling is not overcome; it is carried. The ache does not vanish; it is folded into the rhythm of breathing. Sometimes, being carried means simply not being left alone.

There are saints of survival whose names we will never know—the ones who sat with others through the night, who held the phone line when no words came, who stayed through silence and tremor and doubt. They are the quiet priests of presence. Their testimonies do not fill pulpits or pages, but they keep the world from falling apart.

If this book leaves anything behind, let it be this: that we measure holiness not by resolution, but by return. That we count endurance not in triumphs, but in those who stayed long enough for morning to arrive. And that we remember—the story is not finished because the survivors are still here, still breathing, still believing that being here is enough.

CHAPTER FOUR: YIELDING

There is a difference between giving up and letting go, though from the outside they can look the same. Depression convinces us to collapse; trauma convinces us to clutch everything in sight. Yielding is neither collapse nor clutching. It is the slow, trembling decision to loosen the grip—on fear, on control, on the story that survival depends on constant effort.

Yielding often begins in the body before it reaches the mind. A jaw unclenches in therapy after weeks of holding tight. A hand opens in prayer after months of fists. Shoulders drop when someone whispers, You don't have to carry it alone. The nervous system interprets yielding as permission: the exhale you didn't know you were holding, the cry you didn't want to release, the nap you feared was weakness.

Yet yielding is often mistranslated in faith communities. People hear surrender and imagine defeat. Preachers urge believers to yield to God without acknowledging how dangerous that sounds to trauma survivors, who have already yielded to too many who harmed them. Yielding to abuse is not holy. Yielding to stigma is not healing. Yielding must be reframed: not submission to violence, but release into safety.

Scripture carries this tension. Julian of Norwich yielded to visions in the midst of plague, not as defeat but as opening to love. The psalms yield lament without rushing into resolution, letting the cries remain unanswered. The Prophet yielded to mercy after years of silence, learning that revelation comes not by force but by waiting. Buddhist teachers speak of loosening grasping—not abandoning life, but softening the desperate clench that makes suffering sharper. Enslaved ancestors yielded not to empire but to song, releasing pain into rhythm so it did not devour them. Yielding has always been less about control and more about breathing.

Clinicians echo this wisdom with different words. Trauma locks the nervous system into fight, flight, or freeze. Yielding is the first sign of thaw. In therapy, a survivor clenches their jaw while describing panic attacks; the clinician invites them to breathe, to unclench, to notice the chair holding their weight. At first, yielding feels like danger—if I let go, I will collapse. But slowly the body learns that release can be safety. Muscles remember how to rest. Tears fall without destroying. Yielding is the practice of trusting that collapse is not the only outcome.

For some, yielding happens in prayer. Not the triumphant kind, but the whispered kind: I can't anymore. Hold me. For others, it happens in medication: swallowing a pill after years of shame and discovering that chemistry itself can be mercy. For others still, it is lying down in bed at three in the afternoon, ignoring the voice that says laziness, and listening instead to the body's need. Each act looks small, but each is rebellion against the lie that survival depends on endless striving.

One survivor told of pacing their apartment night after night, too anxious to stop moving. A friend finally sat them down, hand on their shoulder, and said, Rest. At first they resisted. But eventually their body slumped, and tears came. It was the first night they slept in months. Another described clenching fists in church whenever joy was mentioned. One Sunday, they opened their hands. Nothing miraculous happened, but the gesture itself felt like release. Another survivor described months of refusing medication because they thought it meant lack of faith. When they finally swallowed the first pill, they wept, not because the medicine worked instantly but because they had stopped punishing themselves.

Yielding is frightening because it feels like loss of control. And survivors of trauma know that loss of control has often meant danger. To yield requires trust—trust that this space, this moment, this presence is safe enough. Communities fail when they demand yielding without earning trust. Pastors who preach surrender but ignore abuse. Imams who urge obedience but neglect mental illness. Teachers who praise silence but overlook dissociation. To yield safely, survivors must first know they will not be harmed.

But when safety is present, yielding becomes holy. A breath held too long is exhaled. A song rises from a body that thought it had no voice left. A nap becomes survival, not laziness. Medication becomes prayer, not betrayal. Yielding is not giving up—it is remembering we do not have to carry everything alone.

Fragments overheard in moments of yielding:

"I unclenched and nothing broke."

"The pill in my hand felt like mercy."

"When I slept, the world did not fall apart."

"I thought surrender meant defeat. But it felt like love."

One evening, a survivor lay down in a circle of friends. They had carried their panic all day, their shame all week. They expected judgment. Instead, hands rested lightly on their shoulders. No prayers were spoken. No sermons offered. Just breath, quiet and steady, shared in the room. The survivor wept until they slept. When they woke, nothing had changed and everything had. They had yielded, and they had been held.

Yielding was the unclenched jaw.

It was the pill swallowed without shame.

It was the nap taken without apology.

It was the cry that did not end in collapse.

Yielding does not erase struggle. Panic still returns. Depression still presses. Trauma still clenches. But yielding interrupts the cycle long enough for the body to remember: safety is possible, rest is not betrayal, release is not defeat. Yielding is trust, trembling and holy. It is never smooth. The body resists. Muscles tense even while the mind whispers, let go. The nervous system remembers danger before it remembers mercy. For a survivor, the smallest gesture of release—a hand opening, a jaw unclenching—can feel like stepping into fire. Trust does not come easily to bodies trained by trauma. It comes slowly, shakily, often in the presence of another who can carry the weight for a while.

Clinicians see this every day. A client slumps into the therapy chair after weeks of stiff posture. The therapist does not interpret it as laziness but as breakthrough. Muscles surrender to gravity because at last the body senses it will not be attacked for collapsing. This is yielding in its most clinical form: regulation replacing hypervigilance. In those slumps, sobs, sighs, a new liturgy forms.

Faith traditions, when read with trauma-tuned ears, tell the same story. The psalms teach us to collapse into God's silence without apology. Mystics remind us that surrender is not defeat but an opening. In the cave, before revelation returned, the Prophet had to stop striving and simply listen. In Buddhist practice, the unclenching of grasping is itself the first taste of compassion. Diasporic ancestors, beaten and silenced, yielded not to masters but to music—they let sorrow move through rhythm so it would not devour them whole. Yielding has always been tremor before trust.

One survivor described yielding as lying on the floor during a panic attack. They had fought for hours, trying to pray harder, trying to breathe correctly, trying to prove faith strong enough. At last they stopped, sprawled on the rug, and whispered, I can't. They expected collapse. Instead, a strange stillness came. Not joy, not light, but a pause in which breath could return. Another told of years spent refusing medication. They said, I thought it meant defeat. The first time I swallowed, I wept. But afterward, I slept. And the sleep itself felt like God had not abandoned me.

These moments are fragile, easily lost. The panic returns. The stigma whispers. Communities still condemn. But once yielding has been tasted, the body does not forget. It remembers what trust felt like, even if only for a minute. That memory becomes a map back.

Yielding is not passive. It is active trust. It takes courage to soften the jaw, to unclench the fist, to let tears fall, to rest without apology. In a world that prizes control and in communities that mistake striving for holiness, yielding is rebellion. Depression tells us to collapse into nothing. Faith traditions sometimes tell us to push harder. Yielding takes another path: neither collapse nor compulsion, but trembling release into the possibility of care.

Fragments gathered in moments of trembling release:

"I exhaled, and the room did not collapse."

"The pill was not a chain—it was a key."

"I slept, and the world did not fall apart without me."

"Yielding did not erase pain, but it gave me breath inside it."

When survivors yield together, the act multiplies. One body unclenches, another sighs in response, another cries, another steadies. The room becomes chorus of release. No one planned it, no one scripted it, but suddenly the silence is full of holy trembling. This is why communal practices matter: one person's yielding gives permission for another's. What feels impossible alone becomes possible together.

Yielding is trust, trembling and holy. It is the nap taken at midday because exhaustion is too heavy. It is the medication swallowed without shame. It is the therapy appointment kept despite stigma. It is the whispered prayer, I cannot do this alone, followed by the unexpected truth: you are not alone. It is small, fragile, often overlooked. But it is survival.

A Buddhist counselor I met during group therapy called surrender "the softening that saves." She said that when the body unclenches, the spirit remembers it can stay.

And when we look back on our attempts to keep living, we may discover that what carried us was not our striving but these small acts of yielding—holy tremors that taught the body to breathe again.

CHAPTER FIVE: UNLEARNING

"Maybe grace was never a rule to remember.
Maybe it was the breath I kept forgetting to take."

The first time medication eased the darkness, I waited for guilt to follow. It always had.

I'd been taught that strong faith should outpray despair, that courage meant endurance without assistance. So when relief arrived in a capsule, I read it as proof of spiritual failure. My jaw ached from clenching through that contradiction—faith on one side, chemistry on the other.

I once spoke with a young Catholic woman who said, "I prayed harder when I got worse. I thought that meant I was failing God." Therapy, she told me later, was the first time someone said healing and holiness weren't opposites.

In therapy I was asked to describe what "sin" felt like in my body. I said *tight.* My neck locked, my breath thinned. The counselor didn't contradict me; she simply said, "That sounds like pain." It was the smallest reframe, but something inside me shifted. What I'd been calling *sin* was a nervous system screaming for rest. I left the session sore, as though a muscle had finally been named.

Unlearning began there—in the body, not the mind.

Each time the old shame rose, I practiced tracing the ache from jaw to throat to breath, following it like a prayer bead. I stopped asking whether my sadness offended God and started asking what it was trying to tell me. The language changed: sin became symptom; weakness, wound. I didn't need to confess it—I needed to listen to it.

In church, the sermons hadn't changed, but the way I heard them had. When a pastor spoke about endurance, I wondered if he knew the difference between endurance and depletion. When the choir sang *"It Is Well,"* I noticed how many of us whispered the words softly, as though hoping they'd become true by repetition. That tenderness—those quiet throats carrying impossible hope—felt holier than any certainty I'd known.

Unlearning, I realized, was not a theological rebellion. It was consent.

Consent to feel, to question, to breathe without apology. I learned that healing doesn't require permission slips from doctrine. It requires proximity to truth, however uncomfortable. Sometimes that truth arrived through my therapist's dry humor, sometimes through a friend's text that said, *"Don't explain. Just come over."* Grace started sounding less like psalms and more like ordinary sentences that didn't demand improvement.

One afternoon, sitting in traffic, a line of thought surfaced so quietly it startled me: *Maybe strength is what happens when I stop pretending to have any.* It wasn't profound—it was physiological. My shoulders dropped, my jaw released, and I realized the tension had been a prayer my body was tired of saying.

I've kept learning from that silence. When panic presses against my throat, I try not to spiritualize it. I press a hand there instead. Sometimes I recite nothing at all. The absence of words feels honest. Breath fills the space where faith once performed.

It's strange—how much of my recovery has happened in the plainest settings.
A waiting room chair.
The kitchen sink.
A long walk around the block.

In each, I practiced being unheroic. I practiced staying.

The clinical and the sacred began to share vocabulary. "Grounding," my therapist called it. "Grace," I still called it. Both meant: stay in your body long enough for the world to widen again.

And it does widen—slowly, imperfectly. Sometimes I still wake with the old instinct to earn my worth by fixing something. Those mornings, I start small: unclench the jaw, loosen the neck, breathe once, deeply. The act feels secular, but something in me still calls it prayer.

Not the kind of prayer that asks for anything—just the kind that notices. When my breath steadies, it's not reverence I feel first, but relief: the nervous system easing its grip on survival long enough to remember it has other settings. In those moments I don't sense heaven opening; I sense my pulse slowing. Maybe that's all revelation ever was—something physiological mistaken for divine intervention.

For years I thought holiness required transcendence—lifting the spirit above the body, escaping the ache, proving I could rise. But lately I've begun to wonder if transcendence was never the goal. Maybe sacredness is descent: returning to the body I abandoned when pain made it inconvenient. If faith once taught me to ascend, unlearning has taught me to inhabit. In Jewish *Mussar*, the path of ethical refinement, awareness of our own patterns is not punishment—it's invitation. Naming our struggle is itself a moral act, because honesty is the first movement toward compassion.

I catch myself performing less and observing more. Washing dishes becomes a kind of meditation—the warm water over my hands, the rhythm of plate to towel, plate to rack. There's a stillness there, unplanned and unproductive. It doesn't change the world, but it changes the hour. I don't tell myself I'm praying, yet the same quiet awareness settles over me. I think of the psalms that describe the earth itself worshiping: trees clapping hands, rivers singing. None of them asked permission. They simply did what they were made to do. Maybe my body, rinsing a plate, stretching a neck, unclenching a jaw, is doing the same.

Sometimes prayer sounds like conversation, but more often now it sounds like maintenance. Restocking the fridge. Making the bed. Feeding the body I once neglected because I thought spirituality required hunger. I used to equate holiness with deprivation—the fast, the vigil, the ache for meaning through lack. But the longer I live inside recovery, the more I suspect that fullness is also sacred. Eating without guilt. Sleeping without apology. Smiling without pretext. These are tiny sacraments of existence.

The psychologist in me, the one shaped by therapy and repetition, would say I'm retraining neural pathways. The believer in me still calls it grace. Neither of us is wrong. I'm learning to let those languages overlap without fighting for translation. Maybe prayer has always been an early form of neuroplasticity—the mind rehearsing trust until the body believes it.

There's an evening ritual I've fallen into without planning it. Before bed I sit on the edge of the mattress, feet flat on the floor, palms resting loosely on my thighs. I breathe in until my chest expands, and exhale until it softens. Sometimes I count. Sometimes I don't. The room is quiet except for the hum of the refrigerator down the hall. In the absence of words, the body does its own liturgy: inhale, release, pause. The heart keeps time. I think of all the nights I used to pray for escape. Now I pray for endurance—not the kind that grits its teeth, but the kind that keeps returning to presence, breath after breath.

I don't always feel grateful. Some nights I'm just tired. I sit in the dark and let exhaustion say its piece. The act itself feels secular, nothing mystical, no vision, no surge of divine energy—but something about the ordinary rhythm feels like communion. I've begun to suspect that what I once called faith was just attention, and attention is enough. When I attend to my body, I attend to life. When I attend to life, I meet whatever I used to call God.

Therapy gave me tools for this—grounding techniques, somatic awareness—but it also did something quieter: it gave me permission to blur the boundary between the sacred and the scientific. The old me would have needed to choose. The new me doesn't. I can quote my counselor and the psalms in the same breath and mean both. I can see medication as mercy. I can recognize that serotonin and Spirit might be co-conspirators in my survival.

That realization has softened how I speak to others about healing. I no longer try to reconcile their language with mine. Whether they call it mindfulness or mercy, grounding or grace, what matters is that they're still breathing. Sometimes the vocabulary doesn't need agreement; it just needs gentleness. I've learned that empathy, when practiced long enough, becomes its own dialect of prayer.

And so my days are filled with small liturgies that no one else would name as such. The sound of water hitting the sink. The hum of a car engine idling while I gather myself before driving home. The faint vibration of a phone in my pocket reminding me I'm not alone. Each gesture a syllable, each moment a verse. The old prayers were loud and scripted; these new ones are quiet, improvised, bodily.

There's humility in that. I used to think faith was about certainty; now I think it's about repetition—returning to presence again and again, even when it feels empty. Every time I breathe intentionally, I'm repeating a truth I can't yet articulate: that I belong to life, and life hasn't given up on me.

It's strange to realize that this is what belief has become: not a creed, not a doctrine, not a list of things I affirm, but an embodied routine that keeps me tethered to existence. The act feels secular, yes. It happens in traffic, in therapy, at the sink, in the half-light before sleep. But somewhere beneath those ordinary motions hums a quiet acknowledgment—something older than religion and younger than reason. It's the body whispering what the soul once shouted: *Still here. Still breathing. Still held.*

And maybe that's the most honest prayer of all.

Reflection

Unlearning isn't about losing belief; it's about letting belief grow up.
It's the process of retiring old scripts that mistake exhaustion for devotion.

It's remembering that the body is fluent in truths theology forgets to translate.

And maybe holiness begins there—
in the breath that finally stops apologizing for being human.

✦ INTERLUDE II – *AFTER THE THRESHOLD (ECHO FRAGMENT)*

We stand at the threshold of transformation,
breathing in the liminal air of this in-between.
O Sacred Mystery, accompany us as we pass.
Guide our steps over fear's last frontier into hope's dawn.

May our hearts open to the new light,
and our voices find the prayer beyond words.
As we cross from Unlearning into becoming,
hold us in the space between who we were and who we will be.

Holy Source of Peace, let our passage be gentle.
May blessings come in the silence of new beginnings,
may strength rise quietly in our bones.
And so, with breath and intention, we move forward
into the next chapter of our living story.

Amen.

PART TWO
THE MIDDLE SPACE

CHAPTER SIX: RESTING

Rest has always been contested. The body craves it, but trauma resists it. Capitalism devalues it. Communities often misunderstand it. Survivors are left caught in the crossfire—exhausted, ashamed, unable to stop moving for fear that collapse will come if they do. Yet rest is not laziness, not failure, not selfishness. Rest is survival. Rest is resistance. Rest is holy.

Trauma survivors know how difficult rest can be. The nervous system trained by danger does not easily unclench. Even when the body lies down, the mind races. Even when sleep comes, it is shallow, interrupted by nightmares or jolted awake by imagined alarms. To rest requires trust, and trust is precisely what trauma erodes. The survivor lies awake, heart racing, body braced, even when there is no threat. Rest feels like danger.

Depression complicates rest in the opposite way. The body collapses under fatigue so heavy it feels impossible to rise. Sleep stretches for hours, yet it does not restore. Shame whispers: you are lazy, you are worthless. Communities sometimes echo the lie, mistaking the body's exhaustion for moral failure. Survivors live between two accusations: when they cannot sleep, they are faithless; when they cannot wake, they are weak. Either way, rest is framed as failure.

Yet traditions have always insisted otherwise. Sabbath was commanded not as luxury but as necessity. Stop working, not because everything is done, but because your body is not a machine. Friday prayer interrupts the flow of labor, calling worshippers to step away, to breathe, to remember they are not defined by production. Monastic communities ordered their lives around rhythms of rest and prayer, insisting that ceaseless striving is unsustainable. Ancestors forced into endless labor still carved out moments of song and silence, teaching that even a stolen breath could be holy. Rest has never been optional; it is survival written into the sacred.

Clinicians confirm what faith proclaimed long ago: the body cannot heal without rest. Trauma therapy begins by teaching the nervous system to pause, to notice safety cues, to enter windows of tolerance where recovery can take root. Survivors who refuse rest collapse into burnout. Those who embrace it find resilience. Rest is not retreat from healing—it is the soil where healing grows.

One survivor described their first full night's sleep after months of insomnia. They wept upon waking, not because the depression had lifted, but because the night had carried them without interruption. Another described canceling plans to nap, expecting judgment, but discovering compassion in friends who said, sleep is prayer too. Another survivor took medication that finally allowed their body to quiet at night. They said, I thought pills meant I was weak. But now I see rest as holy gift.

These moments are not dramatic. They do not make headlines or testimonies in sanctuaries. But they are survival. And survival is sacred.

Communities that shame rest do profound harm. Pastors who preach productivity as proof of faith, imams who valorize ceaseless striving, teachers who dismiss exhaustion as laziness—these leaders reinforce trauma's lies. Survivors pushed beyond their capacity collapse harder. But communities that bless rest become sanctuaries. Congregations that build naps into retreats, families that encourage sleep, circles that refuse to shame missed prayers because of fatigue—these communities embody mercy.

Rest is also rebellion. Against systems that value us only by what we produce. Against trauma that demands hypervigilance. Against stigma that calls exhaustion weakness. To nap is to refuse capitalism's lie. To sleep deeply is to resist trauma's grip. To Sabbath, to pause, to retreat into stillness is to declare: I am not a machine. I am not only my wounds. I am a body worthy of rest.

Fragments overheard in the practice of rest:

"I slept, and the world did not collapse without me."

"My nap became my prayer."

"I laid down because my body begged, and that was holy."

"Rest is the proof I do not have to earn survival."

One evening, survivors gathered for a retreat. Not for constant sessions, not for productivity, but for rest. They lay on mats in silence. Some dozed, some wept, some simply breathed without rush. Leaders had prepared no sermons, only blankets. Someone played a soft drum, heartbeat steady. Hours passed with no agenda. When the retreat ended, participants said it was the first time they had been given permission to rest without shame. For many, it felt like the most spiritual experience of their lives.

Rest was the nap taken without apology.

It was the Sabbath table set in the midst of deadlines.

It was the silence that held instead of accusing.

It was the body remembered as holy, even in stillness.

Resting will not erase depression. Fatigue will return. Panic will wake us some nights. But each moment of rest interrupts despair. Each pause teaches the body that safety is possible. Each nap, each Sabbath, each still breath, becomes survival. Rest is not absence of faith—it is faith in practice. To stop moving is to trust that the world will not collapse without you, that God does not require your exhaustion, that holiness does not demand endless striving. For trauma survivors, this trust feels almost impossible. Their bodies have been trained that stillness equals danger. Their minds race with the conviction that if they let go for even a moment, something terrible will happen. Yielding to rest requires a faith deeper than certainty—it requires faith that safety can be real, if only for a breath.

Communities rarely understand this struggle. Too often, they frame rest as luxury, as laziness, as self-indulgence. They preach productivity as virtue, busyness as devotion, exhaustion as proof of commitment. Survivors already drowning in fatigue absorb these messages as condemnation. They lie down and immediately hear the accusations: You should be doing more.

You are failing. You are letting God down. The irony is cruel: rest, which could be medicine, becomes another site of shame.

Unlearning these messages requires more than individual determination; it requires communal blessing. When congregations pause liturgy to breathe in silence, they declare: rest is holy. When imams encourage worshippers to nap after Friday prayer, they declare: rest is holy. When synagogues gather for Shabbat meals and forbid work, they declare: rest is holy. When meditation halls teach lying-down practices, they declare: rest is holy. And when families tell their children, sleep, we will keep watch, they declare the same. Survivors need these declarations until their nervous systems can believe them.

One survivor remembered the first time a pastor said from the pulpit, If you need to sleep during this service, do so. God is not offended by your fatigue. They wept in the pew. Another recalled a retreat where leaders provided cots instead of lectures; participants napped, and no one was shamed. They said it was the most spiritual weekend of their life. Another survivor remembered when their therapist reframed their midday naps as sacred pause rather than laziness. That reframe kept them alive.

The body knows rest as prayer even when the mind doubts. Muscles loosen. The breath deepens. Tears rise. Sometimes survivors dream, sometimes they wake startled, sometimes they lie still without sleep. But in each case, the body is learning to inhabit safety. Rest is not wasted time. It is embodied theology. When I finally let my spine touch the bed, it felt like confession. The body's release is its own liturgy: breath as absolution, stillness as prayer.

Rest is also protest. Against capitalism that insists bodies are machines. Against trauma that demands hypervigilance. Against stigma that names fatigue as failure. Every nap is an act of rebellion. Every Sabbath is refusal to be consumed. Every retreat is defiance of the world's demand to keep producing. Rest is faith not only in God but in the worth of one's own survival.

Jordan told me he hadn't rested in seven years. Rest felt like permission he hadn't earned. When his therapist prescribed a weekend of nothing—no volunteering, no worship team, no phone—he panicked. He said silence made him feel unemployed from God.

The first day he tried, he folded laundry just to hear the dryer spin. By day two, his hands shook from stillness. On day three, he sat on the porch and realized the tremor was not weakness—it was the sound of his nervous system learning trust.

The room was silent except for the sound of breathing. I led the group in a simple exercise we called "Sanctuary Breath." We sat or reclined comfortably and inhaled slowly through the nose, as if inviting a warm light into the body. Then we exhaled through parted lips, imagining every ounce of tension melting away. Some participants pressed hands against their chest or belly to feel the rise and fall. After a few moments, one woman opened her eyes and whispered, "I can feel the weight lifting." She later said it was the first time she'd experienced her body pause **without anxiety**. In that quiet, clinical and spiritual met: neuroscience calls this a regulated state, faith might call it peace descending.

The nervous system had been trained for danger, but here it found proof of safety. As a trauma therapist once explained, grounding techniques like breath work help expand the *window of tolerance*—the zone where learning and healing can occur. In the circle, we practiced together: a long inhale, a slow exhale; lingering silence between. Muscles that had held their story of panic unwound just a little. For the first time that day, some of us felt the *body forget to tremble*. This stillness was not escape; it was revolt against the lie that our worth depended on being "on." It was rest as active, embodied prayer.

Later, I asked each person to note any physical sensations. One survivor wrote: *"My jaw unclenched. My hands loosened. All I did was breathe, and suddenly I remembered what my body felt like when it wasn't fighting."* Another wrote: *"I didn't say words out loud, but inside I was chanting a quiet poem of gratitude for this pause."* These fragments became their own kind of liturgy, small prayers in kinetic form. The body's response — slackened skin, slower pulse, steady breath — testified that healing starts when survivors give themselves permission to rest. **Resting, we learned, is not passive. It is practice.**

His story stayed with me because it mirrored my own. I once mistook exhaustion for devotion. Every time I pushed past my body's limits, people called it strength. No one saw the collapse that followed.

A trauma-informed therapist once said, *"Rest is not what happens when you finish healing; it's how healing begins."* I wrote those words on an index card and taped it to my mirror.

These days I practice rest like prayer: slow breath, open palms, surrender without apology. Sometimes it feels sacred; other times it feels impossible. Either way, it is worship.

Testimonies of Rest

"I slept through prayer, and it was the first holy thing I had done in months."

"My grandmother's lullaby felt more like scripture than any sermon."

"The silence of Shabbat was the only place my anxiety loosened."

"The nap I took in therapy saved my life."

Communities can embody this truth more deeply. Trauma-informed sanctuaries could provide rest stations instead of only sermons. Clergy could normalize silence, naps, pauses. Families could teach children that exhaustion is not failure. Friends could bless one another with words rarely spoken: Rest. We will keep watch. Sleep, and you are still loved. These small changes alter nervous systems. They make survival possible.

Sabbath is not absence—it is alignment. In Buddhism, rest is called *samatha*: the stilling of agitation. Both remind us that rest is rebellion against the tyranny of exhaustion. To rest is to return to trust.

Each nap, each Sabbath, each still breath, becomes survival. And survival itself is holy. In a world that demands constant motion, the body that rests is already practicing resurrection.

Sacred Pause:

- Find a quiet space where your body can rest. Lie down or sit comfortably, feet on the ground.
- Close your eyes gently and place a hand over your heart and one on your belly. Take three slow, deep breaths, feeling each inhale and exhale.
- Notice any tension in your body. With each exhale, imagine letting that tension melt away. If thoughts come, let them float by like clouds.
- Silently say to yourself, "In this moment, it is safe to rest." Repeat quietly if it helps.
- Listen to your body's needs without judgment. Are you thirsty? Tired? Breathe and trust what your body is telling you.
- When you are ready, begin to bring awareness back to the room. Wiggle your fingers and toes, stretch gently, and open your eyes with kindness.

Sacred Pause Practice: Use this simple practice whenever you feel overwhelmed or disconnected from your body. It is a sacred moment to pause, breathe, and remind yourself that rest is a gift you deserve.

CHAPTER SEVEN: RETURNING

Return is not a single act. It is a rhythm, often clumsy, often reluctant, often repeated until the body remembers what the mind resists. Survivors know this rhythm well. Depression loosens for a season, then returns. Panic recedes, then surges again. Shame is unlearned, then whispers itself back. Faith is embraced, then doubted, then embraced again. Healing does not move in straight lines. It circles, spirals, retraces steps. Each relapse feels like failure, but in truth it is part of the path. Returning is survival in motion.

A client once told her therapist, "Every relapse feels like betrayal." The therapist replied gently, "Or rhythm." Healing moves in circles, not ladders.

Clinicians describe relapse not as catastrophe but as recurrence. Symptoms resurface. Behaviors return. But each recurrence happens in a different body than before—a body that has already learned some regulation, already practiced yielding, already tasted rest. The recurrence is not the same as the first collapse. The spiral may feel endless, but in its turns there is learning. What once lasted months may last days. What once destroyed may now only disrupt. Returning is not shameful; it is evidence that survival has not ceased.

Faith traditions tell similar stories. The prodigal son left home not once but many times in his heart. His return was not triumph but desperation, and yet the story frames him as beloved. Judaism names teshuvah—return—as the core of spiritual life. To turn again and again toward God, toward self, toward community, even after failure. Islam calls tawbah the same—repentance as return, repeated as often as needed, welcomed without limit. Buddhism teaches that lapses in mindfulness are expected; the practice is not to never wander but to keep returning to the breath. Diasporic ancestors, displaced and fractured, returned to memory, to song, to ritual, even when their bodies could not return to homeland. All of these traditions agree: holiness is not in perfection but in the rhythm of return.

For survivors, this rhythm often feels unbearable. They celebrate progress—weeks without panic, months with steady mood, years with new practices—only to find themselves again weeping in bed, again canceling plans, again drowning in shame. Communities often deepen the wound by demanding permanence: Didn't you say you were healed? Didn't you testify that God delivered you? Didn't therapy fix you? The relapse is framed as failure, the return as weakness. Survivors internalize these accusations, believing they have disappointed everyone—family, community, God, themselves.

But relapse is not failure. Relapse is rhythm. Returning is holiness. To fall again into despair and still choose to rise, still choose to breathe, still choose to show up to therapy, still choose to pray in whispers—this is the miracle.

One survivor described their first major relapse after a year of stability. They said, I thought I had failed. But my therapist told me, this is proof you are healing. Your body is showing you where more care is needed.' Another survivor described relapse not as collapse but as rehearsal: I practice surviving each time, and the practice makes me quicker to return. Another spoke of prayer: I left it for months. When I came back, I expected judgment. Instead, I felt held. That is when I knew return is always possible.

Communities must learn to bless returning. To welcome relapse without shame. To hold survivors when symptoms resurface. To preach that healing is not one-and-done but cyclical. Imagine if churches celebrated not only testimonies of sudden deliverance but also testimonies of slow, stumbling returns. Imagine if mosques and synagogues normalized relapse as part of spiritual life, not exile from it. Imagine if therapists integrated liturgy into relapse prevention, reminding clients that return is not regression but rhythm. Such blessings could transform despair into hope.

The body, too, learns to interpret return differently. Panic no longer feels like total annihilation; it becomes a familiar wave, terrifying but survivable. Depression no longer feels endless; it becomes a valley with memory of light beyond it. Each return strengthens resilience, even when survivors do not see it. The spiral remains painful, but it is no longer the same as the first collapse.

Fragments overheard in the rhythm of return:

"I left prayer for a year, then whispered one line. That was enough."

"I relapsed after six months, but it lasted days instead of years."

"Each time I return, I come back with more tenderness for myself."

"I thought relapse meant failure. Now I see it means I'm still alive."

One evening, survivors gathered in a circle to mark their returns. They lit candles for each relapse, not as shame but as testimony. Each flame represented a time they had fallen and risen again. The room glowed with dozens of small lights. No one pretended the relapses had been easy. They spoke of hospital stays, medication changes, broken relationships, crushed hope. Yet as the candles burned, they saw their survival made visible. The glow was not perfection. It was persistence.

Returning was the whispered prayer after silence.

It was the therapy session attended after weeks in bed.

It was the relapse survived without collapse.

It was the candle lit for another cycle of survival.

Returning will always feel fragile. The spiral may never straighten. Symptoms will come and go. But each act of return is sacred. Each relapse survived is miracle. Each step back toward breath, body, community, God, is holiness in motion. Healing is not the absence of return—it is the rhythm of it.

To walk this path is to carry contradiction. You may sit in a pew or a mosque one week and find your body steadied, then wake the next week unable to rise from bed. You may meditate with full attention one morning, then find yourself dissociating by evening. You may return to therapy ready to engage, then cancel the next session in shame. And yet, every time you come back—even halting, even half-hearted, even exhausted, you are inscribing survival into your story. The return is the sacred act, not its permanence.

Communities often struggle with this truth because they prefer linear narratives: once lost, now found; once sick, now healed; once broken, now whole. These stories are neat, inspiring, easy to preach. But they betray the messiness of real survival. Survivors know that "once" and "now" are often tangled. You can be found and still wander, healed and still aching, whole and still splintered. To return is not to erase what came before; it is to fold it into the rhythm of being alive.

The nervous system mirrors this rhythm. Breath itself is a cycle: inhale, exhale, pause, return. There is no shame in breathing out and needing to breathe in again. No one condemns the lungs for repetition. And yet we condemn survivors for relapsing, forgetting that healing is patterned the same way. The inhale of stability will always give way to the exhale of collapse. What matters is not preventing the cycle but allowing its return without shame.

One therapist described relapse as breathing out: "You are not losing progress—you are completing a cycle. When you breathe in again, it will be because your body trusts you can." Survivors who grasped this reframe stopped punishing themselves for returning. Instead, they began to track the rhythm as proof of life, not failure.

Traditions hold echoes of this truth. The Jewish calendar marks time in cycles, returning each year to the same feasts, the same laments, the same prayers. Islam gathers its faithful each week for Jumu'ah, knowing that one prayer will never be enough. Buddhist practice instructs the wandering mind not to avoid distraction but to return, over and over, to the breath. African diasporic rituals repeat call and response until the body remembers what history tried to erase. None of these practices demand once-for-all permanence. They sanctify return as the essence of faith.

Survivors testify in fragments:

"I keep coming back, even when I don't believe."
"I relapse, but I rise sooner each time."
"My therapist said, 'The rhythm itself is holy,' and I cried."
"God has not asked me for perfection—only return."

Returning reshapes memory. Survivors begin to look back and see not only collapses but patterns of endurance. What once felt like failure now appears as continuity. They realize they have returned dozens, even hundreds of times, and each time survival deepened. The relapses did not erase the healing—they became part of it. This is the paradox: the spiral looks like repetition, but it is actually growth. Each circle carries you further, even if you cannot see it.

After a long stretch of stability, one survivor—let's call her Maya—found herself spiraling back into panic. She had been managing well: attending therapy, praying in the mornings, and volunteering in her community. Then, without warning, fear clamped her chest like a vise. Plans unraveled; sleep disappeared. Stifled shame whispered, *"You failed."* Maya felt as if she'd lost the entire progress of the past year.

In our next session, her therapist listened quietly as Maya cried. She recalled the poem "The Seed's Return" and read: *"Even buried, a seed longs to see the light."* The therapist offered a lens: *"This moment is not defeat, Maya. It's the earth shifting around your growth."* Together they built a "Relapse Map": Maya charted what happened, where and how the panic returned. They identified triggers and noted her body's reactions. With each detail, Maya realized it was **consistent with trauma patterns**—not some new, personal failure.

Then came a poem of her own making. Quietly, Maya wrote in her journal:

"The spiral turns,
Night follows day.
In falling, I learn:
there is always a way."

This became a personal liturgy against hopelessness. She read it aloud once a day as a commitment: each return would teach her something.

Clinically, Maya's journey was part of what therapists call "titration" — allowing grief or fear to resurface in smaller, manageable waves. Spiritually, it echoed the Psalmist's cycles of lament and hope. One morning, Maya knelt in prayer and confessed her fear. Instead of rebuking her, her community prayed *with* her words, softly echoing, *"We will help you rise."* That morning she left her apartment carrying a folded page of her spiral notes and her poem in a wallet. Each step felt like a small return: back to street, to sunlight, to herself.

Returning became a ritual of grace. Maya's relapse didn't mean she was back at square one. It meant she was learning where the ground beneath her still shook. Each time the spiral brought her down, she took a breath, looked at her map, and chose one simple step: a walk, a call to a friend, a glass of water. These were her "anchors of return." By morning, the panic lessened; her body remembered how to trust even in trembling. Eventually Maya could say, *"I fell, and something inside me held gently—their hand."* In that holding, she found the courage to breathe, again and again, back toward the light.

Communities that embrace this paradox become places of safety. A church that welcomes members back after absence, without questions or condemnation, embodies grace. A mosque that makes space for those who struggle to pray, acknowledging lapses without judgment, embodies mercy. A sangha that teaches distraction is not failure but practice embodies compassion. A synagogue that calls teshuvah not weakness but core spiritual work embodies truth. When survivors find these places, their bodies finally believe they can return without shame.

One evening, a circle of survivors gathered with paper and ink. They were asked to write not only their relapses but also their returns. The paper filled with dates, moments, breath marks: August 12—hospitalized. September 3—returned to therapy. January 15—relapsed. February 2—lit a candle in prayer. At first, the relapse dates screamed louder. But as the papers filled, the returns multiplied. Survivors saw, maybe for the first time, that their lives were not defined by collapse but by the endless rhythm of coming back. They pinned the papers to the walls, a litany of return. The room glowed with witness.

Returning was the inhale after exhale.

It was the hand lifted after months clenched.

It was the step into a sanctuary after weeks of silence.

It was the body remembering its own rhythm.

To return is to keep breathing. To return is to insist on survival even when despair insists otherwise. To return is to join the chorus of traditions, ancestors, and survivors who have always known that holiness is not perfection—it is persistence. Healing is not the end of return. Healing is the return itself.

No one tells you that relapse can wear a suit. Mine did—every time I smiled through meetings, fluent in the language of competence while my body whispered panic. Depression doesn't always come as collapse; sometimes it comes as overachievement.

Imposter syndrome sits beside me like a coworker I can't fire. In predominantly white spaces, my Blackness becomes both armor and exhaustion. Every sentence is translated twice—once for clarity, once for survival.

There were weeks I arrived at work polished and hollow. Code-switching became its own form of prayer: *Let them see me as harmless; let me make it through the day.*

The relapse wasn't the return of darkness—it was the return of pretending. Healing means I now recognize that performance for what it is: fear dressed as excellence.

I'm learning to measure progress not by productivity but by softness. Some days that looks like crying at my desk and still answering emails. Other days it's leaving on time. Either way, I return.

Graceful Return Ritual:

- Sit comfortably and close your eyes. Bring your attention to each breath, acknowledging the journey you have taken.
- Recall moments when you stumbled or relapsed. Without judgment, see each misstep as part of your path and your learning.
- Place a hand on your heart or belly. Repeat softly to yourself: "I am here now. I am still learning, and I am loved."
- Remember that every breath carries you back to the present. With each inhale, welcome healing; with each exhale, release guilt and shame.
- If it feels right, write down one small step you will take today to care for yourself. This is your promise as you return.
- Give yourself the gift of forgiveness. Whisper a word of grace or comfort—perhaps "I am whole," or a phrase from your faith—to honor your courage in returning.

Ritual Practice: Use this ritual when you feel lost in doubt or relapse. Allow it to guide you gently home to your own care and compassion.

CHAPTER EIGHT: PARASURVIVAL

Survival is not always life. Sometimes what looks like survival is only disguise, a thin shell of functioning wrapped around a nervous system in collapse. Parasurvival is what happens when the body refuses to die but forgets how to live. It is fasting not as devotion but as avoidance. It is prayer not as communion but as panic ritual. It is busyness that masks despair, religious zeal that hides anxiety, discipline that numbs rather than heals. Parasurvival is not fake faith or false practice—it is faith hijacked by trauma, devotion shaped by fear.

Clinicians might call it maladaptive coping. The body, flooded by trauma, invents strategies to endure. It clings to rituals, repetitions, compulsions. It performs strength while hollow inside. It mimics aliveness without allowing the vulnerability of rest. To the outside world, parasurvival looks impressive—disciplined, devout, productive. But the body knows the truth: the jaw is locked, the stomach in knots, the breath shallow, the heart racing. Parasurvival exhausts. It is survival on borrowed breath.

Faith traditions, distorted by stigma or fear, can enable parasurvival. The person who fasts every week not from joy but from terror of eating. The one who prays aloud for hours not from intimacy but to drown out panic. The student who memorizes every verse not to understand but to silence intrusive thoughts. The activist who never stops moving because stillness would mean collapse. Communities often praise these practices as holiness, mistaking hypervigilance for devotion. They do not see the trembling hands, the insomnia, the panic hidden beneath the piety. Parasurvival is rewarded even as it erodes the soul.

But traditions also contain antidotes. Sabbath interrupts compulsive labor. The psalms legitimize cries of exhaustion rather than ceaseless praise. Prophetic mercy names hypocrisy when devotion masks harm. Mindfulness teaches not doing, but noticing. Ancestors preserved survival not by erasing pain with ritual but by embedding lament into it. These practices remind us that faith is not meant to harden trauma but to soften it. Yet survivors must often unlearn what they were taught and reclaim rituals for healing rather than hiding.

In Islam, the self's struggle is called *jihad al-nafs*—not a war of destruction, but of discipline. It is the work of untangling fear from faith, of learning that avoidance is not surrender but exhaustion. Healing, too, is a sacred struggle.

Late one night, a survivor named Faisal sat awake doing the *Ruqya* prayers over and over, hoping to banish his terror. Instead of the peace he sought, his hands shook with each verse. We paused this story: I asked Faisal to place a hand on his chest and breathe quietly with me. His breath was shallow, barely moving his body. Softly I explained, "Your body is in *survival mode*, Faisal. Even your prayer has become a shield, not a sanctuary." We practiced a grounding exercise: naming safe things in the room as he inhaled, saying "Allah's peace" as he exhaled. Slowly his breath broadened.

I told him about the *polyvagal theory*, a framework clinicians use to describe how trauma locks us in alert. "Your prayer beads are moving faster, because your nervous system still expects danger," I offered gently. "Let's teach it trust again." We created a new ritual together: every verse Faisal recites, he will follow with one breath aloud. Inhale: recite the line. Exhale: "Ashhadu" (I bear witness) softly, feeling the air move. This simple rhythm — prayer paired with conscious breathing — began to turn a panic-laced ritual into a breathing meditation.

Over weeks, Faisal noticed changes. He found that when fear spikes, delaying rituals for just one breath would often calm the storm. In our sessions, he brought the language of clinic and Qur'an: "My diaphragm used to tremble with fear; now it lifts in *dhikr* (remembrance) and calm." We celebrated each small victory. His fasting, once driven by compulsion, became more mindful. If anxiety came, he would quietly eat a morsel and whisper a short prayer, showing himself compassion instead of punishment. In therapy terms, he was **differentiating** the trauma from the faith: now he fasted with intention, not avoidance.

Healing named parasurvival as strategy, not sin. Faisal's transformation was testimony: routines that once felt like grave demands became gestures of self-care. In one reflection, he wrote: *"I've been praying with shaking hands, but now I pray with an open heart."* His body's rhythms softened; the panic's grip loosened. The "completer" in him began to say, *"It is enough."* This was not failure—it was freedom. Together, we taught his community to honor that freedom. When mosque leaders heard Faisal's story, they instituted a short silent pause after every service: a moment for anyone to just breathe or rest as needed. In that pause, many bodies found breath that had long been held — healing woven into ritual, faith made whole again.

One survivor described fasting compulsively during anxiety. "If I was hungry enough, I couldn't feel panic," they said. But over time, their body collapsed under malnutrition, and the practice left them hollow. Only when a counselor reframed fasting as optional—not obligation, not punishment—did they learn to eat again without terror. Another survivor recounted memorizing scripture as shield against despair: "If I knew enough verses, maybe the pain would disappear." But when relapse came anyway, they felt betrayed. Therapy helped them see that verses are not weapons but companions. Another survivor kept vigil every night, refusing to sleep because nightmares haunted them. Community praised their "discipline," never knowing it was fear. Only when they learned to rest without shame did they begin to live again.

Parasurvival thrives in communities that confuse exhaustion for holiness. Leaders who preach discipline without tenderness, families who reward endless busyness, peers who valorize burnout—they all reinforce parasurvival. Survivors collapse under applause. Their nervous systems fry under constant demand. Their faith warps into performance. Healing requires unveiling parasurvival, naming it not as weakness but as trauma response, and creating space for survivors to reclaim faith without fear.

Clinicians remind us that parasurvival is not failure. It is strategy. It kept the survivor alive when no other tools were available. The person who fasted to numb panic survived another day. The one who drowned sorrow in prayer survived another night. The one who buried themselves in activism survived another season. Parasurvival may not be sustainable, but it is proof of resilience. The goal is not to condemn it but to help survivors shift toward practices that bring rest, joy, and connection. Parasurvival is survival that has forgotten its way home. Healing is remembering.

Fragments overheard in the edges of parasurvival:

"I prayed until my throat ached, not because I believed, but because silence terrified me."

"I worked until collapse because stopping meant feeling."

"I fasted because hunger was easier than despair."

"I kept smiling in church, but inside I was gone."

One evening, survivors gathered and shared the rituals they had used to keep going. They named them without shame: fasting, overwork, memorization, ceaseless prayer, endless volunteering. At first, they feared judgment. But the group nodded, each recognizing their own survival strategies. Then they asked a different question: what practices bring life rather than numbness? Slowly, answers emerged—rest, song, silence, touch, shared meals. They realized that parasurvival had been necessary, but it did not have to be final. Together, they began to imagine devotion not as disguise but as breath.

Parasurvival was the prayer shouted to drown out panic.

It was the fasting that numbed despair.

It was the activism that erased exhaustion.

It was survival disguised as holiness.

And healing was the remembering: that faith can be softer, that rituals can be gentler, that survival is more than disguise.

Some of us were taught to pray our pain away, not through it. We learned early that silence made us appear faithful. So we over-prayed, over-served, over-volunteered—anything to prove our worthiness.

I once believed fatigue was a love language. If I wasn't tired from serving, I assumed I hadn't given enough. The truth is, I was addicted to spiritual anesthesia. Devotion became my drug of choice because no one condemns the over-spiritual.

A Muslim chaplain I interviewed called it *"religious bypassing."* She said, "When prayer becomes avoidance, God waits outside the ritual for us to feel again."

Her words wrecked me. For years I'd hidden behind liturgy to avoid grief. My fasting was hunger for control. My worship was a negotiation for relief.

Parasurvival is the liminal space where trauma pretends to be obedience. Healing, I've learned, is learning to distinguish the two—and forgiving yourself for not knowing sooner.

Courageous Naming:

- Find a comfortable space and a notebook or piece of paper. Light a candle or lamp if it helps create a sacred feeling.
- Close your eyes and take a few deep breaths. Think of a fear or pain you have carried, and also a strength or survival skill that has carried you through.
- On the left side of the page, write the name of your fear (e.g., "Fear of Being Alone," "Pain of Betrayal"). On the right side, write the name of your strength (e.g., "Brave Survivor," "Loving Courage").
- If it feels right, say each name aloud. Notice the shape of the words, the sound of them. Let the fear-name rest on the page and watch it quiet down. Let the strength-name rise in your chest.
- Feel gratitude for the part of you that has survived. Acknowledge

the pain without judgment.

- Close the practice by folding the page or drawing a line underneath. Carry the named strength with you, and let the named fear be witnessed so it may lessen in silence.

Naming Practice: Use this ceremony whenever fear feels too large or your strength needs recognition. Each time you name them, you bring them from shadow into light.

CHAPTER NINE: BELONGING

"Healing began the day I stopped trying to fit in
and started letting myself be held."

The first thing I remember is the noise.
Not the loud kind, but the layered kind—a low tide of voices, chairs shifting, doors clicking shut, the soft percussion of people arriving. I was early to a peer-support group that met in the church basement, though it could just as easily have been any room with folding chairs and burnt coffee. There were no icons, no altar, no promises of transformation—just a circle waiting to be filled.

I sat near the back, hands pressed between my knees. The fluorescent lights flickered once, then steadied. Someone laughed across the room, not at me, but near enough that my body flinched. Years of performing composure had trained my muscles to misread proximity as threat. I took a breath, felt the jaw tighten, the shoulders lift. Then a stranger—a man with kind eyes and a stutter—offered a simple *"Glad you made it."*

That was it. No sermon, no invitation to share. Just recognition. My shoulders dropped half an inch. It startled me, the way warmth can disarm faster than explanation.

For most of my life, belonging had meant earning my seat. I learned the choreography of approval: nod at the right time, volunteer for the hard shifts, pray aloud with conviction even when the words felt foreign. Community was conditional; love came with performance notes. When I finally unraveled, I expected exile. What I found instead was quieter—a handful of people who didn't ask for proof of progress, who simply stayed long enough for my breathing to find theirs.

We rarely talk about what happens to the body in a safe room. Heart rates synchronize. Muscles mirror. The brain interprets presence as permission. Clinicians call it **co-regulation**; Scripture calls it where two or three are gathered. In that basement, neither language mattered. The science and the sacred were describing the same thing: survival made communal.

A woman named Elise once described it this way during group: *"When I walk in here, I don't have to brace for impact."* Everyone nodded. That collective nod was its own benediction. Belonging wasn't a creed; it was the sound of twenty nervous systems remembering they could exhale together.

I began to notice how small gestures carried the weight of liturgy.
The passing of a pen to someone whose hands trembled.
The refill of a paper cup before anyone had to ask.
The shared silence after someone admitted they'd thought about ending their life that week.
No one rushed to reassure. We simply stayed. The stillness felt holy, though no one named it.

Later, when I tried to explain the experience to a friend who didn't attend, I reached for familiar metaphors—body of Christ, household of faith—but none of them fit exactly. What we had wasn't doctrine; it was respiration. We were learning to breathe in one another's direction without shame.

Sometimes the church upstairs hosted choir practice while we met below. The harmonies drifted through the vents—half muffled, half luminous. The songs were about triumph and resurrection, but what reached us were the in-between notes, the ones that wavered slightly before finding pitch. Those wobbles felt honest. They matched us. We were the unsteady chorus beneath the sanctuary, the echo that refused to disappear.

As months passed, I realized how much of healing depended on proximity. Solitude had its place—reflection, rest—but recovery demanded witnesses. Pain metabolized differently when named aloud. Not performed, just spoken. The first time I said *"I thought about dying"* without whispering, I watched half the room nod in recognition. Nobody gasped. Nobody prayed over me. The room simply expanded around the words, making them survivable.

One evening I asked the facilitator why he kept doing this work year after year. He smiled, rubbed his temples, and said, "Because every time someone new walks in, the rest of us remember why we stayed." That sentence rearranged something in me. I'd always thought belonging was about being accepted. Now I saw it was about accepting the responsibility of witnessing someone else's return.

Belonging, I've learned, doesn't erase loneliness; it gives it context. There are still nights I feel untethered, scrolling through messages I don't answer, standing at the kitchen sink wondering who would notice if I vanished. But even then, I can feel the phantom outline of that circle—the chairs, the laughter, the hum of fluorescent light. My body recalls the calibration. Shoulders lower. Jaw softens. Breath steadies. The memory of being seen becomes a kind of present tense.

Sometimes I try to recreate that presence outside the group: holding eye contact a heartbeat longer with the cashier, asking the coworker who looks distant if they want to eat lunch together, texting a friend "thinking of you" with no expectation of reply. They're small things, barely measurable, but each one widens the circle a little more. Each one reminds me that community is not a place you join; it's a rhythm you keep practicing.

I don't pretend belonging is easy. It's messy, human, full of awkward silences and unmet expectations. Yet every time I choose to stay—through discomfort, through doubt—I feel the quiet click of connection, like a door unlatching inside my chest.

The act still feels secular: sitting in chairs, sharing coffee, repeating each other's names. But something in me recognizes the pulse underneath. This is communion, stripped of ritual but not of reverence.

Maybe that's what the sacred was always trying to show us:
that God hides in proximity,
that love is a nervous system event,
that to belong is to keep breathing in rhythm with others who haven't given up yet.

In all the years I spent chasing belonging, I mistook proximity for presence.
I learned how to stand beside people without ever letting myself be seen. I could harmonize, volunteer, lead prayers, fill pews, teach classes, and still feel like a ghost in the room. I had mastered togetherness while remaining untouched.

It wasn't malice—it was protection. When you've been shamed for feeling too deeply, you learn to edit yourself for comfort. You learn to withhold. I carried that withholding into every space that claimed to welcome me. And the more fluent I became in fitting in, the more foreign belonging felt.

Real belonging, I've come to realize, isn't about merging; it's about being recognized as whole while still allowed to change. It's the freedom to arrive disassembled and know the room won't rush to rebuild you.

In the group basement, that truth unfolded slowly, not through conversation but through calibration. Each week, I'd find my usual seat—third from the left, near the old radiator. The heat clicked on in uneven bursts. Someone would cough. Another would shuffle papers. Nothing remarkable, except that nobody required me to be remarkable either. My worth was assumed in my arrival.

At first, I didn't know what to do with that kind of quiet acceptance. My body, trained for vigilance, kept waiting for correction: the theological nudge, the spiritual diagnosis, the polite distance after confession. None came. The room simply held.

Therapists call this *attunement*. Faith traditions might call it grace. But I think it's older than either language. It's what happens when one nervous system tells another: you are safe enough to stay.

I began noticing it elsewhere—on the bus ride home, when a stranger caught my eye and smiled without reason; in the grocery line, when an elderly man dropped a coin and someone bent to pick it up for him; in the therapist's office, when I couldn't finish a sentence and she waited without impatience. These moments were small, nearly invisible, but they registered in my chest like light touches. A pulse of belonging that asked nothing except acknowledgment.

It changed how I prayed. I stopped asking to be delivered from isolation and started asking for the courage to notice connection when it appeared. Most of the time it didn't look religious at all—it looked like shared air. Like synchronized exhale.

Sometimes, when I enter a church now, I watch the congregation instead of the altar. I study how people lean toward one another during song, how their shoulders shift unconsciously in time, how grief and hope make the same posture. I think about the science of it: the way oxytocin floods when we make eye contact, the way communal rhythm regulates breath. It's not desecration to see the physiology in worship; it's revelation. The Spirit, if she moves at all, must love the way bodies align to one another's breathing.

I remember once visiting a friend's home during Ramadan. At sunset, when the call to prayer sounded from her phone, she spread a small mat and gestured for me to sit nearby. I didn't know the words, so I just matched her pace: bowing when she bowed, pausing when she paused. Afterward she smiled and said, "You prayed." I started to protest, to explain that I hadn't spoken, but she shook her head. "You were here. That's enough."

That night, on the train back, I thought about all the rooms where I had spoken every right word and still been unseen, and this one moment where silence had said everything. Presence, not performance, is what sanctifies space.

Belonging doesn't always feel euphoric. Sometimes it feels awkward, even raw. True presence exposes the parts of us that imitation can hide. I've cried mid-sentence in front of near-strangers and hated myself for it, only to find their faces softening, their eyes meeting mine with something that felt like quiet permission. The body knows safety when it sees it; the throat releases accordingly.

There are still places where I don't belong—rooms too narrow for contradiction, faith circles allergic to ambiguity, friendships that can't hold silence. But I'm learning to grieve exclusion without confusing it for unworthiness. Some doors stay closed because they must; some communities can't yet hold nuance. That doesn't mean there's nowhere left to stand. It means I keep walking until I find the ones who can breathe with me.

I used to equate belonging with unanimity—everyone believing the same, behaving the same, bowing at the same time. Now I think belonging looks more like a choir rehearsal: off-key voices, tentative starts, adjustments mid-song. We tune ourselves to each other not by erasing difference, but by listening harder.

On my worst days, when loneliness flares like fever, I replay the simplest gestures: a hand on my shoulder, a friend's voice saying, *"You don't have to explain."* My body reacts as if the touch were happening now. This, too, is the physiology of grace—the brain's capacity to store warmth and recall it as medicine.

One evening during group, a new participant sat rigid, eyes fixed on the floor. No introduction, no story—just presence. Halfway through, someone passed him a cup of water. He didn't drink it, but he didn't refuse it either. At the end, as chairs scraped back, he whispered, "Thanks for not asking me to talk." The facilitator nodded, saying, "You belonged the moment you walked in."

I carried that line home and wrote it on a scrap of paper: *You belonged the moment you walked in.*

I keep it tucked inside my journal. On days when isolation returns, I read it aloud. Sometimes it feels true; sometimes it doesn't. But even when I doubt it, my pulse slows, as if the body knows the truth before belief catches up.

It took me years to understand that belonging doesn't begin with acceptance; it begins with **not being disqualified**. No matter how far gone, no matter how inconsistent, the invitation remains: *stay.*

In that circle, I saw belonging happen as co-regulation. Neuroscience confirms it: when calm people gather, their nervous systems **entrain together**. One teen named Rosa realized this during a check-in: she said she felt the room slow down as others nodded along with her breathing. She later called it "our silent heartbeat." This is not magic but biology: our muscles and breath unconsciously sync, and stress hormones drop.

To practice this intentionally, we introduced a simple exercise at the end of group: **"Shared Breath Prayer."** Sitting in a circle, everyone closed their eyes and settled their spine. I led them: *"Inhale peace together, hold it, exhale love together."* On each inhale, each person thought of one word or image of comfort; on the exhale, they shared that word aloud with the group. The effect was immediate. One member, crying softly, said, "I felt wrapped in their words." Another smiled: "It was like we built an invisible blanket around me." In clinical terms, this is **mirror neuron activation**: watching a friend breathe calmly teaches the brain it's safe to do the same. In spiritual terms, it felt like everyone quietly praying together with one voice.

Afterward, participants quietly discussed what each word meant: *"hope," "I'm here," "you are loved."* These small testimonies became modern psalms of belonging. One young man admitted he'd never spoken aloud the sentence, *"I missed you"*—not to a friend, not to God—until this circle. Saying it into the still air, and hearing nods of empathy, made it real.

Outside the room, survivors took these lessons to daily life. It could be as simple as holding a coworker's steady gaze for a count of five or placing a gentle hand on a sobbing partner's shoulder without words. These actions enacted what clinicians call *secure attachment cues*: they reminded the body, "You are seen, you are safe." One woman began every Sunday by texting her small support group a "weekly check-in ritual": three sentences – how she really felt, one gratitude, one intention to connect. This small act kept her tethered. Sometimes the group would all share a photo of their morning coffee together via video call, simply witnessing each other's normal. It was ordinary, yet holy.

Belonging became practice. It wasn't the lofty creeds or songs that saved these survivors, but these rhythmic, relational acts: synchronized breath, shared silence, loyal returnings. Over time, their bodies learned a new foundation: the familiar warmth of another's presence. They proved that a trembling heart can settle when another heartbeat is nearby. The circle taught them that to belong is not merely to be in a place, but to breathe in harmony with others who refuse to let them break.

Reflection

Belonging is rarely an arrival; it's an ongoing calibration.
It happens each time we risk being seen, each time we let another person's steadiness steady us.

It's the moment when proximity becomes presence and presence becomes peace.

The sacred hides in that small exchange—
the hand extended,
the nod returned,
the synchronized breath that says, without words,
You still matter here.

Shared Breath Prayer:

- Find someone you trust to sit or stand with. If you are alone, imagine a circle of friends or loved ones around you.
- Place one hand on your heart and one on your belly. Close your eyes and take a slow breath in. Feel your chest rise and your heart expand.
- As you breathe out, silently speak a blessing or affirmation, such as "You are held," or "We are together." If you are with others, you can say it out loud or simply share the silence of that intention.
- Continue breathing together. Inhale the courage of those who came before you; exhale the blessing of love to those beside you. Let each breath become a shared prayer.
- When you are ready, gently open your eyes and offer a smile or touch of peace to your companion. If alone, place a hand on your heart again and feel the love that still surrounds you.

Community Practice: Use this prayer when you long for connection and grounding. Each shared breath is a reminder that none of us truly stand alone.

Communal Breath Ritual

Inhale: We are not alone.
Exhale: We are allowed to stay.

(The breath is the proof.)

Echo Fragment – Echo of Return

We gather on the tide of returning,
breath by breath, together.
Our bodies remember the rhythm of healing.
In each exhale we come home to one another.

✦ CHAPTER 9.5: THE DAYS I DON'T WANT TO BE HERE

There are still days I wake up and wish I hadn't.
Not dramatically. Not in panic. Just with a kind of quiet resignation—like a body that has decided it's tired of pretending to be fine.

Some mornings, the thought slips in before my feet hit the floor: *Maybe I could just stop trying today.*
It's not that I want to die. It's that I'm tired of performing life for systems that don't know how to make space for me to live inside them.

The Weight of Two Worlds

Being a Black man in professional spaces means carrying two languages in one body: the one I speak out loud, and the one I swallow.
It means learning how to make my pain sound palatable enough for white ears to hear without flinching.
It means code-switching even in grief, trimming my rage into something that sounds like professionalism.

There's a certain violence in translation.
You begin to wonder if anyone has ever heard your native tongue, your sighs, your silences, your refusal to shrink just to survive the room.

Imposter syndrome isn't just self-doubt. It's historical memory.
It's walking into every meeting feeling like your ancestors are watching, hoping this time you'll be seen as human. It's sitting in spaces that call themselves diverse but still expect gratitude for letting you exist there.

Sometimes I wonder if my anxiety is just centuries of hypervigilance coded into my nervous system.
PTSD, after all, is the body remembering too much.

The Office That Never Learned My Name

I've sat through meetings where people talked over me, borrowed my ideas, corrected my pronunciation of my own name.
I've smiled politely while my competence was questioned, my tone monitored, my presence tolerated.

After a while, it seeps in: maybe I really don't belong here.
Even when I achieve, the voice in my head whispers, *You're only here because they needed someone like you.*

I've learned to hold that voice without obeying it.
Because the same world that doubts my worth has benefited from my brilliance.
Because the same system that bruised me couldn't function without the quiet labor of people like me, holding it together at the seams.

The Therapist and the Mirror

My therapist once asked me what safety looks like.
I said, "It looks like a day where I don't have to translate myself."
She smiled, then said softly, "That's not safety. That's freedom."

I think about that a lot. How freedom feels like an impossible request.

Even in church, I code-switch. I translate my lament into acceptable theology. I filter my despair through verses that sound victorious.

It's exhausting—trying to be a person, a symbol, and a survivor all at once.
Sometimes the pressure to *represent* outweighs the permission to *exist.*

So yes, there are days I think about disappearing.
Not because I want to die—but because I want to rest from all the versions of me I've had to keep alive.

The Ache That Wears a Suit

Depression doesn't always look like darkness.
Sometimes it looks like a well-dressed man replying to emails with tears still drying behind his eyes.
It looks like sitting in a staff meeting, body present, spirit elsewhere, nodding through the ache.
It looks like an inbox full of reminders of how much you owe the world just to be taken seriously.

When PTSD flares, it's not always flashbacks.

Sometimes it's the way my heart accelerates when someone raises their voice in a meeting.
Sometimes it's the way I plan every sentence three times before I speak.
Sometimes it's the way I still look for exits in rooms that call themselves "safe spaces."

This is what survival looks like when you can't afford to fall apart.
It's functional depression, masked by a good work ethic.
It's professional composure disguising existential exhaustion.

The Tether That Keeps Me

But even in the exhaustion, there are reasons I stay.
Writing keeps me tethered. Words are a form of witness—I write to remember that I'm still here, even when my mind tells me otherwise.

I write to name the ache before it names me.
Every sentence is a small act of defiance against the silence that depression demands.
Sometimes, the page is the only place where I can exist without translation.

And my family—they are the pulse beneath the noise.
My wife's laughter, my daughter's voice calling "Dad" like it's both greeting and grounding—those moments pull me back from the edge.
They remind me that my story is still unfolding. That love is still

happening around me, even when I can't feel it in me.

We go for walks. We eat dinner together. We talk about everything and nothing.
And sometimes that's enough—to be alive inside ordinary life.

The Wins I Don't Always Believe

I've built things that matter. Books. Art. Work that echoes.
People write to tell me that something I said helped them choose to live another day.

Sometimes I want to believe them.
Sometimes I can't.
But I keep showing up anyway, because I've learned that purpose doesn't require certainty, it just requires presence.

There's a strange grace in surviving what should have ended you.
It doesn't feel like triumph. It feels like breath.

Reflection: The Practice of Staying

When the darkness presses close, I remind myself of three things:

1. I have felt this before, and it passed.
2. I am not the voice that says I shouldn't exist.
3. There are people who love me enough to wait until I remember why.

Grounding looks different every time.
Sometimes it's kneeling on the floor until my heartbeat slows.
Sometimes it's repeating my daughter's name like a prayer.
Sometimes it's writing the word *stay* on a scrap of paper and keeping it in my pocket until I believe it again.

(Inhale) I am still here.
(Exhale) I am still becoming.

Liturgy for the Split Selves

For every version of me that learned to shrink—
may I remember that survival was never a sin.

For the voice that whispers *you don't belong,*
may I answer, *I already do.*

For the days when the mask feels safer than the truth,
may grace find me beneath the disguise.

For the boy who thought success would silence the pain,
may the man he became finally rest in his enoughness.

(Inhale) All my selves.
(Exhale) Still one body.

(Inhale) Black and breathing.
(Exhale) Worth staying for.

Closing Reflection Practice

Write down one lie depression tells you.
Then write one truth you've lived in spite of it.
Hold both on the page at once.
That tension—the space between—is where survival lives.

CHAPTER TEN: INTEGRATING

Integration is less about fusion than about companionship. It does not erase the split between faith and illness, between prayer and panic, between devotion and diagnosis. Instead, it insists these realities can sit in the same body without exile. The work of integrating is not to make despair disappear, but to refuse to fracture yourself because of it.

For survivors, fracture is the default. They learn to compartmentalize: prayer in one corner, panic in another. Faith on Sundays, medication on weekdays. Hymns sung aloud, intrusive thoughts hidden. Smiles presented to community, sobs carried in private. The split is protective—if one part collapses, maybe the other can carry on. But over time, fracture drains. It demands energy to maintain the walls between selves. Integration begins when survivors whisper: I am one body. I cannot divide myself to survive.

Theological language sometimes deepens fracture. Communities praise spirit while shaming flesh. They exalt joy while condemning sadness. They demand holiness while pathologizing struggle. Survivors hear: faith and illness cannot coexist. If you are depressed, you are not spiritual. If you panic, you are not trusting. If you take medication, you are not faithful. The message is exile: you must choose which part of yourself is allowed to belong. Integration begins when we reject that lie.

Clinicians describe dual diagnosis—faith and mental illness, spirituality and therapy—as complex but possible. Survivors do not need to abandon belief to engage medication. They do not need to reject prayer to attend therapy. They do not need to hide their panic from their pastor or their faith from their psychiatrist. Integration is the work of building bridges, of translating across languages, of letting one body hold many truths.

Traditions, read carefully, offer resources for this work. The incarnation insists that divinity and humanity can coexist in one body. The psalms show lament and praise braided in a single prayer. The Prophet embodied both revelation and exhaustion. Buddhist practice teaches that compassion arises not by erasing suffering but by accompanying it. Diasporic ancestors sang songs that held rage and hope in the same breath. Integration has always been possible; what is needed is permission to live it.

One survivor described the first time they brought their medication bottle into church. They placed it in their bag beside their hymnal. They said, It felt like blasphemy. But also like truth. Another survivor told of reading psalms aloud during a panic attack, not as cure but as companionship: I realized I could pray and panic at once. They were not enemies. Another survivor recalled therapy sessions where their counselor asked about their faith. It felt like integration: my story did not have to split between clinic and church.

Integration requires imagination. Communities must imagine worship that includes restless bodies, therapy that honors prayer, sermons that name depression, rituals that bless medication. Families must imagine dinner tables where silence is allowed, holidays where grief is remembered, conversations where diagnoses are spoken without fear. Integration is not assimilation but hospitality—each part of the self-welcomed home.

The body testifies when integration begins. Shoulders drop because shame no longer weighs them down. Breath deepens because panic is not exiled. Tears flow without accusation. Survivors describe feeling more whole even when symptoms remain. Integration is not cure. It is coherence.

Fragments overheard in integration:

"I can be faithful and depressed."

"My panic and my prayer sit beside each other."

"The pill bottle on my nightstand is not exile—it is covenant."

"I am no longer split. I am still whole."

One evening, survivors gathered for a liturgy of integration. They brought objects from both sides of their fracture: hymnals and journals, pill bottles and prayer beads, therapy notes and candles. They placed them on a single table. Together, they spoke words of blessing over the whole. No object was condemned. None was shamed. Each was acknowledged as part of survival. The table became altar. Integration became visible.

Integration was the psalm whispered through panic.

It was the pill bottle carried into sanctuary.

It was the therapist who honored prayer.

It was the refusal to split survival into separate rooms.

Integration will never be finished. Fracture will tempt again. Communities will still demand division. But once survivors taste wholeness, they know it is possible. And each act of integration—each therapy session that includes prayer, each prayer that includes panic, each medication swallowed without shame—becomes survival. Integration is not perfection. It is persistence in wholeness. Not once-for-all, not tidy, not without relapse. Wholeness here is fragile, trembling, often incomplete. But it is real enough to steady breath for another day. When survivors resist the pressure to fragment—when they allow faith and illness, body and spirit, grief and hope to inhabit the same room—they are already practicing a kind of resurrection.

Persistence is not glamorous. It rarely makes a sermon illustration. It looks like showing up to therapy with shaking hands. It looks like taking medication at the same time every morning, even when despair insists it is useless. It looks like whispering a psalm into the dark when panic claws at the chest. It looks like returning to community after weeks of absence and choosing to sit in the back row. Persistence is not dramatic. But it is sacred.

Communities often miss this holiness because they look for spectacle. They celebrate sudden healing, loud deliverance, visible triumph. But the quiet rhythms of persistence go unnoticed. The survivor who still breathes after suicidal ideation. The congregant who keeps returning even when joy feels impossible. The family member who sits in silence rather than demanding cheer. These are small acts of survival, but they are miracles of coherence.

In clinical terms, persistence rewires. Each time a survivor chooses not to fragment, neurons strengthen new pathways. Shame loosens its grip. The body learns that panic does not exile prayer, that medication does not erase faith, that despair does not end belonging. Slowly, the nervous system begins to trust itself again. In theological language, this is sanctification by survival—holiness revealed in repetition, in ordinary acts of refusal to divide.

A survivor once described placing their Bible, their pill bottle, and their therapist's business card on the same nightstand. "I used to hide them from each other," they said. "Now I see them as my altar." Another survivor described sitting in church while panic rose, refusing to leave in shame, and whispering, I am still here. Another described falling apart mid-prayer and realizing that the collapse itself was prayer. These stories are not about neat endings. They are about coherence—fragile, partial, yet real.

The work continues because fracture never disappears fully. Old voices resurface: Faith should be enough. Illness means weakness. You do not belong here if you despair. Communities sometimes echo those voices, urging survivors to pick one identity, one truth, oneself. But each time survivors resist, each time they persist in holding their multiplicity together, they embody wholeness. Not finished, but unfolding. Not seamless, but real.

Fragments overheard in persistence:

"My pill and my prayer are both covenant."

"I broke down mid-service, and no one asked me to leave. That was healing."

"The altar I built was not in a sanctuary—it was on my nightstand."

"I am not done, but I am not divided."

At the close of a gathering, survivors laid their survival objects on a single table again—candles, journals, photos, pill bottles, prayer beads, scraps of psalms, therapist notes. This time, they did not name them with shame. They blessed them. They called them holy. They lit the candles and sat in silence, no longer fractured between sacred and secular, between spiritual and clinical. The table glowed with witness: persistence made visible.

What persists is not certainty. What persists is not unbroken joy. What persists is the refusal to exile parts of the self in order to be accepted. To carry despair and devotion side by side, to honor panic and prayer in the same breath, to let faith and therapy share the same altar—that persistence is already wholeness.

Integration is not a miracle moment. It's the slow, unglamorous practice of staying—one refill at a time, one therapy session you almost cancel, one breath that doesn't end in panic.

For months I resisted medication. I wanted prayer to be enough, wanted my faith to prove its strength through endurance. But depression doesn't negotiate with doctrine. When the pills finally steadied me, I realized healing can look chemical and divine at once.

My therapist called this "both-and faith"—the courage to let science and spirit share custody of your sanity.

These days I practice integration like liturgy. Morning meds, evening prayer, water in between. Sometimes the prayer is only "thank you." Other times it's "please don't let me fall apart again." Both are sacred.

The miracle isn't that I never break down. It's that I keep returning—to breath, to therapy, to God, to myself.

✦ INTERLUDE III
BETWEEN THE MIDDLE AND THE SACRED WORK

When you live long enough in the middle, even peace starts to feel suspicious. You wait for the next collapse, the next phone call, the next loss that reminds you recovery is not linear—it's tidal.

The middle is its own country. You learn to speak its slow dialect: the language of "almost okay," the quiet endurance of showing up again. It's where you measure progress not by joy but by gentleness—how softly you can meet yourself when the day unravels.

There's a point where exhaustion becomes devotion. You keep showing up for your appointments, for your community, for yourself, even when belief is small. That's what sacred endurance looks like—habit as holiness. Faith becomes something you do, not something you feel.

A therapist once told me that healing is repetition performed with compassion. A monk once told me that even doubt can bow. I didn't understand either lesson at first. But maybe that's what this part of healing is—the quiet bow in the middle, the body recognizing it has not fallen apart completely.

Some days, the only prayer you can manage is motion: washing dishes, answering messages, breathing on purpose. Every act becomes a small liturgy of persistence. The middle teaches us that holiness often hides inside monotony.

There's grace in the ordinary rhythm of survival—the way the breath steadies itself even when the mind trembles. This is faith as physiology: muscle remembering mercy.

Liturgical Echo:
Inhale: Still broken.
Exhale: Still breathing.
Inhale: Still uncertain.
Exhale: Still here.

Because faith, too, is an autonomic response—quiet, involuntary, but alive.

And maybe endurance itself is prayer: not the loud, confident kind, but the soft pulse that keeps the heart from closing completely. In this sacred middle, we do not ascend—we continue.

PART THREE
THE SACRED WORK

CHAPTER ELEVEN: HOLD ME WHILE I BREAK

Breaking is not the opposite of healing. Breaking is part of it. Bodies collapse before they rest. Voices crack before they sing. Faith falters before it finds new ground. Survivors know this intimately: the nervous system holds too much until it cannot hold anymore. The rupture comes—panic overwhelming, depression flattening, grief unbearable. And in those moments, the deepest need is not for answers, not for theology, not for quick repair. The deepest need is to be held.

Holding here does not mean fixing. It does not mean cheering up, silencing sobs, or supplying solutions. It means presence. A therapist who stays steady when tears flood. A friend who sits through the shaking. A community that does not turn away from rupture. To hold is to make space for breaking without abandoning. Survivors who are held in their breaking discover something astonishing: safety does not require composure. Love does not require performance. Belonging does not require strength.

Clinicians name this therapeutic alliance. In the sacred language of psychology, it is the trust that emerges between survivor and therapist, a bond that allows risk, collapse, honesty. Without alliance, no treatment can work. With it, even the most fragile body can begin to heal. Survivors often describe their therapist not as healer but as holder: someone steady enough to contain their breaking until they can breathe again.

Faith traditions, too, testify to the holiness of holding. The psalms cry aloud, but what makes them bearable is that they were sung together. Jesus wept at Lazarus' tomb not alone but in the company of friends. The Prophet endured grief surrounded by community. Buddhist practice honors compassion as presence, not solution. Diasporic ancestors held one another in song when they could not hold themselves. Across traditions, the act of being held transforms breaking from isolation into survival.

One survivor remembered collapsing in therapy after years of composure. They sobbed until words disappeared. The therapist did not interrupt. Did not explain. Did not pathologize. They simply said, I'm here. The survivor later said that moment felt more like prayer than any sermon. Another survivor described breaking down in church, expecting to be asked to leave. Instead, a friend wrapped arms around them and stayed through the whole service. They said, I thought faith meant never breaking. That day I learned faith meant breaking together.

Breaking is terrifying because it feels like loss of control. Trauma survivors have often been punished for showing weakness. Communities sometimes reinforce this fear, demanding strength, composure, joy. Survivors internalize the message: if I break, I will be abandoned. But when breaking is met with holding, the message rewrites itself: if I break, I will still belong. This is the heart of healing.

The body confirms it. In co-regulation, a trembling nervous system steadies by syncing with another's. A shallow breath deepens when it matches the rhythm of a calm companion. A racing heart slows when a hand rests gently on the arm. Breaking does not destroy when someone else carries part of the weight. Survivors learn that collapse does not equal death. Breaking can be survived—if they are not alone.

Fragments overheard in the breaking:

"I shattered, and she stayed."

"He held my hand while I sobbed, and I lived."

"My therapist said nothing, and that silence saved me."

"I thought breaking meant failure. Now I know it meant I was still alive."

One evening, survivors created a ritual of being held. They paired up, one resting against the other, breathing together. Some cried, some trembled, some laughed nervously. But slowly, bodies softened. The ones being held realized they did not have to stay composed. The ones doing the holding realized they did not need to fix anything. The room filled with a quiet holiness. Breaking was no longer exile. It was communion.

The work is sacred rupture. Faith and therapy agree on this point: safety is not the absence of breaking but the presence of care within it. Communities must learn to bless breaking, not shame it. To say: You can fall apart here, and we will not turn away. To train clergy and therapists alike to recognize tears not as interruptions but as liturgy. To create sanctuaries where sobs echo as prayer.

Closing Fragments

Breaking was the sob that did not end in abandonment.

It was the collapse held in steady arms.

It was the silence that did not exile but embraced.

It was the holiness of being carried when I could not stand.

Breaking will return, as surely as panic, depression, grief. But each time it is met with holding, survivors learn to trust again. Each time, the nervous system rewires: collapse can be survived. Each time, faith re-anchors: love does not leave when I am undone. To be held while breaking is not weakness. It is sacred survival.

The first time it happened, it was not dramatic. An emergency room at 2:17 a.m., fluorescent light numbing the edges of the room, a monitor ticking out a measured proof that the body was still here. The chaplain slid a chair to the corner—not too close, not far away—angled so the door was visible and the exit easy to reach. "We don't have to talk," they said, lowering their voice until it matched a calm no one in the room yet felt. The air changed. Not better—just less alone. A cup of water, a blanket that didn't itch, the permission to stare at the floor. The body, which had been braced for judgment, measured the room again and let two muscles release. It wasn't rescue. It was anchoring.

Holding is not a metaphor here; it is a set of decisions. The quiet chair.

The slower prosody. The way a hand is offered palm-up (so it can be refused) rather than reaching to take. The presence that doesn't flinch at sobbing or speed up when silence lengthens. The small, ordinary cues of safety speak to parts of the nervous system that words can't reach. And when the break crests—shaking, breath snagging on the way out—those cues keep the moment from becoming an edge that someone falls from.

To hold another person through pain is not a metaphor—it is a clinical act, a sacred practice, and a discipline of presence. In the language of therapy, "holding" means containment and co-regulation. Containment is what allows the wound to stay within a boundary; it ensures that the distress does not flood every corner of the room or of the self. Co-regulation is subtler. It is the quiet lending of one nervous system to another until the body in crisis remembers the tempo of safety. The helper's slower breath becomes the bridge; the survivor's body, entrained to that rhythm, begins to return from the edge. This is what holding actually does: it steadies the autonomic storm long enough for the mind to find the body again.

What it does *not* do is fix. Holding does not persuade, reason, or argue the despair into retreat. It does not locate silver linings or press anyone back into composure. Fixing can become a form of flight—an anxious move to escape helplessness. Arguments masquerade as empathy but often function as avoidance, a way to sidestep another's pain and our own discomfort with powerlessness. True holding tolerates that helplessness; it stays long enough for the body in front of us to survive the crest of its own breaking.

From an attachment lens, every rupture asks for reliability. The body, faster than thought, asks three questions within seconds: *Am I safe? Am I seen? Will you stay?* Safety is proximity without pressure—the gentle closeness that does not demand performance. Seeing is naming without diagnosing, acknowledging without analyzing. Staying is measured not in declarations but in the slow passage of minutes that take the shape of patience rather than urgency. Polyvagal theory gives the physiology behind what love already knows: softer tone, open posture, warm facial expression, predictable pacing—each one tilts the nervous system from defense toward engagement. The content of our words matters less than the music of our presence.

But there are risks few name aloud. Holding can wound if done without awareness. **Premature soothing**—rushing to calm too soon—teaches the sufferer that their brokenness is intolerable. **Boundaryless empathy**—flooding the space with our own tears or stories—pulls the attention away from the person breaking and forces them to hold us instead. **Savior drift** turns care into control; the helper's need to rescue overshadows the survivor's right to agency. **Uninvited touch**, even meant in comfort, can detonate like a landmine; consent is not courtesy—it is the container itself. And **spiritual bypass**, the reflex to coat pain in theology—"It's all in God's hands"—shuts down grief that was meant to move through the body, not be sealed away.

The ethical edges differ by role. Therapists owe containment through boundaries, confidentiality, and informed consent. Clergy owe spiritual presence that complements, not replaces, medical care. Friends owe companionship that resists the impulse to perform therapy. What every role shares is humility—knowing where one's skill ends and where another professional or community circle must begin. Timely referral is not abandonment; it is a form of love.

For those standing at the edge of another's rupture, a quiet field guide can help. Begin with consent: *Do you want company right now, or space with me nearby?* Follow with capacity: *I can stay forty-five minutes and come back tomorrow—will that help?* Containment follows: *Can we ground together for two minutes—feet on the floor, name five things you see—and then decide what's next?* Culture matters too: *Is there a word, ritual, or boundary that feels sacred in moments like this?* And always, continuity: *If tonight gets hard again, what will our plan be, and who else is in the circle?* These questions are not scripts but scaffolds; they build ecosystems of care instead of heroic moments.

Micro-rituals often bridge where words cannot. Slow breath pacing—counting longer on the exhale—signals safety to the vagus nerve. Gentle orienting—scanning the room, naming colors, locating the door—tells the brain the danger is not now. Temperature shifts, like a cool cloth or a warm mug, reintroduce the body to safe sensation. Object anchoring—a stone, a string of beads, a note in the pocket—gives the hands something to remember when memory itself fractures. And time-boxing—"for two minutes, we only breathe; then we reassess"—teaches that feelings, even unbearable ones, have edges and duration.

When holding belongs to a room—when breath, tone, and ritual conspire toward safety—something profound occurs. The one in pain does not need to believe in healing yet; their body only needs to believe it can stay. The one offering presence does not need to know what to say; their steadiness is the language. Holding, done well, transforms helplessness into communion. It becomes the quiet architecture of survival—the liturgy of staying.

We keep imagining a single pair of hands. Often it is a room that holds. An usher who knows which pews are near an exit; a greeter who has learned to recognize the stare that means not today, please no questions; a side-chapel with lamps instead of bright lights and chairs that sway a little so restless bodies don't feel like failures. A posted statement: Crying is welcome; pacing is welcome; step out and return as you need. Architecture that tells the truth reduces the number of words the body demands from us.

There was a congregation that quietly set aside a "soft space"—the last few rows with dimmer lights, weighted lap blankets, a small basket of earplugs, a card that read, Stay as you are, leave as you need. People began lingering there after services. Less confession, more exhale. The change was measurable, if you are the sort who measures: fewer early exits, more returns after absence, an uptick in requests for peer support instead of disappearing.

We resist metrics because the sacred resists spreadsheets. Presence cannot be graphed. Yet accountability protects everyone. In both therapy and ministry, we assess not to quantify compassion but to ensure safety—to make sure that care, however holy, is also effective. The nervous system, after all, keeps its own data.

The first signs appear in the body. Breath begins to slow. Shoulders, once locked in defensive vigilance, descend by degrees. The gaze widens; the voice regains contour and cadence. These are not small changes—they are physiology returning from exile. Within forty-eight to seventy-two hours, the signs extend outward: a meal eaten, a night of real sleep, a returned message, a kept appointment. These acts may look mundane, but they are clinical gold—indicators that the system is stabilizing.

Across a few weeks, subtler shifts emerge. Avoidance decreases; the survivor revisits places once charged with shame. Help-seeking rises; a phone call is initiated instead of delayed. Narratives loosen; the vocabulary moves from absolutes—*always, never, ruined, hopeless*—to temporal realism: *sometimes, this week, for now.* The body is learning flexibility again. The theology of despair—*I am beyond repair*—gives way to a smaller, holier confession: *I am still here.*

Even organizations display markers of effective holding. A crisis conversation ends with a plan instead of panic. Volunteers report that they feel supported rather than stranded. Referrals are used responsibly, boundaries kept intact, repairs initiated after missteps instead of avoided. Systems that hold well begin to resemble the very nervous systems they hope to heal: responsive, elastic, humble in recovery.

When the data reverse—when isolation deepens, appointments lapse, meals disappear, risk rises without a plan—it signals a fracture in containment. The holding may be insufficient or misapplied. That is not failure; it is feedback. The task then is to adjust the model: widen the circle, clarify roles, refer out, or slow the tempo. Even care needs calibration.

Two scenes, both true in essence if not in detail, illustrate what this looks like in practice.

Rain against the clinic window. The clock slides past the hour. The client who never cries sits folded into herself, shoes half-off, one heel tapping like a metronome for panic. "If I let go," she says softly, "I don't know who I am." The therapist doesn't reach for a technique—they reach for time. "Then for two minutes, we won't let go. We'll just breathe." They count silently on their fingers where she can see, not hear, because numbers spoken aloud can sound like grading. On the third minute the tapping slows. On the fourth she asks for the blanket. On the ninth she weeps. Later, the notes read plain and uneventful: *Affect modulation improved. Risk unchanged but contained. Plan co-created.* Boring notes mean the body found a floor.

Another night, a different room. The sanctuary is empty except for a line of votive lights. Two friends sit cross-legged on the carpet, backs against the dais. "I can't do Sunday," one says. "The songs lie." The other nods. "Then we hum nothing." And they do—just breath, the faint buzz of the exit sign, city noise drifting through an open door. Twelve minutes, then fifteen. "Okay," the first says. "I didn't drown." No testimonies. No verse. A hinge stops squeaking when you oil it; no one applauds the hinge.

Holding, like hinges, only matters when it works quietly.

But holding also requires edges. Without them, compassion turns into collapse. Touch, if used, must be asked for, named, and time-bound—*Would pressure on your shoulders help for thirty seconds?* Time itself is a boundary: starts and stops honored, extensions negotiated. Role clarity protects both sides: *I can stay tonight and next Tuesday. I can help you reach the clinic. I can't be your only nighttime call.* And afterward, the holder must be held—through supervision, debrief, rest. Compassion without replenishment curdles into resentment or rescue.

Power, too, demands vigilance. A microphone, a collar, a badge, a key—each adds leverage to presence. What begins as "staying with" can, if left unchecked, become "keeping." The difference is consent. Holding without choice is not care—it is captivity.

Even with skill, holding fails. Someone arrives late, says too much, stays too long, touches without asking. Repair, then, is not a footnote; it is the covenant. *Last night I rushed you. I'm sorry. I won't do that again. What would feel safer next time?* The nervous system registers sincerity more than eloquence. Communities that practice apology without defensiveness become generators of trust. Survivors do not need flawless spaces. They need honest ones.

To make holding sustainable, design for repeatability. If care depends on charisma or one heroic volunteer, it will collapse at scale. Build scaffolding instead: short crisis-literacy trainings on suicide risk and de-escalation; trauma-informed hospitality through lighting, signage, seating, sensory supports; story stewardship practices that replace extraction with gratitude—*thank you for trusting me* instead of *at least...*; referral ecosystems with warm hand-offs, not cold lists; care for the carers through rotations, debriefs, sabbath equivalents. When holders are forbidden to break publicly, the model is already exploitative.

Presence, when designed well, becomes infrastructure. Breath becomes policy. Boundaries become theology. Repair becomes culture. The economics of presence are simple: one breath steadies another. And in that exchange—the sacred, measurable and not—healing keeps finding its way back.

There is a cost to this work. Time that could have been spent on programs gets spent on people. Budgets favor what can be counted. A coffee station is easier to fund than a quiet room; a new projector is more exciting than chair glides and weighted blankets. But the outcome we claim to value—lives steadied—grows in spaces that look boring on spreadsheets. The analysis is simple: if we underwrite aesthetics and starve containment, we will get performance and lose people.

The body banks safety. It does not store it in words or doctrines but in tissues, in rhythms, in breath. One night of being held will not prevent the next rupture—but it becomes recallable. In panic, a breathline reappears. In depression, a muscle remembers how to soften. In shame, a sentence returns unbidden: *You can break and still belong.* These are not thoughts; they are imprints—somatic data written in the language of the nervous system. Therapy multiplies them, layering safety into neural pathways that once only knew collapse. Community rehearses them until belonging becomes reflex. Over time, enough imprints form a map—not out of the woods, but through them. Healing does not erase danger; it teaches the body which paths lead home.

There is a house three blocks from the bus stop with a deep front porch and a single lamp that glows like the inside of a chest at rest. On wet evenings, someone always sits there with a thermos, steam unspooling into the night air. Neighbors know what it means. It's not a shelter, not a program, not an intervention—just a place to land for a few minutes before continuing. There is no form to fill out, no script to recite. Only a bench, a wicker chair, a dog that sighs like an old accordion. Sometimes two people share the silence, watching the rain bead on the railing. Sometimes no one speaks at all. You can measure pulse. You can chart return visits. You can call it hospitality. Or you can let it remain what it is: a body remembering it was not made to carry itself alone.

Fragments, collected after:
a hand offered and not taken, yet still counted as care;
the sentence, "I will stay until the clock says ten," and someone believing it;
a chair that rocks just enough for the foot to find a rhythm;
an apology that arrived with no defense, only repair;
a door left open to the night air because breath needed sky.

None of this looks like triumph. It looks like time—unhurried, gentle, exacting in its patience. It looks like tone—voices low enough for the body not to flinch. It looks like rooms arranged for staying: a chair angled toward the window, a lamp that says *you are still welcome.* The art of holding has never been glamorous; it is the humble craft of not leaving. And when it is present, breaking stops being a cliff. It becomes a wave that crests, then recedes—because something on shore is steady.

My therapist once told me, "A patient's breakdown is never failure; it's language finding form." I think about that every time I watch a body tremble before words appear. The collapse is not rebellion; it is translation. The body speaks first when language has fled. It tells the truth in tremor, in tears, in breath that catches before it steadies.

In sacred terms, this is revelation by nervous system—grace made visible through the body's surrender. Meaning breaking through muscle before theology can catch up. Every tear, every stuttered inhale, is both data and prayer. When someone holds that moment without interpreting it, without rushing to theologize or fix, something holy happens: the body learns it can speak without being silenced.

That is liturgy—the lived sacrament of survival.
That is what it means for being held to become memory.
And memory, when blessed by safety, becomes the quiet architecture of faith.

CHAPTER TWELVE: A GOSPEL FOR THE WOUNDED

The word *gospel* means good news. But for many who live with depression, trauma, or relapse, the news they have been handed has never been good. It has come in sermons that mistake panic for sin. In families that whisper about suicide as scandal rather than sorrow. In communities that celebrate survival only when it looks like triumph—never when it looks like limping. What most survivors have received is not gospel at all; it is judgment wrapped in scripture, exile masquerading as theology.

And yet across history the real gospel has always begun with the wounded. Not the triumphant. Not the polished. Not the ones who arrive spotless at the altar. The first recipients of divine attention were the broken, the barren, the leprous, the possessed, the ones gasping for breath on the margins. The gospel has never been about performance; it has been about proximity—Love choosing to draw near to pain. To reclaim a gospel for the wounded, then, is not innovation. It is recovery. It is the remembering of what faith has always known but keeps forgetting: that wholeness begins in fracture, and holiness often limps.

The Architecture of Exclusion

Too often, religion becomes a sorting machine. The joyful are platformed, the grieving hidden. The disciplined are praised, the fragile corrected. People with chemical imbalance or trauma history are told to pray harder, fast longer, believe stronger—as though the serotonin receptor were a moral muscle. The implicit curriculum is cruel but clear: if your body breaks, your spirit is suspect.

Clinically, the results are predictable. Shame intensifies symptoms. Exile magnifies risk. People begin to conflate diagnosis with defect. The internal monologue turns liturgical: *If I were stronger, I'd be healed. If I had more faith, I'd be free.* Neurobiology tells us that shame tightens the amygdala; theology reminds us that shame is the oldest exile story we know. Both agree—it isolates. And isolation kills.

If faith communities confine grace to the unbroken, they betray their own creed. Because if salvation excludes the trembling, it ceases to be salvation at all.

Good news does not erase pain. It refuses premature closure. It walks into the fracture and sits down. It names the wound without turning away. True gospel insists that survival is not failure, that relapse is not exile, that despair does not forfeit belonging.

One survivor told me of the first time a preacher said aloud, *"Some of you could not get out of bed this morning. That does not make you less beloved."* She wept, because it was the first sermon that called her depression by name and did not call it sin. Another remembered a hospital chaplain who whispered, *"You do not need to perform faith right now. You are already held."* That single sentence rewrote years of doctrine.

Gospel is not about triumph—it is about witness. It does not require resurrection to name life sacred; it begins wherever breath still rises. In womanist theology, survival itself is testimony. A friend in Nairobi once told me, "We shout because we're still alive." That, too, is gospel enough. To still be here is liturgy.

The Anatomy of Wounding

To preach to the wounded, we must first name the wounds.

Spiritual bypass — Scripture wielded to silence grief instead of accompany it. "Don't be anxious" becomes an indictment rather than an invitation.

Pathologizing pain — Depression labeled rebellion; panic reframed as disbelief. A misreading of faith as emotional control rather than relational trust.

Community exile — Absence met with gossip, relapse met with withdrawal, suicide whispered instead of lamented. The body of believers amputates its own limbs.

False testimony economy — Congregations rewarding only victory narratives. Survivors must lie or vanish to stay included.

Clergy overreach — Leaders claiming to "cure trauma" through prayer alone, displacing clinical help and deepening harm.

Each wound is preventable. None require divine intervention—only humility, literacy, and love. These are not failures of faith; they are failures of formation.

Toward a Gospel That Heals

A gospel for the wounded must do five things.

It must **name wounds without shame**—speak the words *depression, panic, suicide, addiction* in the sanctuary until they lose their stigma.

It must **honor relapse as rhythm**—not moral lapse but evidence of persistence. Falling is not apostasy; it is gravity.

It must **reframe medication and therapy as mercy**—not substitutes for prayer but sacraments of care, extensions of divine wisdom through science.

It must **celebrate presence over victory**—the testimony of trembling attendance as equal in holiness to the testimony of triumph.

It must **practice communal lament**—crying together, not as spectacle but as solidarity, until grief becomes shared breath instead of private shame.

These five practices are not sentimental—they are strategic. Communities that embody them measurably reduce suicide risk, increase treatment adherence, and strengthen belonging. Neurobiology calls it co-regulation; theology calls it incarnation. Both describe the same mystery: love taking physiological form.

Fragments Overheard in Wounded Spaces

"I thought faith meant pretending—then someone said I could pray while sobbing."

"The pills I take each morning are gospel in my body."
"They remembered the anniversary of my relapse without shame. That was good news."
"The sermon that saved me was three words: *You are loved.*"

Each of these is a verse in the new psalter—a canon of survival hymns. They are not metaphors but evidence: liturgies born from the pulse, not the pulpit.

The real gospel is not for the flawless; it is for those still negotiating breath. Its promise is not that we will never break again, but that breaking will not exile us from love. The wounded gospel does not say, "Be whole and you will belong." It says, "Belong, and you may yet become whole."

Clinical science and sacred story converge here: regulation and redemption are both relational. The nervous system heals through safe presence; the soul heals through steadfast love. Both require someone who stays.

So the next time you hear good news, listen for who it includes. If it cannot be sung by the exhausted, if it cannot be whispered by those still afraid to wake, if it cannot be prayed through tears or silence, it is not gospel yet.

The gospel for the wounded begins in the dark,
and calls the darkness holy until morning comes.

In a small congregation, a woman stood up during testimony time and said, "I relapsed last month. I missed therapy. I drank too much. I thought of ending it. But I am here." The room fell silent—not in judgment, but in reverence. Then someone began to clap. Not loud, not triumphant, but steady. Others joined. The applause was not for perfection; it was for presence. For showing up. For surviving. That moment was gospel: the community saying together, *We do not exile you for breaking.*

Good news was the chair saved for the relapser.
It was the pill blessed as provision.
It was the grief spoken aloud without scandal.
It was the survivor saying, "I am here," and the community replying, "We are too."

But good news cannot remain contained in a single moment of recognition or one act of mercy. It must become rhythm—something breathed, lived, and embodied daily. A gospel for the wounded cannot be reduced to a one-time liturgy of inclusion. It must become the grammar of relationship, the syntax of belonging that makes space for fracture, for relapse, for silence, and for rage. Too many congregations collapse gospel into performance: a crescendo of joy divorced from sorrow, a tidy testimony that edits out the ache. Yet joy without sorrow becomes brittle; triumph without memory becomes cruel. What makes good news *good* is its capacity to stay in the room with despair and still remember its name.

The measure of a gospel is not how it resounds beneath stained glass, but how it carries in a hospital corridor at midnight. How it speaks in the quiet of a panic attack that will not yield to prayer. How it holds the exhausted body that cannot rise for morning worship. If it cannot travel into those spaces, it is not gospel—it is a conditional bargain dressed in holy words. Survivors learn quickly which kind of gospel they've been handed. They can feel its weight, or lack thereof. Many discover that what they were offered cannot bear the gravity of their pain. That discovery becomes its own wound: the realization that their faith community, the very place meant to cradle them, has no language for their breaking. That absence of language is a second exile.

And yet the stories that endure are the ones in which a different word was spoken—quietly, without ceremony, yet enough to alter the landscape of survival. A hand that stayed on the shoulder when the sobs grew louder. A line in a sermon that named relapse without euphemism. A friend who wrote down a therapist's number and said, "I'll go with you if you're afraid." These moments are not grand gestures, but they rewire the soul's circuitry. They teach the wounded what doctrine forgot: that belonging does not require composure, that love is not revoked by relapse, that the holy table always has room for the shaking hand.

What makes this gospel trustworthy is not its ability to erase despair but its refusal to forget it. *Memory itself becomes sacrament.* The community that remembers anniversaries of loss, the therapist who remembers the shape of a story told months ago, the family who remembers to set a place even when the loved one still cannot emerge from their room—these small remembrances keep faith tangible. Forgetting isolates. Remembering heals. Survivors live in the constant fear of erasure: of being too heavy to hold, too inconvenient to include. But when they are remembered—even in absence, even in silence—something inside them loosens. Breath deepens. The nervous system releases its grip. Healing takes root not in the absence of pain, but in the assurance that pain does not erase belonging.

There is a kind of collective courage required for this remembering. Communities must resist the seduction of neatness—the pressure to package every story with a resolution. They must be willing to host testimonies that end mid-sentence, to allow the sob itself to be the liturgy, to let silence linger as prayer. This is not failure of faith; it is faith unguarded, faith incarnate. The gospel that pretends wounds do not exist collapses under its own denial. The gospel that names wounds and remains in their presence can bear anything.

So much of this gospel is ordinary. It is not found in dramatic rescues or sweeping reforms, but in the quiet accumulations of presence. The neighbor who drops off soup when depression makes cooking impossible. The coworker who covers a shift without commentary. The friend who replies to a midnight text with "Still here." These gestures do not solve the wound; they surround it with recognition. And recognition is often the first form of healing.

Each act, however small, becomes liturgy: a living theology written in kindness. Over time, these gestures form a theology of continuity—a gospel stronger than words, one that tells of a God, or a Love, or a

Presence that does not disappear when we do. The wounded gospel is not abstract doctrine; it is embodied memory. It is mercy practiced until it becomes muscle memory. It is the patient work of saying to one another, again and again, in voice and silence alike:

You are still here.
And so are we.

✦ LITURGICAL ECHO — *After Wounding, We Still Breathe*

After the sermons broke and the noise faded,
we learned to breathe again—
not as praise,
but as proof.

After relapse, after the shaking hands,
after the silences that split prayer in two,
we found that grace still entered
through the unguarded places.

After the body refused performance,
after the voice cracked mid-psalm,
after the faith we were told should never falter did—
we discovered that love did not withdraw.

The gospel for the wounded is not shouted;
it hums quietly beneath the ribs.
It moves like breath between those who remain,
whispering: *You are not beyond the reach of mercy.*

So, we exhale what shame once held.
We inhale what courage requires.
And together, we keep repeating the first and truest prayer:

Still here.

Still breathing.

Still beloved.

CHAPTER THIRTEEN: FAITH ACROSS TRADITIONS

The instinct, when speaking of faith traditions, is to line them up like items on a shelf: this practice here, that teaching there, a neat comparison of how one tradition approaches despair versus another. But real life refuses such neatness. The survivor pacing their apartment at 3 a.m. does not parse a comparative chart of theology. They reach for what is at hand: the verse they half-remember, the breath prayer their grandmother whispered, the song hummed in childhood, the silence they learned on retreat, the drumbeat still echoing from ancestral memory. Faith does not arrive sorted by tradition. It arrives as fragments—carried through bodies, received across generations, mixed and overlapping in ways no scholar could ever catalog.

Survivors live in this mixture. A Christian raised on hymns finds comfort in Buddhist meditation. A Muslim raised on dhikr finds rest in the cadence of psalms. A Jewish survivor of panic learns to breathe through metta phrases from another tradition. None of this is contradiction; it is survival. What matters is not the taxonomy of traditions but the way these practices keep bodies alive when nothing else will. Faith, in trauma, becomes bricolage—an improvised architecture of mercy assembled from whatever pieces remain standing.

At the core, the question is not which tradition is "right." The question is: *what helps the nervous system remember safety?* What loosens shame's grip? What allows despair to be named without exile? When seen this way, traditions converge—not because they teach the same words, but because they know the same human body. Breath is breath whether it rises in mosque or synagogue. Tears are tears whether they fall before icons or in meditation halls. Lament is lament whether sung in Hebrew, Arabic, Pali, or the hum of a slave song. Survival recognizes kinship beneath doctrine.

Yet traditions are not neutral. They wound as well as heal. Every lineage carries both medicine and weaponry. Each faith bears its stories of exclusion: sermons wielded to shame depression, rituals turned into tests of worth, communities that banish the struggling in the name of purity. Survivors learn to live with this double edge—finding nourishment in one corner of a tradition while resisting harm in another. A psalm comforts until it is preached as cure-all. A fast disciplines until it disguises avoidance. A chant steadies until silence is mistaken for absence. Integration requires discernment: to ask, *which parts of my tradition give life, and which strip it away?*

A survivor once described sitting in synagogue during Yom Kippur, stomach gnawing from the fast, anxiety amplified by hunger. "I realized I wasn't fasting to return to God," they said. "I was fasting because I didn't know how else to manage my panic." Another spoke of repeating surahs through the night, not in devotion but to drown intrusive thoughts. "It kept me alive," they admitted, "but it left me hollow in the morning." A Buddhist practitioner recalled years of retreat where her depression was misread as attachment: "I almost drowned in that silence," she said. "Later, I learned to use the breath differently—more gently." These are the paradoxes of faith under pressure: where the same practice that sustains can also suffocate, depending on how it's held.

Faith across traditions, then, is not about comparing creeds. It is about honoring how bodies reach for what steadies them. A survivor who kneels on a prayer rug finds the forehead's pressure against the ground easing the panic in the chest. Another lights a candle before an icon and finds the flicker anchoring their breath. Another chants metta phrases until compassion touches their own skin. Another drums in a circle until rhythm pulls grief through muscles too tight to weep. These are not abstractions. They are nervous systems learning regulation through ritual, through rhythm, through repetition.

Clinicians often miss this because training divides "faith" from "treatment." But rituals are embodied interventions. A prayer repeated with steady cadence slows a racing heart as effectively as paced breathing exercises. A psalm recited aloud externalizes despair much like cognitive reframing. A song sung communally co-regulates bodies more powerfully than any worksheet. When therapists dismiss faith, they discard ancestral technologies of regulation. When clergy dismiss clinical care, they risk turning ritual into repression. The healing work is not to choose one over the other but to weave them wisely—each enriching the other.

A group of survivors once gathered for a retreat where each brought a practice from their own faith. One lit candles and read psalms of lament. Another led dhikr, the gentle repetition of divine names. Another offered metta meditation. Another sang a spiritual passed down from enslaved ancestors. At first, the practices clashed—different tones, different cadences, different languages. But as the weekend unfolded, participants began borrowing. The Christian whispered metta phrases. The Muslim hummed the spiritual. The Jew swayed to the chant. The Buddhist joined the psalm reading. No one converted; all expanded. What scholars debate, the body resolved: healing prefers inclusion.

This blending is not dilution—it is translation. In Hindu *bhakti*, devotion is not escape but intimacy. In Sikh *simran*, remembrance of the Name is rhythm restored. In African-diasporic tradition, drumming is not entertainment—it is regulation, calling scattered souls back into sync. Breath, repetition, and remembrance link them all. Across faiths, the sacred keeps time with the heartbeat.

Still, honesty requires caution. Not all borrowing is benign. Appropriation wounds when practices are stripped of lineage or used without reverence. Metta without Buddhist ethics becomes sentimentality. Spirituals sung without memory of enslavement become performance. Sacred phrases used for productivity hacks cheapen the very breath that birthed them. The call is not to flatten differences into interchangeable "tools," but to honor each practice as a living inheritance. Every ritual carries the body of a people—its suffering, its endurance, its survival. To borrow across traditions must be to remember that one is touching holy ground.

does it mean, then, to speak of faith across traditions for mental health? It means acknowledging that no single language is sufficient for despair. Depression exceeds doctrine. Trauma exceeds creed. Panic exceeds liturgy. Only a chorus of voices—a polyphony of prayer, silence, song, and breath—can meet the complexity of pain. A survivor might need the psalmist's lament on Monday, the dhikr's rhythm on Tuesday, the metta's compassion by Friday, the ancestor's drum always. Healing is not unison—it is harmony.

And yet the deeper question remains: *why does ritual heal at all?* Neuroscience offers part of the answer: repetition re-patterns the brain. Predictable sequences regulate the vagus nerve, re-establish safety, and reduce hyperarousal. But ritual also carries memory—ancestral, historical, embodied. To light a candle is not just to anchor breath; it is to remember those who lit candles through centuries of darkness. To kneel is not merely to stabilize posture; it is to join the procession of bodies that have bowed before mystery. Rituals do not simply regulate individuals—they bind generations, stitching the nervous system into a lineage of survival. This is why traditions matter: they remind us we are not inventing endurance alone. We stand in a river of witness.

The good news of faith across traditions is not that they share identical truths, but that each holds a fragment of the whole. The psalmist teaches lament. The Prophet teaches mercy. The Buddha teaches compassion. The ancestors teach resistance. Survivors weave them together into a patchwork strong enough to bear the weight of their lives. It is not seamless; it does not need to be. Wholeness was never the goal—continuity was.

One night in a hospital, a patient who had survived a suicide attempt asked a chaplain, "Do you think God forgives me?" Unsure of the patient's tradition, the chaplain replied, "Do you want me to pray, or to sit?" The patient whispered, "Sit." Nothing doctrinal was resolved. But the silence between them became liturgy. Sometimes faith across traditions looks exactly like that—presence stripped of form, but full of meaning.

The work, finally, is not comparative theology. It is survival. It is learning to borrow breath where it's found, to reclaim rituals once distorted, to weave fragments into a living theology of endurance. Faith across traditions is not neat—it is broken, borrowed, reassembled. But so is recovery. So is resurrection. What makes it holy is not coherence but continuity.

The theological debates still rage—who owns what, whose God speaks where—but the survivor's question remains simpler: *What helps me breathe?* A body in panic does not care if its breath prayer is canonical. A body in despair does not ask if its chant is doctrinally pure. It asks: *Will this keep me alive for one more hour? Will this keep me connected to the living?*

Faith across traditions answers yes—not through uniformity, but through chorus. Each ritual, each rhythm, each word in every tongue, adds one more voice to the song of survival.

Still, we must remember that reverence is protection. To stitch together practices without honoring their origin risks turning sacred survival into a consumer's toolkit. It is possible to light a candle and forget the centuries of women who kept that flame. To chant without remembering the community that breathed those words first. To drum without acknowledging the enslaved whose rhythm carried hope through chains. Memory guards against misuse. Survivors deserve not only tools but lineage—the knowing that their healing participates in something larger, older, communal.

The invitation, then, is not to strip traditions for parts but to receive them as living gifts. When a Christian whispers a Buddhist phrase, let them do it with reverence. When a Muslim joins a Hebrew lament, let them do it as a guest who honors the host. When an atheist lights an ancestral candle, let them name the hands that passed it down. Reverence transforms borrowing into belonging.

And still, the miracle remains: survival happens even within fractured faith. Survivors build altars from scraps—the psalm of their childhood, the chant of their adulthood, the drum of their ancestor, the silence of their therapist. What emerges is not confusion but coherence born of mercy. The patchwork itself becomes the proof: wholeness need not mean uniformity. It means the capacity to live amid fragments that sustain.

A gospel of survival cannot belong to one tradition alone, because despair recognizes none. Panic visits mosque and monastery alike. Depression walks through synagogue and temple, through cathedrals and clinics. If despair is ecumenical, healing must be too. That is why the patchwork works: it mirrors reality.

The analysis ends where faith begins: survival is polyphonic. One voice cannot hold the weight of grief; a chorus can. When survivors borrow across traditions, they do not betray faith—they deepen it. They testify that truth is larger than language, that mercy is multilingual.

And the survivor who endures through this patchwork becomes, in turn, a bearer of witness for others. They become the one who lights the candle for someone else, hums the chant into another's panic, sits in silence when words fail. The patchwork multiplies. Survival ripples outward. The fragments become gospel again—not for the perfect, but for all who live in the fracture.

I paused here, between traditions, and wondered if faith's real work was never conversion but translation.
Every prayer, in every tongue, was trying to say the same thing:
I am still here.

But translation alone is not enough. Something happens after survival—the slow work of re-rooting what was once scattered. After despair, faith asks a harder question: how do we live together again, across wounds, across stories, across the memories of exclusion that still hum beneath our rituals?

Every tradition bears a map of human tenderness, but most of those maps were drawn before trauma was named. Now we live in a world where despair has vocabulary, where neuroscience meets mysticism, and where belonging must be built, not assumed. Faith across traditions must therefore become an act of civic imagination: how do we create sacred spaces where everyone, regardless of creed, can breathe without fear of correction?

At a trauma recovery center in Chicago, the weekly group is a constellation of faiths. On Tuesday evenings they sit in a circle—an imam, a priest, a therapist, a rabbi, a Buddhist nun, and a retired nurse who calls herself "spiritual, but mostly tired." Each week, someone opens with a text from their lineage. A psalm about crying in the night. A verse from the Qur'an about mercy. A teaching from the Dhammapada about impermanence. Then the group breathes together, not to homogenize their languages, but to hear what compassion sounds like when spoken in six accents.

After months of meeting, one participant noticed that the words mattered less than the cadence. "It's like our prayers started listening to each other," she said. "The spaces between them began to sync." This, perhaps, is what healing faith looks like: not erasing distinction, but learning resonance.

Interfaith work at its most honest is not a diplomatic exercise; it is a spiritual experiment in nervous system attunement. When people of faith breathe together, they begin to share regulation. When they share stories of despair, they begin to dismantle the myth of isolation. What unites them is not creed but capacity—the mutual capacity to remain present with pain, to let another's truth exist beside one's own without collapse.

And yet, the wounds of history complicate this intimacy. There are hierarchies of who gets to define "the sacred." The colonial mission that once imposed conversion as salvation still echoes in modern missionary logic. Theologies that justified slavery, genocide, and patriarchy linger as unexamined frameworks inside the very traditions now seeking reconciliation. To speak of "faith across traditions" without acknowledging those histories is to build a bridge over an unhealed grave. The interfaith future must therefore begin with confession: before we can pray together, we must name the damage done in the name of prayer.

Reckoning is itself a form of worship. When a church publicly names the survivors it once silenced, that is repentance in motion. When a mosque invites a queer Muslim to lead dhikr, that is reformation embodied. When a synagogue lights candles for Palestinians as well as Jews, that is covenant renewed. The sacred is not lost—it is redefined by courage.

What makes these moments holy is not their harmony but their honesty. They prove that faith can evolve—not by abandoning its roots, but by deepening them into truth. This is what the mystics of every tradition already knew: the divine is not fragile. It does not shatter when touched by difference. It multiplies.

In this way, trauma survivors are theologians of the future. They know that rupture does not mean absence. They live the paradox that every faith claims: resurrection, return, awakening, repair. They embody the truth that healing, like holiness, is never complete—it is continuous. Their very survival becomes a new form of scripture: not written on parchment, but in breath and scar and endurance.

One might say that we are all mid-translation. Between faiths, between selves, between centuries. The words fail, but the impulse persists: to reach for meaning, to reach for each other.

And so the chapter ends not with a conclusion, but a convergence.

Faith across traditions is not a compromise—it is an ecosystem. It thrives on plurality, reverence, and reciprocity. It invites us to see the divine not as property, but as presence. It teaches that survival, when shared, becomes liturgy. And it reminds us that no matter how far apart our languages begin, the body always knows the same refrain:

Still breathing. Still beloved. Still here.

✦ INTERLUDE
PRAYER WITHOUT BORDER

There are prayers that wear names, and prayers that wander unnamed. Some are written in scripture, some are carved into bone memory, some are only breath.

A mother in Lagos hums the same melody a monk in Kyoto chants at dawn.
A survivor in Detroit whispers "help me"
and an elder in Kathmandu breathes the same plea through another syllable.

Language divides; ache unites.

When you strip the ornament from every ritual,
you find the same movement underneath:
inhale what is unbearable,
exhale what might redeem it.

There is no monopoly on mercy.
No single tongue owns the sacred.
Every cry for wholeness is translation.
Every act of care is theology spoken through touch.

Perhaps what we call faith
is just the world learning to speak its hope in every dialect of pain.
And perhaps what we call survival
is what happens when those dialects finally recognize each other.

Let this be the borderless prayer:
no creed, no flag, no hierarchy—
only breath shared across the distance,
only presence that refuses to end at the skin.

You have crossed into the place
where faith becomes bridge,
and bridge becomes invitation.

CHAPTER FOURTEEN: BRIDGING THE DIVIDE

"The sacred and the clinical were never enemies.
They were two languages trying to describe the same wound."

The first time I saw Dr. Lewis and Reverend Martin work together, I understood why the world keeps trying to build bridges between disciplines that were never meant to be islands.

The hospital chapel wasn't beautiful. The carpet smelled faintly of disinfectant; half the chairs didn't match. A small wooden cross hung crookedly above an old piano beside a framed poster of emergency hotlines. Someone had taped a handwritten sign to the door: *Grief Support — All Are Welcome.*

I'd been invited to observe how the hospital's chaplaincy and behavioral health units were experimenting with "integrated care." The phrase sounded bureaucratic, but the intent was simple: patients were tired of being divided into body and soul.

When the first attendees trickled in—patients, family members, and nurses off-shift—the tension was immediate. A woman in a headscarf sat apart, eyes lowered. An older man in scrubs folded his arms. No one seemed sure if this was going to be a prayer service or a therapy session.

Dr. Lewis, the psychologist, opened with something neither group expected. She didn't cite research or suggest coping skills. She said quietly, "Let's start with a breath. You don't have to believe anything to breathe."

There was a shuffle of hesitation, then compliance. Shoulders lifted, dropped. The air shifted—barely, but enough.

When she finished, Reverend Martin stepped forward, voice soft, deliberate. "In my tradition," he said, "we call that a prayer without words." He didn't quote Scripture. He didn't translate it into theology. He simply named the overlap.

For the next hour, I watched their rhythm—two forms of care taking turns without competing. When Dr. Lewis spoke about the body's stress response, the reverend listened as though he were hearing a psalm. When Reverend Martin spoke about lament, she nodded like a colleague reviewing data. Between them, the room began to breathe differently.

A nurse named Anthony broke the silence. "My brother died last year," he said. "People at church told me God needed another angel. People at work told me to take two days and move on. I don't know which was worse."

Dr. Lewis leaned forward, hands open. "Both tried to erase your pain." Reverend Martin added softly, "Neither stayed long enough to carry it."

Something in the pairing landed. Anthony's face folded. No one filled the silence. Only the low hum of fluorescent light kept time with their breathing.

Later, during debrief, I asked how they planned their sessions.
"We don't," Dr. Lewis said. "We listen for what the room needs."
"And if we can't name it," Reverend Martin added, "we breathe until it names itself."

They laughed—an exhausted, knowing laugh—but beneath it was reverence. Both understood that grief isn't solved by doctrine or diagnosis. It's eased by accompaniment.

Centuries of mistrust had kept their professions apart. Clergy feared psychology would strip the mystery from the soul. Clinicians feared religion would shame patients back into silence. And between them, the wounded kept falling through the cracks.

But here, in this plain chapel that smelled faintly of antiseptic, the wall had a door.

At one point a participant asked, "So which of you is right—does healing come from God or from the brain?"
Dr. Lewis smiled. "Yes."

The room laughed—genuine, startled laughter that carried relief.
Reverend Martin added, "Sometimes the brain is how God reaches the body."

The man blinked. "I've never heard anyone say it like that."

That was the moment I realized what the bridge actually was: translation. Not conversion, not compromise—translation. The act of saying the same truth in two dialects until it makes sense to the listener's nervous system.

After the session ended, the participants lingered. Some exchanged numbers. One woman asked the reverend if it was okay that she hadn't prayed in months. "If you're breathing," he said, "you're already halfway to prayer." Dr. Lewis nodded approval; her language for it would have been self-regulation, but the meaning was the same.

Walking out, I thought about how many people still imagine healing as a choice between two camps—science or spirit, pills or prayer, logic or mystery. The divide feels authoritative because institutions have codified it, but most of us live somewhere in between: swallowing medication with one hand and lighting a candle with the other.

I used to feel guilty about that contradiction, as if coherence were proof of faith. But I've learned that wholeness often sounds like dissonance at first. The body and the soul play in different keys until they learn to harmonize. What bridges them isn't certainty—it's rhythm. It's remembering to breathe while the notes collide.

Dr. Lewis once told me, "Healing happens in relationship, not in isolation."
Reverend Martin later phrased the same thing differently: "Where two or

three gather, presence abides."

Different vocabularies, identical anatomy. Both depend on proximity, breath, voice.

That insight has changed how I listen. When someone tells me about panic or despair, I no longer search for the right verse or diagnosis. I start by slowing my breathing, matching theirs unconsciously. Sometimes that's all it takes for conversation to open. Maybe that's the real integration: less argument, more attunement.

In later months, the hospital expanded the program. They created mixed teams—clinician and chaplain co-facilitators for every ward. The results weren't miraculous, just measurable. Patients stayed in treatment longer. Fewer relapses, fewer readmissions. But the most telling feedback came handwritten on an evaluation form: *"It felt like everyone spoke the same language, even when they didn't."*

I keep thinking about that sentence. Maybe bridging the divide isn't about inventing unity. Maybe it's about trusting that unity already exists beneath our competing grammars.

When the session's memory returns to me—the mismatched chairs, the scent of disinfectant, the half-crooked cross—I remember not the arguments resolved but the breathing synchronized. A roomful of strangers inhaling at once, proof that life still wants to continue.

Weeks later, I found myself walking past that same chapel on the way to another meeting. The door was cracked open. Inside, the chairs had been stacked against the wall. The cross had been rehung straighter this time, though one arm still leaned slightly, as if in quiet defiance of perfection. The faint hum of the HVAC filled the silence. The air smelled like lemon cleaner, sharp but clean.

I stood in the doorway longer than I meant to. I could still feel the residue of that earlier evening—the way the room had changed temperature once everyone settled, the collective quiet that came after tears, the fragile warmth of shared exhale. It struck me how quickly rooms forget their miracles, and how quickly people forget they were part of them.

Hospitals are built on rotation. Staff change shifts, patients move floors, grief disperses into new corridors. But some moments stay imprinted. You can feel them when you enter—a pressure behind the ribs, a whisper in the air. Not haunting exactly, but memory metabolized into space. The room had absorbed something that day. Maybe it wasn't holy in the way churches intend, but it was sacred in the way hospitals need.

I thought about how often we separate sacredness from maintenance. We imagine holiness in candles and choirs but rarely in mop water and quiet repairs. Yet this chapel, with its scuffed linoleum and faint antiseptic tang, had become a temple precisely because it served grief without glamour. The janitor who cleaned it was, in his own way, a keeper of that sanctity—restoring order after revelation, turning chaos back into possibility.

As I walked on, I passed Dr. Lewis in the hallway. She was leaning against the wall, scrolling through patient notes, her coffee going cold beside her. I asked how the new group was going. She smiled tiredly. "It's messy," she said. "But it's good. They keep teaching us how to stay human."

That line stayed with me: *how to stay human.*
It reminded me that bridging disciplines is less about merging ideas and more about remembering what both were made for. Theology asks what it means to be human before God; psychology asks what it means to be human, period. The bridge isn't an intellectual exercise—it's a humanitarian one.

A week later I joined Reverend Martin for coffee at the small diner across the street. He looked out the window at the hospital sign and said, "You know, for all our theories, most of what we do is just making sure people don't feel alone while they heal." He stirred sugar into his mug, watching it dissolve. "Presence," he said, almost to himself, "that's the oldest medicine we have."

I thought about how presence isn't passive. It's an act of endurance. Sitting beside suffering without trying to dominate it requires stamina of its own. The body reacts to another's pain; heart rate spikes, breath shortens, muscles tighten. To stay with someone in distress means regulating your own system enough to keep them safe. Maybe that's why clergy and clinicians both burn out so easily—they mistake proximity for presence, forgetting that presence is work.

The more I observed the partnership between Dr. Lewis and Reverend Martin, the more I noticed their choreography. She often watched body language; he watched tone. She would name anxiety before it spiraled; he would name grace before it disappeared. Together they made space wide enough for contradictions to coexist—guilt and gratitude, faith and frustration. Each left room for the other to speak without fear of correction.

That partnership became my model for how institutions—and people—might heal. Not by agreement, but by rhythm. Integration isn't a merger; it's a conversation where each side retains its accent but learns to listen for harmony.

One afternoon, months later, I attended the funeral of a patient who had joined that very session. Her family asked both Dr. Lewis and Reverend Martin to speak. The sanctuary was fuller than expected—nurses, techs, volunteers, patients, even the janitor from the chapel. Reverend Martin read from the psalms, his voice catching at the line, *"You have collected all my tears in your bottle."* Then Dr. Lewis stepped up to the podium and, without notes, spoke about the brain's capacity for resilience—how mourning, when shared, reshapes neural pathways toward connection. The two speeches should have clashed. Instead, they overlapped like two halves of a benediction: one naming the mystery, the other naming the mechanism.

After the service, the family thanked them both. "You helped her find peace," the daughter said. "I don't know if it was God or therapy, but it worked." They smiled. Neither corrected her. They didn't need to. Peace, in that moment, belonged to everyone.

Driving home that evening, I realized I no longer cared about where one discipline ended and the other began. All the boundaries I once defended—sacred vs. secular, clinical vs. spiritual—felt artificial against the immensity of human need. The divide had never been real, only inherited. The body doesn't distinguish between holy and helpful; it only knows relief.

I started paying attention to smaller bridges afterward. A social worker holding a patient's hand during intake. A rabbi sitting beside a physician reviewing test results. A nurse humming softly while adjusting an IV. Every profession names the gesture differently—rapport, pastoral care, bedside manner—but underneath, it's the same pulse. The same breath. The same declaration that pain will not have the final word.

In my own work, I began practicing what that partnership had taught me: when someone speaks from faith, I listen for emotion; when someone speaks from emotion, I listen for faith. They often arrive braided together anyway. Language becomes less important than the sincerity beneath it.

Sometimes I still replay that evening in the chapel. The room full of strangers inhaling at once. The way grief briefly synchronized us into choir. I used to think of it as a singular miracle, but now I see it as rehearsal. Every community—every family, every ward, every congregation—is capable of that collective breath if it stops policing vocabulary long enough to listen.

A trauma chaplain once told me, "You can't pray someone into regulation. But you can breathe beside them until their body remembers safety." That line has stayed with me longer than any sermon. Presence is often the only theology that works.

I imagine what would happen if seminaries required courses on trauma physiology, or if medical schools taught lament alongside diagnostics. Maybe then we'd have fewer walls to bridge. Maybe then a pastor's hand on a shoulder and a therapist's reminder to breathe would be recognized as the same sacrament, delivered in different tongues.

Even now, when I sit in new circles—boardrooms, classrooms, living rooms—I test the air for that possibility. Does the space invite honesty? Does the rhythm allow breathing? Sometimes yes, sometimes no. But every time I help make it possible, even briefly, I feel that same pulse from the chapel: the heartbeat of integration, the sound of compassion learning its own anatomy.

The world doesn't need more bridges built on theory. It needs people willing to walk across the shaky ones that already exist, holding out a hand to whoever waits on the other side. The plank may creak, the rope may sway, but crossing together is still safer than watching from shore.

Reflection

Integration is less about consensus and more about courage.
Courage to stay in the room when language fails.
Courage to translate hope into whatever vocabulary survival understands.
Courage to let breath be prayer,
to let science be mercy,
to let two different truths hold the same body at once.

And maybe that is the final bridge:
not between faith and medicine,
but between the parts of ourselves
that have been speaking past each other all along.

✦ ECHO FRAGMENT AFTER BRIDGING, WE LEARNED TO STAY

After bridging, we learned to stay.

After the sacred work came the silence—
the strange stillness where miracles looked like maintenance.
Healing no longer shouted its arrival;
it moved quietly through laundry folded, meals made,
mornings faced without ceremony.

Recovery stopped being a story of rising
and became a practice of remaining—
staying home in the body that once felt uninhabitable,
staying kind to the self that once felt impossible to love.

I learned that sustaining faith was harder than finding it.
Hope glittered in the beginning,
but staying demanded something deeper—
a daily tenderness that no audience would applaud.

Recovery did not shimmer; it simmered.
It asked for patience instead of passion,
consistency instead of conquest.

And in that quiet endurance,
I began to recognize the sacred in the ordinary—
the holiness of showing up again tomorrow,
of brushing my teeth when I didn't want to,
of answering a friend's text when isolation beckoned.
Small faith, practiced often, became devotion.

In the end, healing was not a finish line.
It was a homecoming—
a gentle agreement with myself to keep returning.
The miracle was not in crossing the bridge;
it was in deciding to stay.

CHAPTER FIFTEEN: THE PULSE OF BELONGING (REPRISE)

When I first wrote about belonging, I meant the kind that happens between people—the sanctuary that forms when another nervous system meets yours without judgment.
But this belonging is different.

This is the belonging that happens inside the body once it learns to trust its own rhythm again—the architecture of breath, pulse, and sacred safety that can exist even when no one else is in the room.
The first belonging was communal; this one is cellular.
Together, they form the architecture of return.

Belonging is not an idea. It is a pulse. You feel it before you name it—how a room hushes when you enter, how a hand lingers on your shoulder without rushing, how silence expands instead of contracts. Bodies register belonging before the mind interprets it. The nervous system relaxes, the breath deepens, the shoulders unclench. The opposite is just as visceral: the glance that looks away, the chair that is not saved, the sermon that ignores the wound everyone knows is in the room. That pulse—or its absence—can determine survival.

One woman described the first time she entered a church after her hospitalization. She expected whispers, judgment, avoidance. Instead, an elder moved over on the pew and said simply, "I've been saving this seat for you." Nothing else—no questions, no pressure. Her body knew before her mind did: she belonged. Later, she said, "I think that's why I didn't give up again. They left a space, and I filled it." The gesture was not large, but her nervous system took it as gospel.

Belonging is built not only in gestures but in spaces. A synagogue redesigned its sanctuary so that there were chairs at the edges for those who needed easy exits. A mosque added a quiet corner where children with sensory sensitivities could play with soft blocks during prayers. A clinic waiting room placed a sign that read, All emotions are welcome here. Tears are honored. These are not aesthetic decisions; they are theological ones. They proclaim, without saying it, that the body in distress is not a disruption but a participant. Survivors entering these spaces find their hearts pacing less, their breath less jagged. Architecture itself becomes liturgy.

In contrast, exclusion wounds most deeply when it hides behind neutrality. A therapist's office that has no sign of cultural or spiritual recognition tells the client silently: your other identities do not belong here. A congregation that never mentions depression in its prayers tells sufferers: your pain is not fit for liturgy. Survivors notice. Their bodies tense. They learn to mask. Belonging evaporates. Without it, even the most eloquent sermon or the most skilled therapy cannot take root.

A young man who lived with bipolar disorder said he used to sit in the back of his church, leaving before the last hymn. "I thought if I left early, no one would see the shake in my hands." One Sunday, a fellow congregant followed him out, walked beside him without comment, and said as they reached the parking lot, "You don't have to leave alone." He cried in the car afterward, not from shame but from relief. Belonging had caught up with him before he could run from it.

Belonging also pulses in sound. A group of survivors gathered in a trauma-informed choir. Some had never sung in public, ashamed of shaking voices. But when they sang together, the imperfections blended into harmony. One described it as "therapy that sounded like prayer." Another said, "For the first time, I believed my voice could belong." Neuroscience explains it—choral singing synchronizes breathing, releases oxytocin, calms the vagus nerve. But the survivors did not need science to know they had been steadied. The pulse of belonging was in their chests, carried by sound.

Communities often underestimate how small adaptations create large belonging. A church that announces, "If you need to step out for panic or tears, the ushers will guide you back when you're ready," removes shame from leaving. A clinic that allows clients to bring prayer beads or sacred texts into session signals, all of you belongs here. A temple that names depression in its prayers signals that despair is not an exile but part of the human condition. Each gesture becomes a metronome, steadying the pulse of those who would otherwise fracture.

But belonging is not only about what is offered; it is about what is withheld. Spaces that refuse gossip, that resist the urge to diagnose from the pew, that protect the privacy of those who weep—these spaces safeguard belonging. Survivors carry radar for danger. They know instantly if their story will be safe. When they sense judgment, they retreat. When they sense protection, they risk staying. Belonging grows where protection is visible, practiced, and dependable.

One man recounted the moment he returned to group therapy after a relapse. He expected disappointment. Instead, the group leader said, "We saved your chair." That sentence re-anchored him. The group had not erased his absence but preserved his place. He later said, "I didn't know belonging could wait for me." That waiting was not indulgence—it was survival. The pulse of belonging had a memory longer than his relapse.

Even rituals of exclusion can be reclaimed as rituals of belonging. A community once accustomed to whispering about suicide began lighting a candle each service for those lost. The silence was awkward at first. But eventually, the ritual shifted: those grieving felt their loss honored; those surviving felt their pain named; those fearful felt less alone. The candle became a pulse in itself, a heartbeat carried forward each week, declaring that no wound disqualified one from belonging.

Belonging is not sentiment. It is as concrete as oxygen. Survivors who feel they belong are less likely to attempt suicide, more likely to stay in treatment, more likely to return to community after relapse. The data confirms what the body already testifies. The question is not whether belonging matters but whether we will build spaces where its pulse is audible.

The most striking truth is that belonging cannot be faked. A community may speak welcome but still radiate judgment. Survivors know. They know when the hug is forced, when the invitation is conditional, when the silence around their pain is loudest of all. But they also know when welcome is real. They feel it in the unhurried glance, the saved chair, the song sung together. Belonging is not declared; it is enacted.

And when it is enacted, something shifts. Survivors begin to trust not only the community but themselves. The body that once trembled in panic begins to believe it can stand. The mind that once whispered, you are too much, begins to hear, you are enough. The soul that once hid begins to risk showing up again. This is the pulse of belonging—not a metaphor but a rhythm that keeps survivors alive.

Belonging sometimes arrives in places where no one expects it. A psychiatric unit held a weekly community meeting. Most patients dreaded it, convinced it was a bureaucratic exercise. But one week a nurse brought in a guitar, strummed softly, and asked if anyone knew a song. A man who had not spoken in days whispered the name of an old hymn. Slowly, voices joined—fragile, uneven, some off-key, but together. The effect was immediate: shoulders dropped, eye contact returned, even laughter flickered. Later, the man said, "It wasn't the hymn itself. It was that my voice was allowed to matter." That moment stitched the unit together. Belonging pulsed in a room no one thought could hold it.

There was another community where the opposite was true. A woman sat in Bible study and mentioned she was on antidepressants. The leader frowned and said, "We should pray you off those." She left the group and never returned. Months later, she found a secular support group where no one prayed, but everyone listened. "I don't even share their worldview," she said, "but they saved my life because they didn't flinch." That story is not just about exclusion—it is about the body's relentless search for belonging. When one place wounds, the body will keep searching until it finds somewhere to breathe.

Belonging is also shaped by memory. In diasporic traditions, belonging is carried through ancestral songs, foods, and rituals that survived despite oppression. One survivor described how hearing a drumbeat at a community gathering instantly stilled her panic. "It was the sound of home," she said, "even though my body had never been to that home." The drumbeat was not nostalgia; it was nervous system memory passed across generations. For her, belonging did not come from words but from vibration, from being joined to a pulse older than herself.

Children understand belonging instinctively. In one congregation, a boy with autism often paced during services. Some congregants whispered disapproval. But one Sunday, the pastor paused the sermon and said, "His body belongs here as much as mine." The boy's mother wept. The boy kept pacing, but now the pacing was liturgy. His belonging became a signal to everyone else: holiness does not require stillness. Later, families of children with disabilities began joining, drawn by the safety of that declaration. A whole community shifted because one child's pulse was honored instead of silenced.

A therapist told of a patient who could not attend group because crowds triggered her panic. Instead of insisting, the therapist arranged for a small circle in a quiet room. After weeks, the patient asked if she could join the larger group, "just to hear the hum." She discovered she could sit at the edge and feel part of it without being forced into the center. "It felt like being at the table without being on display," she said. That edge space became her sanctuary. Belonging does not demand uniform participation; it demands freedom to remain at the edge without exile.

Sometimes belonging is carried in food. A recovery group held potlucks, and one member always brought stew from her childhood. "I can't pray anymore," she confessed, "but I can cook." Others ate in silence, tasting memory, tasting care. In that stew, theology and therapy met. Belonging had flavor, warmth, aroma. Survivors who had lost words still found themselves fed.

At a vigil for suicide awareness, candles were lit in a public park. People gathered who had never entered therapy, never joined church, never admitted their pain aloud. Yet as the flames multiplied, strangers looked at each other and nodded. One woman whispered, "For the first time, I'm not hiding." Belonging pulsed not in shared doctrine but in shared flame. It was enough.

Communities sometimes mistake belonging for uniformity. They imagine everyone must believe the same, heal the same, speak the same. But real belonging is precisely the opposite—it is the space where difference is carried without fracture. Survivors describe the relief of hearing someone else confess a panic attack, or relapse, or doubt. "It made me feel human again," one said. "Not because they fixed me, but because they were broken too." Belonging is not erasure of wounds; it is companionship in them.

A congregation once invited members to write laments anonymously and place them in a basket. Each week one was read aloud, without names. "I want to die." "I feel abandoned." "I am angry at God." The first time, the room held its breath. But slowly, the practice became normal. People began nodding instead of flinching. Belonging grew, because the most unspeakable truths were now part of the community's liturgy. No one was forced to disclose, but everyone was allowed to be carried.

The body remembers belonging longer than the mind. A man said his most healing moment was not therapy, not prayer, but the time a friend sat beside him in silence for an hour while he cried. "I can't remember what she said," he admitted, "but my body remembers she stayed." This is the essence of belonging: not the eloquence of words but the endurance of presence. Survivors do not need communities to solve their pain; they need them to stay.

And staying is itself a theology. It is the refusal to exile, the commitment to remain when others break. The pulse of belonging is the echo of that theology in flesh—hands that do not release, chairs that do not vanish, songs that do not exclude. When communities live this way, they become more than gatherings. They become safe nervous systems. They become the place where bodies can rest.

The greatest measure of belonging is not attendance but return. Survivors come back to the places that held them without condition. They return not because they are healed, but because they are still welcomed in their unhealed state. That return is testimony: belonging saves.

In a city shelter, a weekly circle formed for residents struggling with both housing instability and mental illness. There were no credentials in the room, only lived experience and a facilitator who had herself survived years of depression. At the start of each gathering, she lit a single candle and said, "This flame means you belong, no matter what story you bring." Over time, people who once avoided eye contact began arriving early, eager to sit close to the candle. One man said, "I didn't think I belonged anywhere. But when I saw the same light waiting for me every week, I started to believe I belonged here." That candle outlasted several facilitators, even changes in the shelter's leadership. It became the heartbeat of the group, a steady pulse that kept survivors tethered when everything else shifted.

Belonging often grows in rituals of return. A woman with a long history of relapse came back to her support group after weeks of silence. She was braced for scolding. Instead, the group leader smiled and said, "We're glad you're here. Your chair missed you." She burst into tears. "I thought you wouldn't want me back." But the chair had waited. That empty seat was a quiet covenant: even in absence, she was not erased. This is the subtle genius of belonging—not only honoring presence but remembering those who are absent, refusing to let absence translate into exile.

There was a small parish that began naming anniversaries of loss out loud during services. "Today we remember that it has been one year since we lost David." "Today we remember that it has been three months since Maria's relapse." At first, the practice unsettled some, who preferred to leave grief in silence. But over time, the community realized these acts of remembering were lifelines. Survivors no longer feared being forgotten. Families no longer feared shame. The act of speaking names aloud became a communal pulse, each remembrance a beat that stitched the fractured body back together.

One therapist told of a client who carried an old hymnal into session each week. She rarely opened it, but it rested on her lap like armor. The therapist asked one day, "Would you like to use it?" She opened to a page and began humming softly. "This was the song my mother sang when I was sick," she explained. "When I hum it here, I feel like she's with me." From then on, the therapist made space for the hymnal, even letting it rest on the desk between them. The client later said, "I didn't just feel like I belonged in therapy. I felt like my whole history belonged." The bridge between belonging in family, faith, and clinic was not theoretical—it was physical, made of paper and song.

Sometimes belonging is secured not by words or rituals, but by architecture itself. A community center repurposed an old gymnasium as a gathering place for those navigating grief. Instead of rows of chairs facing a podium, they placed chairs in a circle with open space in the middle. People came and went, sitting for minutes or hours, sometimes speaking, sometimes not. One man who had lost his son said, "When I sat in that circle, I didn't feel watched. I felt included without pressure." The physical shape of the room carried what words could not—the pulse of belonging built into the geometry of space.

There are failures, of course, and they teach us just as much. A woman joined a church hoping for refuge after her hospitalization. At a potluck, someone asked casually, "You're better now, right?" She never returned. The question was meant kindly, but it reduced her belonging to her recovery status, as if presence required progress. Survivors remember these moments for years, their nervous systems registering exclusion even when minds try to forgive. This is why communities must be vigilant: belonging dies quickly in the presence of conditionality.

But belonging also revives quickly in the presence of honesty. In another congregation, a pastor began his sermon by confessing, "I have struggled with depression. I have taken medication. If you are here today carrying the same, you belong with me." The sanctuary was silent, then filled with tears. People came forward afterward, not for prayer of deliverance but for prayer of solidarity. That honesty widened the circle of belonging, because it told the wounded they were not alone in the pulpit or the pew.

A youth counselor once asked her group to bring objects that made them feel safe. Some brought blankets, others photos, one brought a small carved statue of an ancestor. As each shared, the room filled with a collage of memory. One boy who had never spoken whispered, "I don't have anything." The group leader offered him a pen. "You belong here, so you can use this." He clutched it for the rest of the session. Belonging had found him not in possession but in participation—the gift of being recognized when he thought he had nothing to offer.

Even laughter can pulse with belonging. In a group for trauma survivors, someone made a joke about how awkward panic attacks can be in public. At first, there was hesitation, then the room erupted in laughter. "I thought I was the only one," someone said, gasping through tears. Laughter, too, became liturgy—shared nervous system release, proof that joy was still possible in wounded bodies. That laughter was not trivial; it was a survival beat, the heart finding rhythm again in community.

Belonging is the opposite of invisibility. It says: we see you, we remember you, we will wait with you. And when belonging is consistent, survivors begin to internalize it. They carry the memory of the chair saved, the hymn hummed, the candle lit. These memories become anchors for nights when belonging feels impossible. The nervous system recalls safety even when the mind doubts it. That recall is what keeps many alive.

Communities that master belonging do not erase difference; they hold it tenderly. They make space for the pacing child, the relapsed parent, the grieving elder, the skeptical visitor. They do not demand assimilation; they offer sanctuary. The circle began with silence. A rabbi adjusted his glasses. An imam folded his hands. The chaplain closed her eyes. No one tried to fix anyone. We just breathed together.

We met in a hospital chapel where the fluorescent lights flickered like hesitant faith. Each week, new stories arrived—grief that spoke different languages but shared the same pulse.

A woman recited Psalm 13 in Hebrew; another followed with the Fātiḥa in Arabic; someone whispered a Buddhist metta prayer for those "caught in the storm." By the end, we sat in a hush so thick it felt like fabric.

That's when I understood belonging was never about agreement. It was about co-regulation—the miracle of multiple heartbeats finding tempo.

Afterward, the imam told me, "You don't have to believe alike to breathe alike." I wrote it down, because my body needed to remember what my theology sometimes forgets.

And in that sanctuary, the pulse of belonging becomes steady enough to carry those who cannot yet carry themselves.

A young woman in her twenties spoke of how she had always sat near the back of her church, timing her arrival to avoid greetings and leaving before the final hymn. She described it not as cowardice but as survival. "Every handshake felt like a question: are you normal again? Every hug felt like a test: do you belong here?" After her third hospitalization, she stopped going altogether. Months later, she returned one Sunday and found that the same pew where she had once sat had been draped with a scarf she had left behind long ago. An older member had kept it, waiting for her to come back. "I thought you'd want to see it waiting," the elder said. That scarf became more than fabric. It became the physical testimony that belonging can be stored for us until we are ready to return.

In a secular community center, a mental health support group met weekly around long tables. Attendance fluctuated, stories shifted, but one rule held constant: if someone missed a week, the group saved their seat with a folded paper bearing their name. One man who had attempted suicide later said that seeing his name written down in ink kept him alive. "It meant they expected me back. That I still belonged somewhere." Sometimes belonging pulses in the smallest artifacts—paper, ink, the presumption that your absence is temporary, not final.

There was an older woman who described belonging not in spaces but in seasons. She had lived through cycles of depression, each winter heavier than the last. What kept her tethered, she said, was the memory that spring always brought the same ritual: neighbors planting flowers in the shared courtyard, children laughing in the grass. "Even when I couldn't step outside," she said, "I could hear the sound of belonging through my window." Belonging was not a matter of direct contact but of knowing the world was still pulsing around her, still saving a place for her when she could rejoin.

In one congregation, a group of widows began hosting dinners for anyone who was struggling. They did not ask for diagnoses or backstories. They simply cooked and sat together. "We didn't heal their pain," one widow said, "but we made sure no one ate alone." For the participants, those dinners became sacraments. Food passed hand to hand, grief shared without explanation, silence punctuated by laughter. Belonging was not preached—it was served.

Another story unfolded in a therapy practice that intentionally wove cultural rituals into treatment. A patient from a diasporic community brought incense to each session, lighting it before speaking. "It reminds me I'm not alone," he explained. The therapist allowed the ritual, and soon the scent of smoke became synonymous with safety. Years later, he said, "I healed not because I was fixed, but because I was allowed to bring all of me." Belonging pulsed in the shared air, smoke curling upward as if carrying his fractured body into wholeness.

Sometimes belonging is transmitted by refusal. A survivor once recounted the night he confessed to his friend that he wanted to die. The friend did not panic, did not rush to fix him, did not leave. Instead, the friend said, "You're staying at my place tonight. You belong in my house more than in the dark." The survivor laughed bitterly but agreed. He later said, "I think that night is why I'm still here. He didn't let me disappear." Belonging does not always speak softly; sometimes it is fierce, a refusal to let someone slip away.

Belonging is not always warm. Sometimes it is gritty, stubborn, the insistence of a group that you keep showing up. One recovery circle had a practice: when someone relapsed, they were welcomed back with applause. Not congratulation, but recognition: you made it back, you crossed the gap. A man who returned after a particularly dark stretch said, "I thought they'd be ashamed. Instead, they clapped like I'd won a medal. It was the strangest thing—shame turned into pride. That applause still echoes in me." For him, belonging was the sound of hands striking together, rewriting what return could mean.

One more portrait: a mother who lost her child to suicide returned to the same sanctuary week after week, even when people avoided her eyes. She said she kept coming because of one usher who greeted her each Sunday with the same words: "It's good you're here." No questions, no platitudes, just presence. Years later, she said that greeting was what kept her tethered. Belonging sometimes pulses in repetition, the same phrase offered again and again until the heart believes it.

Theologically, belonging echoes ancient patterns. The psalms are filled with refrains: His steadfast love endures forever. Litanies across traditions repeat: We are one body. We return and are forgiven. These repetitions are not ornamental—they are nervous system regulation, liturgical reassurance that the story will not abandon us. Survivors hear such refrains not only as theology but as survival: a reminder that their fracture is not exile.

Clinically, belonging is measurable. Studies show reduced cortisol levels in those who feel embraced by community, lower relapse rates in groups where inclusion is explicit, longer survival for those with networks that welcome rather than stigmatize. But survivors often put it more simply: "I stayed because someone wanted me here." The science validates what bodies already know: belonging is medicine.

The final image belongs to a survivor who once sat at the edge of a crowded vigil. He carried scars on his arms and silence in his throat. As candles were lit, a stranger offered to hold his flame while he steadied his shaking hands. He whispered later, “I thought I didn’t belong anywhere. But for one night, my light was carried by another.” That act became his anchor. Years later, he still speaks of it: “It wasn’t just a candle. It was proof that I belonged to the living.”

✦ PART FOUR
RECOVERY AS RETURN

CHAPTER SIXTEEN: TIME WE REMEMBERED TOO LOUDLY

Memory is rarely polite. It does not knock before entering, does not wait until the sanctuary is quiet or the therapist's office is ready. It bursts in, loud and insistent, carrying images we thought we had buried. Sometimes it arrives as a smell—incense from a funeral years ago, hospital antiseptic, the stew simmering in the kitchen of a childhood home. Sometimes it comes as sound—screams un relived, hymns once sung at full voice, silence that pressed too hard. Survivors often describe memory not as past but as present, invading without consent. To remember is to be caught in recurrence. And when memory is too loud, it can threaten survival.

Communities, too, wrestle with memory. Congregations remember tragedies unevenly. Some whisper them into oblivion, hoping silence will erase pain. Others canonize them, retelling the story so often that survivors cannot breathe without hearing their grief rehearsed. Both extremes wound. Silence exiles. Repetition suffocates. Survivors stand between the two, longing for a place where memory can be named without weaponized, where remembering does not become captivity.

A man described attending a church service the Sunday after his friend's suicide. He expected lament, honesty, tears. Instead, the pastor offered a vague prayer "for those who are hurting" and moved on. The absence was deafening. "I wanted to stand up and scream his name," the man said, "because it felt like the church had erased him." The memory was loud, but the sanctuary demanded quiet. That clash left him exiled not only from his friend but from his faith.

Another community erred in the opposite direction. Each year on the anniversary of a youth group member's death, the church held a dramatic service with photos, videos, testimonies. At first, it was comforting. But after years, survivors of other losses began to feel invisible. "It was as if only one death mattered," one woman said. "The rest of us were ghosts." Memory, when performed without discernment, can fracture belonging. It amplifies some voices while silencing others. The loudness of one memory can erase the quiet of another.

In Jewish tradition, memory is sacred command—zikaron, remembrance, woven into liturgy and ritual. To forget is to betray covenant. But memory is not merely recitation; it is embodied. The taste of matzah, the sound of chanting, the lighting of candles—these are ways of remembering without drowning. Survivors who grew up in these rhythms describe how ritual allowed them to carry memory without being consumed by it. "I could cry," one woman said, "but I could also eat. I could wail, but I could also rest." Ritual gave memory boundaries, a container strong enough to hold grief.

In diasporic traditions, memory is carried across oceans and centuries. Drums, songs, names whispered at altars become acts of defiance against erasure. Yet even here, survivors speak of the burden of memory that is never allowed to rest. "Every gathering," one man said, "was about struggle. I longed for joy that wasn't tethered to trauma." His words remind us: even sacred memory must allow space for breath. When remembering is relentless, it risks re-wounding the very people it seeks to honor.

Clinically, memory that intrudes too loudly is trauma. Flashbacks, intrusive thoughts, nightmares—these are the nervous system remembering without permission. Therapy seeks to help survivors integrate memory, to quiet it without erasing it. Communities can learn from this: remembrance must be integrated, not imposed. When churches, mosques, or synagogues build rituals of lament, they must do so in ways that steady rather than destabilize. The question is not whether we will remember but how.

One story stands out. A small town lost several teenagers to suicide in a single year. At first, the schools and churches organized constant memorials—candlelight vigils, assemblies, plaques. Parents of survivors began to panic. "Our children are drowning in funerals," one said. "They need hope, not just memory." The community shifted. Instead of annual vigils, they built a community garden. Each plant carried a name, but the garden itself grew food for the living. "Now," a parent said, "our children see memory feed them, not haunt them." It was still remembrance—but it pulsed differently, quieter, life-giving.

Time remembered too loudly can become time that never moves forward. Survivors describe anniversaries as traps, days when memory takes over the body. "Every year," one man said, "my chest tightens on the date of my brother's death, even if I don't look at the calendar. My body remembers louder than my mind." Communities that honor anniversaries wisely can help soften this trap. Lighting a candle, naming the loss, then blessing the survivor into the present can transform the day from endless return into gentle passage. Without that support, anniversaries can fracture time into perpetual mourning.

Theologically, remembering too loudly risks idolizing pain. Communities may unintentionally build shrines to tragedy, forgetting that memory is meant to point toward life. Yet forgetting is no cure. Survivors who are told to "move on" find themselves exiled from their own history. The balance is delicate: to remember truthfully but not destructively, to honor grief without enthroning it. Faith traditions offer hints—laments that end in hope, rituals that close with blessing, fasts that are broken with feasts. These patterns teach us that memory is not static. It moves, it arcs, it releases.

In therapy, survivors often practice grounding when memory intrudes—naming five things they can see, four they can touch, three they can hear. Communities can offer collective grounding too. After one congregation named the suicide of a beloved member in prayer, they followed immediately with communal breathing, the whole sanctuary inhaling and exhaling together. "It steadied me," a survivor said, "to know we could remember without drowning." This is remembrance not as re-traumatization but as nervous system regulation.

And yet, even with rituals, memory resists containment. It surfaces at inconvenient times, in grocery aisles, in subway cars, in classrooms. Survivors often carry private rituals to manage it. One woman carries a smooth stone in her pocket, rubbing it when intrusive thoughts come. "It reminds me that I am here, not there," she says. Communities can normalize such practices by blessing them publicly: "If you need beads, stones, or breath prayers to stay grounded, use them." Belonging means not forcing silence on memory but giving it safe outlets.

The risk of remembering too loudly is not only personal but generational. Children inherit unspoken grief from parents who cannot quiet memory. Trauma studies show how stress echoes in descendants, bodies carrying what minds cannot articulate. Faith communities that refuse to speak of suicide or depression pass the memory anyway—through silence, tension, and shame. But spoken remembrance, carefully held, can break cycles. A rabbi once said, "Our children will inherit our grief either way. Better it be sung than whispered."

In this way, remembering is both danger and gift. When too loud, it drowns. When too quiet, it erases. But when carried with balance—through ritual, community, embodiment—it becomes a steady beat survivors can walk with. The task is not to silence memory but to tune it, to let it join the rhythm of survival instead of overwhelming it.

A mother once told the story of how her son's name was spoken only once in church after his suicide—during the funeral. For years afterward, every mention was avoided. When prayers were said for the sick, for the grieving, for the departed, his name never reappeared. She felt herself grow smaller each week. "I thought if no one remembered him, then I would have to remember twice as hard," she said. "I had to keep his memory loud so he wouldn't vanish." This is what happens when communities silence grief: families are forced to hold memory at unbearable volume, shouting into the void what should have been carried together.

Contrast that with a small group in another city that began each gathering by naming those who had died, whether by suicide, overdose, or illness. The list was long, often painful, but never rushed. One member said, "Hearing the names out loud made me cry every week. But it also made me breathe. I didn't have to scream them inside anymore." The community had absorbed some of the volume, letting survivors rest. Memory had not been erased; it had been shared.

A survivor spoke of how each year, when the date of her brother's death approached, she could feel her body change. Her sleep grew restless, her breath shallow, her appetite vanished. "I thought I was weak," she said, "until a counselor told me my body was remembering even if my mind tried not to." That validation was crucial. It reframed her annual dread not as failure but as memory migration—grief stored in flesh. Naming it did not cure it, but it softened the shame. Communities that make space for such embodied remembrance—lighting candles on anniversaries, blessing the grieving with touch—allow survivors to reframe their bodies not as betrayers but as truth-tellers.

One mosque developed a practice of holding a communal dhikr—a recitation of divine names—for members who had died by suicide. At first, it was controversial. Some worried it would encourage sin. But over time, the practice became a lifeline. "It reminded us that they were still within God's mercy," one participant said. "And it reminded me that I could survive remembering." The rhythmic repetition of names, paired with breath, became a steadying ritual. The pulse of memory aligned with the pulse of prayer, quieting what would otherwise have been overwhelming.

In another community, memory became toxic when it was tied to blame. After a teenager died, adults whispered endlessly about who should have seen the signs, what the family should have done differently. The parents felt suffocated not only by grief but by constant judgment disguised as remembering. "Every time they talked about him, it was really about us," the father said. "We lost him twice—once to death, once to blame." Here is the danger: memory spoken without compassion amplifies pain rather than easing it. Survivors not only carry grief but defend themselves against its weaponization.

And yet memory can heal when communities allow lament to coexist with hope. A church began ending every funeral with the same ritual: after the final hymn, congregants filed past the family, each pressing a hand to their shoulder without words. "The silence was deafening," one widow said, "but it was holy. I felt their memory enter me, steady me." This tactile remembrance did not erase loss. It transformed the memory into communal touch, anchoring her body in belonging even as her mind reeled.

Therapists often speak of "trauma narratives"—helping survivors retell their memories in ways that give coherence instead of chaos. Faith traditions have practiced this for centuries: psalms that recount destruction before ending in hope, laments that turn toward promise. One rabbi explained, "We tell the story every year not because it is bearable, but because it must be borne together." Survivors who encounter this rhythm often describe it as the first-time memory became survivable. It was not the absence of pain but the sharing of it that made the difference.

There was a high school that suffered the death of two students in one semester. At first, the administration forbade mention of suicide, fearing contagion. Students responded by painting the names of their friends on the sidewalks, covering the campus with memory too loud to ignore. Eventually, the school relented and created a remembrance wall, where students could post photos, poems, drawings. "We needed somewhere for our grief to land," one student said. "If they wouldn't give it to us, we had to shout it ourselves." Memory, unacknowledged, always finds a way to speak.

Sometimes the loudest memories come not from words but from absences. A chair left empty at Thanksgiving dinner. A desk unoccupied in a classroom. A birthday uncelebrated. Survivors often describe these absences as the most unbearable form of memory: the quiet so loud it rattles their bones. Communities that notice and name these absences, "we see the chair; we honor the missing"—help soften the roar. Naming the absence allows survivors to breathe in the presence of it. Pretending it is not there only magnifies the silence.

In one family, every year on the anniversary of their daughter's death, they gathered to cook her favorite meal. They did not pray or speak much, but they ate together. "It was our way of letting memory stay at the table," the mother said. That meal became a sacrament of survival. For them, remembering too loudly would have been unbearable—but remembering in flavor, in the quiet clink of dishes, allowed grief to remain without taking over.

A woman described the way her father's cologne haunted her after his death by suicide. She would smell it in hallways, on strangers passing in stores, even when the bottle in his bathroom had long since evaporated. "It was like he was following me," she said. "At first it was comforting. Then it was unbearable." Her therapist helped her see that her body was not betraying her; it was remembering. "Your nervous system holds his scent as a thread to him," the therapist explained.

That reframing allowed her to hold the memory without panic. When she finally poured the last drops of cologne onto her wrists, she wept—not because she wanted to erase him, but because she was ready to let the memory quiet. Communities that honor such embodied memories—through smell, touch, music—help survivors reclaim them as threads, not chains.

A man who had lived through war carried memories that never softened. "Every New Year's Eve, the fireworks sound like gunfire," he said. "My body thinks I'm back in the desert." His mosque responded by inviting veterans to gather during the holiday, offering prayer, food, and quiet. They did not forbid fireworks; they created sanctuaries alongside them. "It gave me a place to go where memory could be loud without destroying me," he said. This is the gift of communal foresight—anticipating the seasons when memory grows loudest and providing shelter.

In one family, grief was remembered through silence at the dinner table. Every mention of their son was avoided. His siblings grew up with an unspoken law: do not speak the name. Decades later, one sister broke it.

She whispered his name into the conversation, and the table froze. Then, slowly, others joined in. They spoke of his laugh, his stubbornness, the way he loved music. The silence cracked open, and memory poured out. "I realized we had all been remembering him too loudly inside ourselves," she said. "It was crushing us. Speaking to him out loud made the memory shareable." For the first time, memory became gentle instead of violent.

A congregation once introduced a "book of names" where members could write down the names of loved ones lost to suicide, depression, or addiction. The book remained on the altar year-round. People flipped through its pages, fingers tracing handwriting. For some, it was a trigger—too loud, too much. For others, it was salvation. "I didn't have to explain my brother," one woman said. "His name was already there." Memory, when given a home, can either overwhelm or sustain. The difference is not in the act itself but in the way it is held—open, without demand, with permission to turn the page when needed.

There was a time when a therapist and a pastor sat together with a grieving family. The pastor wanted to retell the story of the deceased in detail; the therapist warned against re-traumatization. They compromised: the family would write their memories in letters, sealed and placed in a box. Once a year, on the anniversary, the box would be opened. "It gave us rhythm," the mother said. "Memory didn't scream every day. It waited for us." This is how traditions and clinical wisdom can meet—ritualizing memory so it pulses but does not suffocate.

Sometimes memory erupts when least expected. A man walked into a grocery store and saw his friend's favorite cereal. He froze in the aisle, heart racing, grief crashing. Strangers passed by without noticing. Later, he told his therapist, "It felt like my body screamed in public, but no one heard." What he longed for was not advice but recognition. Communities that acknowledge these small eruptions—naming that grief appears in cereal aisles as much as in cemeteries—make survivors feel less alone in their sudden drowning.

Faith traditions often contain wisdom for this. In Buddhist practice, chanting the names of ancestors acknowledges their ongoing presence without clinging. In Jewish yahrzeit rituals, candles are lit annually, not daily, giving grief rhythm and time. In Christian Eucharist, memory is tied to presence—"do this in remembrance of me"—transforming grief into communion. These practices show survivors that memory can be loud without being endless, that it can be honored without destroying.

But memory is not always sacred. Sometimes it becomes spectacle. A community that televises tragedy, repeats names for political ends, or commodifies grief risks exploiting survivors. They are left feeling hollow, their pain used rather than shared. "It felt like they were remembering for themselves, not for us," one father said after his daughter's death became fodder for campaigns. This is why remembrance must be handled with reverence. Without reverence, memory becomes noise. With reverence, it becomes song.

A final portrait: a support group of parents who had all lost children decided to create quilts from their children's clothing. Each patch carried memory, stitched into collective fabric. "I couldn't bear to see his shirt alone in the closet," one mother said. "But sewn into a quilt, it became part of something larger." The quilt was heavy, warm, imperfect. When spread across their laps, it reminded them that memory need not isolation. It can join. It can hold. It can cover.

Time remembered too loudly is not easily quieted. But through ritual, through community, through embodied practices, survivors can learn to let memory become rhythm instead of rupture. The task is not to silence memory but to tune it—to let it pulse in harmony with breath, with community, with life that still continues. When that happens, memory becomes more than a scream. It becomes a hymn.

CHAPTER SEVENTEEN: THE BODY THAT STILL PRAYS

Prayer does not always come from the lips. Sometimes it rises from a trembling hand, sometimes from a back bent beneath the weight of grief, sometimes from the sheer act of waking when the mind begged to stay asleep. Survivors often discover that even when they cannot form words, their bodies are still praying. Breath becomes invocation. Tears become psalms. Silence becomes intercession. What faith traditions have always known, neuroscience now confirms: the body remembers what the soul cannot yet articulate.

A man described how he stopped attending services after his panic attacks worsened. He could not sit through a sermon, could not lift his voice in song. "I thought I had stopped praying," he said. But his therapist pointed out how, every time the anxiety peaked, he placed his hand on his chest and whispered, "Stay with me." That gesture, the therapist explained, was prayer. It was his body's liturgy of survival. The man wept—not because he had been healed, but because he realized prayer had never left him. His body had been carrying it all along.

Communities often misinterpret absence as abandonment. A woman who no longer recited psalms aloud during synagogue services was assumed to have lost her faith. In truth, she swayed silently, tears streaming, letting the rhythm of the community's voices carry her. Later she said, "I was still praying. Just not with words. My body was doing the praying for me." Her survival depended not on eloquence but on permission to be silent within the sound.

Bodies hold ancient postures of prayer: kneeling, bowing, swaying, rocking, chanting. These gestures regulate the nervous system as much as they reach toward the divine. One clinician described watching a patient rock gently during a session. "It looked like prayer," the clinician said. "It was also her body calming itself." To call this survival or prayer is not a contradiction—it is a convergence. The same rocking that soothes trauma echoes the rocking of worshippers at the Western Wall, of mothers holding infants, of monks in meditation. The body does not separate the clinical from the sacred.

The body prays through posture long before the mind forms words. Knees bent, hands open, chest softening—it is a silent sermon of surrender.

Yet bodies also resist prayer when trauma is fresh. Survivors speak of shaking so violently they cannot kneel, of numbness so deep they cannot lift hands. "I felt like a fraud," one man said. "Everyone else was standing to sing. I could barely stand at all." But he later realized that his trembling was itself a kind of prayer: the body speaking what the mouth could not. "I was still reaching," he said. "Just not with words." The sacred is not absent in trembling; sometimes trembling is the most honest liturgy of all.

One community began holding services specifically for those carrying trauma. Instead of sermons, the liturgy was built around breath. The leader would guide the room through slow inhalations, exhalations, pauses. Scriptures were whispered between breaths. Survivors reported that their bodies calmed in ways traditional services never allowed. "It was the first time I felt my panic settle in church," one said. The service did not replace traditional worship but added a space where bodies could pray without strain. Belief did not have to bypass physiology.

Memory, too, is carried in bodies that pray. A woman raised in the Black church said that whenever she rocked in despair, she heard her grandmother's voice humming behind her. "My body hums like hers," she said. "Even when I don't mean to." Her body became archive and altar, carrying ancestral prayers forward. Trauma and faith mingled in muscle memory. Her body kept praying across generations.

And then there is the raw truth: sometimes prayer feels impossible. Survivors describe lying on their backs, staring at ceilings, unable to lift a single word. But even here, the body breathes. Inhale, exhale. The oldest prayer of all. Across traditions, breath is invocation—the divine name whispered in Hebrew vowels, the rhythm of dhikr in Islam, the focus of mindfulness in Buddhism. Even when the mind abandons words, the lungs keep faith. Survivors who notice this often describe it as revelation: "I thought I had stopped praying. But my breath never did."

The body that still prays is not perfect. It stumbles, trembles, doubts. But it persists. Every return to ritual, every survival of panic, every silent sway is testimony: faith is not erased by fracture. It shifts form, lowers volume, changes cadence. Communities that honor this truth—by allowing silence, by blessing tremors, by expanding liturgy beyond words—become sanctuaries where the wounded can still belong.

Prayer is often assumed to be language—a recitation, a petition, a spoken act. But studies in both neuroscience and anthropology suggest something more elemental. The body itself enacts prayer even when words collapse. Andrew Newberg's research in neurotheology has shown that repetitive prayer and meditation alter activity in the prefrontal cortex and calm the amygdala, areas linked to anxiety and trauma. Survivors of depression or panic often discover these effects intuitively: rocking, humming, chanting, bowing. Their bodies rehearse patterns of regulation that traditions have long named as worship. Clinical evidence and liturgical history converge on the same truth: prayer is not confined to the tongue. It pulses through breath, posture, rhythm, muscle.

One striking observation emerges in trauma therapy. Somatic approaches such as Peter Levine's Somatic Experiencing argue that trauma is stored not as narrative but as bodily memory—tight jaws, shallow breath, trembling legs. Survivors may not be able to "pray it away" with words, but their bodies instinctively seek discharge and grounding. When placed in ritual spaces, these movements can be misread as distraction or irreverence. Yet if interpreted differently, they become liturgy. A shaking hand on a pew, a bowed head that will not rise—these are not failures to pray, but the body's own psalms. The task of both communities and clinicians is to recognize them as such.

Theological traditions have always held glimpses of this. The prophet Elijah found God not in earthquake or fire, but in the "sound of sheer silence" (1 Kings 19:12). Silence itself became revelation. Islamic mystics describe dhikr—the remembrance of God through breath and repetition—not only as spiritual discipline but as medicine for the restless heart. In Buddhism, metta meditation regulates the nervous system through compassionate focus, lowering blood pressure and heart rate. In diasporic Black traditions, moans, hums, and embodied swaying in worship have long carried trauma and resilience together. None of these practices rely exclusively on articulate language. They recognize what survivors know: bodies pray even when mouths cannot.

Clinical data reinforces this link. In one study published in the Journal of Behavioral Medicine, individuals who engaged in contemplative prayer showed significant reductions in rumination and depressive symptoms compared to control groups. But survivors often describe it less as clinical improvement than as survival itself. "I couldn't speak to anyone," one man said, "but when I whispered the same word over and over, my body stopped shaking." His experience was less about doctrine than regulation—prayer as physiological anchoring.

Yet we must be honest: not all bodies find prayer safe. Survivors of spiritual abuse may flinch at kneeling, their bodies remembering sermons that weaponized posture against them. Others find that worship songs trigger flashbacks, recalling moments of rejection or shame. Here clinical caution is vital. Judith Herman's landmark work on trauma emphasizes that healing requires safety before memory. For survivors, prayer postures that once felt like safety may now feel like entrapment. Communities must therefore broaden liturgy: standing and sitting, silence and speech, words and no words. Belonging must not depend on uniform posture. The body that prays trembling, or refuses to kneel at all, is still praying.

This raises a deeper theological question: if the body itself prays, then does despair itself become a form of prayer? Survivors often confess, "All I could do was cry." From a purely clinical lens, tears discharge cortisol and oxytocin, regulating stress. From a theological lens, tears have long been read as prayer without words. Augustine wrote of his mother Monica's tears as a river of intercession. Jewish psalms describe "tears in a bottle" as prayers God keeps. In diasporic traditions, keening and wailing are communal acts of survival, voices carrying grief as offering. Despair, embodied honestly, becomes liturgy. This convergence of research and ritual dignifies the body: what medicine calls regulation, faith calls prayer. Both may be right.

There is also evidence that communal embodiment multiplies these effects. Studies of group singing, whether religious or secular, demonstrate synchronized heart rhythms and vagal tone activation—markers of calm and connection. Survivors describe it simply: "When I sang, I didn't feel alone." The body, tuned with others, becomes more than individual survival. It becomes collective liturgy. Clinical measures name it co-regulation; theology names it communion. Survivors often do not care what it is called, only that it steadies them.

One survivor's words illustrate this fusion: "After my attempt, I couldn't say a single prayer. But my church let me sit in the back while they sang. I mouthed the words, sometimes not even that. My therapist later told me my breathing had slowed. I realized I had been prayed for, even by my own lungs." His recovery did not come from eloquence but from embodiment. Communities that recognized this—letting him sit without judgment—gave him space to heal. Prayer was not lost; it had shifted into a lower register, one the body carried until the mind could return.

This convergence demands a shift in how we speak of faith and mental health. Instead of asking, "Do you still pray?" communities and clinicians might ask, "How does your body still carry prayer?" Instead of seeing absence from ritual as abandonment, they might recognize presence in trembling. Instead of dismissing silence as unbelief, they might honor it as one of the oldest liturgies. Research confirms what theology has always hinted: bodies are liturgical archives, carrying survival in every breath.

And perhaps this is the most radical insight: prayer does not stop when words do. Survivors often believe they have lost faith because they cannot speak. But the evidence—clinical and theological—suggests otherwise. The body continues. It rocks, breathes, weeps, hums. It remembers when the mind forgets. This is not weakness. It is persistence. It is the body that still prays.

The human body becomes its own sanctuary when language falters. Survivors often discover this in ways that surprise them. One woman described lying in bed during a depressive episode, unable to rise, unable to eat. She thought she had abandoned faith. Later, her therapist asked her to notice her breath: shallow, but steady. "Your lungs kept you alive," the therapist said. "That was prayer." Her tears fell, not from shame but from recognition. She had been worshiping all along without knowing it—breath as invocation, survival as doxology.

This resonates with research in psychophysiology. Herbert Benson's early work on the "relaxation response" demonstrated how rhythmic breathing and repetition lower blood pressure and cortisol levels.[1] More recent studies link prayerful breathing to vagal tone regulation—the body's ability to return to calm after stress.[2] Survivors who believe they have "failed to pray" may in fact be engaging in the most primal form of prayer their bodies know: breath keeping them tethered when words abandon them.

Survivor testimony often affirms this in lived detail. A man who had been hospitalized for suicidal ideation described how, in his most panicked moments, he would place his hand over his heart. "I thought I was just checking if I was alive," he said. "But later I realized it was prayer. My body was reminding me: I'm still here." Neuroscience calls this interoception—awareness of bodily signals that anchor presence. Theology might call it thanksgiving: a hand pressed to the chest as the simplest hymn.

Yet trauma complicates embodiment. For some, kneeling triggers memories of coercion. Bowing reminds them of sermons that shamed rather than freed. Survivors of spiritual abuse often recoil from postures once taught as sacred. Clinical evidence validates this resistance: trauma is reactivated when the body is forced back into postures linked with harm. Judith Herman's framework insists that safety precedes memory—ritual must adapt rather than retraumatize. For communities, this means welcoming postures of refusal. The one who stays seated during song, the one who cannot lift hands, is not faithless. They are practicing the most courageous form of prayer: honesty in the body.

One survivor put it this way: "Every time the congregation stood, I stayed sitting. At first, I thought I was betraying God. But I realized sitting was the only way I could survive. My body was praying by refusing." This reframing is vital. Refusal can be reverence when it protects the wounded body. Communities that understand this transform shame into sanctuary.

Research on communal prayer further illustrates the power of the body. A study in Social Cognitive and Affective Neuroscience found that synchronized ritual activity—such as chanting, kneeling, or singing—enhanced feelings of social bonding and reduced perceived stress.[5] Survivors describe this experientially: "When I sang with others, I felt my chest loosen. It was as if my body borrowed their calm." Co-regulation becomes liturgy. What therapists call mirror neurons, traditions call shared spirit. The difference in language does not erase the shared truth: bodies heal together.

This is especially evident in diasporic Black traditions, where embodied prayer—moans, shouts, rocking—is not incidental but central. Scholars like theologian James Cone have argued that these embodied practices emerged not just as worship but as survival amid oppression. Clinical research now affirms their wisdom: vocalization and rhythm regulate trauma responses. Survivors who grew up in these traditions often find that even when faith wanes, the body remembers the hum, the sway, the stomp. "I don't believe like I used to," one woman said, "but when the drums start, my body prays anyway."

For others, embodiment is quieter but no less profound. A Buddhist practitioner with PTSD described how focusing on the rise and fall of his abdomen during meditation allowed him to reclaim safety. "It wasn't about belief," he said. "It was about noticing I was still breathing." Research confirms this effect: mindfulness practices reduce amygdala reactivity and enhance prefrontal regulation, calming intrusive memories. The body's prayer—breath, sensation—becomes both clinical intervention and spiritual persistence.

Theologically, this suggests that prayer is not contingent on cognitive assent but on embodied presence. Augustine once wrote, "Our heart is restless until it rests in you." What neuroscience now observes—restlessness settling through rhythm—echoes his insight across centuries. Survivors do not need eloquence; they need rest. And rest itself is prayer.

But what of those who cannot find even breath without fear? Survivors with panic disorders often report that focusing on breath worsens their anxiety. For them, alternative forms of embodied prayer may emerge. One woman with severe anxiety found safety in knitting during church services. "Each stitch was my prayer," she said. "It kept me from bolting." Her therapist affirmed the same: the repetitive motor activity soothed her nervous system. A pastor who noticed her knitting blessed it as liturgy. Communities that expand their imagination to include knitting, walking, drawing, or silence as prayer open doors for those whose bodies cannot conform to traditional forms.

Survivor portraits converge on one truth: the body insists on praying, even when belief falters. Tears, tremors, sighs, refusals—these are all part of the liturgy of survival. Research lends weight, theology lends meaning, but the lived body bears witness most clearly.

The danger is when communities demand uniformity. Survivors forced to kneel when they cannot, or to sing when their throats close, often retreat entirely. They internalize the lie that their fractured bodies disqualify them. The work of bridging faith and mental health requires re-teaching: every body posture is a potential prayer. Clinicians and clergy together must model this truth—by blessing silence, by honoring refusal, by expanding liturgy to include tremor and pause.

This is where the body itself becomes gospel. Survivors testify, without words, that life persists even in fracture. The heart still beats. The lungs still rise and fall. Hands still reach for touch. These gestures are not lesser prayers—they may be the truest. Communities and clinicians who learn to see them as such begin to transform survival into sacrament.

One survivor described how she could no longer fold her hands in prayer. As a child, that posture had been demanded at every mealtime, every bedtime, every Sunday service. After years of living with untreated depression, the simple act of folding hands felt like a trigger—tight, constricting, suffocating. "It felt like shackles," she said. For months she avoided prayer entirely. It was her therapist who reframed the question: What posture feels like freedom to you now? She thought for days, then returned with an answer. "When I spread my arms wide, like I'm making myself bigger than my fear, that feels like prayer." That change was small but profound. It echoed what trauma therapy teaches: the body can reclaim agency by creating new postures of safety. For her, prayer was no longer obligation but expansion—an embodied declaration that she still had room in the world.

Another survivor spoke of tears as her only form of prayer. She had grown up in a tradition that emphasized triumph, victory, and declarations of faith. Tears had been seen as weakness. But after her suicide attempt, she found that tears were all her body could produce. She wept through services, wept through therapy, wept into her pillow. "At first I thought I was failing," she said. "But then I read that tears release stress hormones. My therapist called it regulation. My pastor called it intercession. I decided both could be true." Here research and theology converged: tears as both biochemical relief and sacred petition. Her body had never stopped praying—it had simply chosen a form her childhood church had never named as holy.

The literature supports this reframing. Trauma researchers note that crying activates the parasympathetic nervous system, producing calm after arousal. Faith traditions have long sanctified tears—whether as "the gift of compunction" in Christian mysticism or as lament in Jewish psalms. Communities that bless tears as prayer rather than shame them as weakness create sanctuaries where survivors' bodies can heal. Without this recognition, tears become silenced, and the body's loudest liturgy is forced underground.

There is also the prayer of refusal. A young man who had endured years of sermons that conflated his depression with sin told me, "When I refused to go forward during altar calls, that was my prayer. I was praying: 'God, don't let them erase me again.'" His body stayed rooted in the pew as others streamed forward. Refusal, in his case, was the only way his body could stay true. Clinicians would call this boundary-making, a vital skill for survivors of coercion. Theologians might see in it a form of protest psalm, kin to Israel's cries of How long, O Lord? His refusal was not abandonment but lament embodied.

Communal embodiment intensifies these dynamics. In group therapy, one clinician observed that survivors often synchronize unconsciously—crossing arms at the same time, sighing in unison, mirroring posture. She noted that this co-regulation calmed the room more effectively than any single intervention. Neuroscience confirms this: mirror neuron systems and vagal co-regulation help bodies entrain to safety when gathered. Theologically, this echoes ancient claims that "where two or three are gathered" presence multiplies. What science calls entrainment, faith names communion. For survivors, the experience is simpler: "When they breathed with me, I could breathe again."

It is important to admit that bodies sometimes resist even these softer forms. Survivors of PTSD report that group singing can trigger flashbacks; the swell of voices overwhelms rather than steadies. One woman said, "The hymn felt like shouting in my head." Her therapist advised her to hum quietly instead, to let her body participate at her own scale. She later said, "That hum was my prayer. I didn't need to match them. I just needed to stay." Theological communities must hear this: uniform participation is not a sign of faithfulness. Survival itself is.

A particularly moving story comes from a hospital chaplain who sat with a patient in the ICU. The patient was intubated, unable to speak, eyes half-closed. The chaplain began to pray aloud, but the patient shook their head. Then, slowly, they lifted one hand, pressing it weakly against the bedrail in rhythm with the chaplain's words. "I realized their body was doing the praying," the chaplain later reflected. "It was not my voice they needed—it was their own presence." This scene reveals what both clinical and theological perspectives can miss: prayer is not measured in words spoken, but in life still pulsing, however faintly.

The research on postures reinforces this claim. Studies show that kneeling and bowing lower cortisol and foster parasympathetic dominance. Yet for survivors, the meaning of these postures depends on context. The same kneeling that calms one body can retraumatize another. This is why communities must broaden their theology: the body that still prays may not kneel at all. It may recline. It may rock. It may simply breathe. The holiness lies not in the form but in the survival.

The chapter cannot end without considering lament. Survivors frequently tell of nights when they screamed into pillows, fists pounding against walls, convinced they had lost all faith. But the psalms are full of such cries: My God, my God, why have you forsaken me? Clinical psychology would describe this as externalizing emotion, releasing pressure that might otherwise implode. Theology sees it as faithful protest, an act of intimacy with God who can bear our rage. One survivor later said, "When I screamed, I thought I was cursing. But maybe I was praying all along." Both clinical and theological lenses affirm her truth: her body's loudest protest was also her deepest liturgy.

The body that still prays is not a metaphor. It is a clinical reality, a theological truth, and a survivor's testimony.

Bodies pray in tears that never reach the altar, in silence that no hymnbook records. They pray through rocking in the dark, through refusal to rise, through trembling that holds no words. They pray through breath—the most ancient liturgy of all—when language has failed and willpower has dissolved. Every muscle remembers something holy: the body as its own chapel, the nervous system as its own priest.

In trauma work, clinicians call this regulation and release. In faith traditions, it is surrender. In both languages, it means the same thing: the body finding its way back to safety. Tremors, sighs, tears, the loosening of the jaw—these are not just symptoms; they are sacraments. When therapists and theologians both learn to see them as such, healing no longer divides science from spirit.

The body that still prays is not only the one kneeling in a sanctuary but also the one curled on a couch during therapy, the one clutching medication at midnight, the one whispering "please" to no one in particular. The liturgy of survival happens everywhere—between heartbeat and breath, between holding on and letting go.

When faith communities recognize this, they stop measuring prayer by words spoken or hands raised. They begin to measure by breath that continues, by bodies that stay, by the simple miracle of a pulse that endures. When clinicians recognize it, they stop isolating physiology from meaning. They begin to see that the body's shaking is not weakness but testimony—the nervous system bearing witness to what it survived.

The task is not to teach survivors to pray again.
It is to reveal that they never stopped.

Their bodies have been praying all along—louder than words, deeper than doctrine, longer than any creed could hold. The tears were prayers. The silence was prayer. The breath that refused to stop was prayer.

To honor this is to honor survival.
To honor survival is, finally, to honor God.
And when the body knows it is heard—by therapist, by community, by the sacred itself—it exhales.
That exhale is the first and oldest prayer.

CHAPTER EIGHTEEN: THE ONES WHO KEPT SHOWING UP

Survival is rarely solitary. When survivors speak of what held them through their darkest nights, the refrain is almost always the same: someone kept showing up. A friend who texted without expecting a reply. A nurse who sat at the bedside long after the shift ended. A pastor who knocked at the door and waited in silence. A therapist who said, "I'll be here next week, whether you speak or not." Presence itself became salvation.

Research on suicide prevention underscores this truth. Thomas Joiner's interpersonal theory of suicide identifies thwarted belongingness—the belief that one is a burden and disconnected—as a core driver of suicidal desire. The antidote is not abstract reassurance but tangible presence. Survivors often describe it less clinically: "She didn't give up on me." Presence disrupts the lie that disappearance would go unnoticed. To be shown up for is to be reminded: you still matter in the fabric of the world.

One man told the story of how, after his hospitalization, he expected friends to drift away. Many did. But one colleague brought him coffee every Thursday morning, no matter how awkward the silence, no matter how many times he refused conversation. "I hated it at first," he admitted. "But by the sixth week, I realized he wasn't going to stop. That's when I decided maybe I wouldn't stop either." Clinicians call this consistency. Theological traditions call it covenant. Survivors call it survival.

The psalms echo this need: "Even though I walk through the valley of the shadow of death, you are with me." Presence is the refrain. Theologians have long noted that divine comfort is not described as explanation but as accompaniment. Survivors echo this in their own words: "I didn't need answers. I needed someone in the room." This is where theology and therapy converge. Presence does not erase pain, but it interrupts despair.

In clinical practice, "continuity of care" is a protective factor. A 2014 study in Psychiatric Services found that patients with consistent providers after psychiatric hospitalization had significantly lower rates of suicide attempts than those with fragmented care. The science validates what survivors already know: healing requires people who stay. But what is most striking is how often survivors describe this not in medical terms but in sacred ones. "My therapist became my confessor," one said. "She didn't absolve me, but she refused to leave."

Faith communities have their own versions of this continuity. In Jewish tradition, shiva requires neighbors to sit with the grieving for seven days, often in silence. The act is not to fix but to remain. Survivors of loss describe this as unbearable and necessary. "I wanted everyone to go away," one woman said. "But if they had, I think I would have shattered." Silence was suffocating, but abandonment would have been worse. Presence, even when unwanted, carried her through.

Another survivor spoke of how her imam came to her apartment week after week, bringing no sermon, only sitting quietly with tea. "I kept thinking he would stop when I didn't talk," she said. "But he stayed. It was the first time I thought maybe God stayed too." The theology was not in the words spoken but in the persistence of the knock at the door.

Communities often underestimate how radical this simple act is. In a culture of quick fixes and short attention spans, to keep showing up is countercultural. It mirrors the persistence of grace—unearned, unshaken, unrelenting. When churches or clinics embody this, they become more than institutions. They become places where despair cannot isolate unchecked.

Of course, presence is costly. Caregivers often burn out, friends withdraw, congregations falter. Research on compassion fatigue shows that those who continually bear witness to trauma are at risk themselves. Yet presence does not always require extraordinary effort. Sometimes it is sustained through small gestures: a text, a meal, a seat saved in the sanctuary. Survivors rarely remember eloquent speeches; they remember chairs, blankets, and casseroles. "It wasn't the prayer they prayed for me," one man said. "It was the soup they left at my door."

There are also failures—times when communities proclaim love but vanish in crisis. Survivors of depression frequently describe the silence that followed disclosure. One woman said, "Everyone prayed for me the day I shared. The next week, no one called." Research confirms the danger: perceived abandonment after disclosure increases risk of relapse. Theology confirms it too: James warns against blessing the hungry without feeding them. To proclaim without presence is betrayal. Survivors know the difference.

And yet, even when institutions fail, individuals sometimes embody presence in ways that save lives. A nurse told of a patient who whispered, "Why are you still here?" as she held his hand through the night. "Because you are," she replied. Later, he credited that sentence with his decision to stay alive. Clinicians call this therapeutic alliance. Survivors call it miracle. The body registers it simply: I was not left alone.

Presence also changes memory. Survivors often say that what they recall most vividly about their darkest nights is not the pain but the person who entered it. "When I think of the overdose," one man said, "I don't remember the pills. I remember my roommate knocking on the door and refusing to leave until I opened it." His body remembers not just despair but rescue. Memory is rewritten when presence interrupts absence.

Theologically, this is incarnation—the holy refusing to remain distant. Clinically, it is attachment—the nervous system calmed by another's regulation. Survivors experience it less conceptually: "She breathed, so I breathed." This is the essence of showing up. Not curing, not solving, not explaining. Breathing alongside.

A teenager once said, "I didn't want to be saved. I wanted to be noticed." His suicide note had been written, his plan rehearsed, but the night before, his coach texted, "Practice tomorrow—don't forget your shoes." He told his therapist later, "That stupid text ruined my plan. Someone expected me there." The research on suicide prevention validates this: perceived expectation of presence—someone waiting for you—reduces risk even in high-crisis states. His survival was not born of eloquence or intervention, but of ordinary persistence. The theology of covenant finds its echo here: salvation carried in small, relentless reminders that life is not lived in isolation.

One woman described her first months after discharge from a psychiatric unit. She lived alone and had grown convinced that if she disappeared, no one would know. A friend decided to call her every night at the same time, even if only for two minutes. Sometimes she answered. Sometimes she let it ring. But the calls never stopped. "It was the ringing that kept me alive," she said. "I didn't even have to pick up. I just had to know someone would dial again tomorrow." Research on attachment repair shows that reliability—more than intensity—rebuilds trust in survivors. Her friend had no training, no specialized language, but she embodied the deepest theology of all: love that refuses to vanish.

Communities often miss this ordinariness. They imagine showing up means dramatic interventions or polished words. But survivors speak differently. One man recalled the casserole that appeared on his porch after his son's death: "I don't even like casseroles. But I ate every bite. It tasted like I wasn't forgotten." His testimony matches findings in grief psychology: tangible acts of care—food, transport, presence—buffer against despair more effectively than abstract platitudes. Sacred presence is often measured in spoons, not sermons.

There is also the mystery of silent accompaniment. A chaplain told of sitting beside a mother in the NICU as her infant died. Neither spoke. Hours later, the mother whispered, "I could breathe because you were breathing next to me." Neuroscience explains this as co-regulation: one nervous system steadying another through proximity. Theology describes it as Emmanuel—God with us. Survivors live it as relief: not being alone in the unbearable. Silence, when shared, is never empty.

But showing up is not without danger. Survivors can feel smothered when presence becomes surveillance. One young adult who battled self-harm said, "When my church friends checked on me every hour, I felt like an experiment. It made me hide more." Research warns of this too: intrusive or controlling presence can increase shame and withdrawal. Here theology can guide: presence must imitate divine patience, not domination. Staying must feel like freedom, not captivity.

What distinguishes life-giving presence from smothering presence is humility. Survivors consistently describe the difference: "She asked how she could help. He told me what to do." "They sat with me. They interrogated me." The ones who saved them were the ones who did not presume. Theologically, this is kenosis—self-emptying, the refusal to control. Clinically, it is trauma-informed care: letting survivors set the pace. Survivors experience it simply: "They let me breathe."

One man who relapsed into drinking after years of sobriety said, "I thought everyone would give up on me." But his sponsor knocked at his door the next morning with two cups of coffee. "I didn't even drink it," he said. "But I held the cup. It meant I still mattered." Research on relapse recovery affirms this: continuity of relationship predicts long-term resilience better than absence of relapse. The theology is clear too: return is not disqualification. The prodigal was welcomed because the father kept showing up on the road. Presence is the only soil in which return can root.

And there are those who show up across generations. A grandmother who had lived through segregation told her granddaughter, "You keep breathing because I kept breathing." The girl later said, "Her presence was history walking into my hospital room." Diasporic traditions have long framed presence as ancestral covenant: the dead showing up in the living, survival carried forward by memory. Clinical language would call this intergenerational resilience. Survivors call it inheritance.

Presence alters memory itself. A woman who had attempted suicide said the only image she recalled clearly was her friend's hand gripping hers as the ambulance arrived. "That's the only reason I believe God still holds me," she said. Traumatic memory often imprints strongest at the point of rescue—the nervous system associating safety with the face or hand that entered the chaos. Theology sees this as sacrament: God revealed in human hands.

The cost of showing up is real. Friends leave drained. Pastors burn out. Clinicians carry vicarious trauma. Research on compassion fatigue confirms that without support, those who stay risk collapse themselves. Yet survivors insist the risk is worth it: "If she hadn't stayed, I wouldn't be here to tell you this." Theology affirms the paradox: to bear one another's burdens is costly, but it fulfills the law of love. Communities that sustain caregivers—rotating visits, offering respite—make showing up sustainable instead of heroic.

Perhaps the deepest testimony comes from those who failed to show up but tried again. A father admitted that after his daughter's disclosure, he froze and left the room. "I thought I had ruined everything," he said. But he returned the next morning, sat at the kitchen table, and whispered, "I don't know what to say, but I'm here." She later told him that sentence saved her. Research supports this too: repair after rupture often matters more than perfection. Theology calls it forgiveness. Survivors call it mercy.

The ones who keep showing up are not flawless. They fumble, they fail, they misstep. But they return. Again and again. In their return lies the deepest healing.

Clinical frameworks confirm what the sacred already knew: presence rewires despair. Neural pathways—once carved by trauma—can be softened and reshaped by steady relationship, by consistency, by kindness that does not withdraw. Presence retrains the nervous system to believe safety is possible again.

Theological traditions echo this truth in another tongue. Presence is incarnation—the closest we ever come to embodying love divine. To sit beside someone in silence, to offer a meal, to listen without fixing—these are not small gestures. They are sacraments of survival.

Survivors testify to it in the language of lived grace. Presence—ordinary, patient, sometimes awkward—is what kept them breathing when nothing else could. No doctrine. No brilliance. Just a hand that stayed, a body that did not leave.

The task is not to show up perfectly. It is to show up again. And again. And again. Until presence itself becomes the liturgy that keeps the wounded alive. Until repetition becomes resurrection. Until the act of returning becomes the proof that love still works.

This is the holy rhythm of endurance: presence as prayer, persistence as praise.

CHAPTER NINETEEN: THE UNNAMED PSALMS

There are cries too raw to fit in hymnals. The psalms we inherited give us a language of lament—How long, O Lord? Why have you forsaken me?—but even these do not contain all the tones of anguish survivors carry. Some pain resists melody. Some prayers refuse punctuation. These are the unnamed psalms, written not in words but in scars, in midnight sobs, in the silence that follows a scream no one heard.

A man who lived with bipolar disorder once said, "I stopped praying because my prayers no longer sounded like prayers. They sounded like rage. They sounded like despair." His pastor told him to "speak life," but the words felt dishonest. Later, in group therapy, he discovered that another patient had been crying the same words into the dark: "God, I hate this. God, I hate you. Don't leave me." He realized then that his anger had always been prayer—it was simply an unnamed psalm.

Psychologists studying expressive writing have found that unfiltered lament—raw, unedited articulation of despair—reduces intrusive symptoms and lowers physiological stress.[1] Survivors who give voice to their rage are not failing in faith; they are engaging in a practice that rewires the nervous system toward regulation. Yet religious communities often silence this form of expression. They call it blasphemy, when it is in fact survival. Theological traditions of lament insist otherwise: Israel's psalmists screamed their accusations at God and recorded them in sacred scripture. To weep in rage is to join their chorus.

One survivor of childhood abuse wrote prayers in her journal she would never read aloud: "If you are God, why did you let it happen?" She feared these words damned her. Years later, her therapist handed her Psalm 88, the only psalm that ends without resolution, closing not on hope but on darkness. "Darkness is my closest friend." "I thought I was the only one," she whispered. That night she copied the psalm into her journal and beneath it wrote: "My psalm belongs here." Clinical research on validation echoes this moment: when a survivor discovers that their experience has precedent—whether in scripture or science—the shame of isolation loosens its grip.[2] The unnamed psalms become spaces of solidarity.

Communities that embrace lament become sanctuaries for the unnamed. One rabbi described how his synagogue began including moments of silence during services, inviting congregants to cry out internally in whatever words they had. He said, "Some later told me they cursed God in those moments. I told them, good. You are in the psalms now." This permission changed lives. Survivors who had withdrawn returned, no longer feeling exiled by their despair. Silence, once unbearable, became collective liturgy.

Research on collective grieving supports this. A 2020 study in Frontiers in Psychology found that communal rituals of lament—funerals, vigils, public crying—produce measurable decreases in cortisol and increases in oxytocin, deepening trust and solidarity.[3] When survivors lament together, their bodies heal in tandem. Faith traditions have practiced this for millennia—wailing walls, dirges, keening. Modern psychology now affirms what ancient rituals always knew: grief voiced communally is less likely to consume in isolation.

One of the most powerful unnamed psalms I've encountered came from a veteran who lost three friends to suicide. He could not pray in church. The words of triumph felt false. But one night, sitting alone, he screamed until he lost his voice. The next morning, he whispered: "That was my psalm." Later he told his therapist, "I don't think God hated it. I think God finally heard me." Survivors often find that lament brings not distance but intimacy—when all pretenses fall away, what remains is naked truth, and naked truth is where healing begins.

The danger comes when communities rush to resolve lament. Survivors describe how, after voicing despair, someone immediately responded with, "But God is good," or "But you'll get through this." These phrases, though well-meaning, shut down the psalm mid-verse. They erase the sacredness of the cry. Research on invalidation confirms this: responses that minimize emotion increase distress and reinforce isolation.[4] Theological parallels are clear: Job's comforters did more harm with their explanations than good with their presence. Survivors do not need answers. They need their unnamed psalms to be heard.

One woman with postpartum depression described how she began humming dissonant tones during late-night feedings. They were not songs, not melodies, but guttural moans that matched the exhaustion in her bones. "It felt like I was breaking rules," she said. "But it was the only sound that felt true." She later learned about lament traditions in African diasporic rituals, where moans and wails are honored as sacred utterance. The clinical world might call it vocal discharge. Theology calls it groaning too deep for words. For her, it was survival sound.

What makes these unnamed psalms powerful is their refusal of closure. Survivors often speak of needing to leave their cries unresolved. "If you tell me it will get better, I shut down," one said. "I need to leave it hanging in the air, unanswered." This aligns with trauma recovery theory: healing does not demand resolution but safe space for ongoing expression.[5] The psalms themselves model this—many end unresolved, refusing to tie suffering into neat packages. Survivors need communities that can hold that ambiguity without flinching.

The unnamed psalms also expand theology itself. If scripture records cries of forsakenness, then despair is not outside faith—it is part of it. Survivors embody this when they refuse to sanitize their stories. One man in recovery wrote his own psalm on the back of a napkin: "I want to die. I want to live. Both are true." He never published it, never shared it widely. But that napkin, crumpled and stained, became his altar.

A college student told me about the first time she tried to pray after her suicide attempt. "The words wouldn't come," she said. "I sat there and opened my mouth, but it was just air." She thought she had failed. Weeks later, she stumbled across Romans 8:26: "The Spirit intercedes with groans too deep for words." She began sitting in silence each night, letting her breath be the only sound. "I didn't think of it as prayer," she said, "but my body kept showing up." This is what researchers on trauma call embodied persistence—the nervous system continuing to seek regulation even when language has collapsed. Her silence became an unnamed psalm, a survival hymn without lyrics.

Another survivor, an older man who had battled alcoholism for decades, described writing unsent letters to God during his relapses. "They were full of curses," he admitted. "I told God I hated Him. I told Him I wanted Him to leave me alone." He crumpled the letters and threw them in the trash. Years later, in recovery, he found one tucked inside an old Bible. He read it aloud to his support group, trembling. "I thought it was blasphemy," he said. "They told me it was honesty. They told me it was prayer." His letters echo clinical research on expressive writing, which shows that unfiltered, even hostile articulation of emotion reduces recurrence of intrusive thoughts and supports long-term recovery. Theology, when it catches up, recognizes this as psalmic truth: the cries of David were no less sacred when he accused God of abandonment.

A young mother with postpartum depression described how she began humming to her infant in the dark. "I didn't know any lullabies," she said. "So I just hummed the sound of my exhaustion." She later learned that her moaning hums soothed not only her baby but her own nervous system, activating her vagus nerve and lowering her heart rate. "I thought I was failing as a mother," she confessed. "But I realized I was singing my own psalm." In diasporic traditions, these kinds of wails are not failures but sacred utterances—the moan, the hum, the chant that carries sorrow into collective survival. When clinical evidence meets cultural practice, the unnamed psalms gain new legitimacy: lament is physiology, lament is heritage, lament is prayer.

Communal expressions of lament make this even more visible. In Ghana, women lead funerals with dirges—wailing songs that name the dead and the pain of loss. Anthropologists have found that these dirges regulate grief by giving collective form to individual sorrow. Survivors who witness such rituals often carry them back into personal life: a whispered dirge in a kitchen while washing dishes, a moan carried in traffic. One Ghanaian immigrant woman said, "When I cry alone, I know my mother cried the same way. I am not the first. My cry belongs to the chorus." The unnamed psalms are never truly solitary—they are fragments of ancestral lament still echoing in modern bodies.

One veteran described his unnamed psalm as silence. "After the war, I couldn't talk about it. People asked, and I just shut down. My silence was my psalm." At first, he believed this made him faithless. Later, in therapy, he discovered that silence can itself be ritual. Studies of contemplative practices confirm that silence activates similar neural pathways as meditative prayer, reducing amygdala reactivity and increasing tolerance of distress. His silence was not absence. It was sacred protest, too deep for words.

Faith communities sometimes stumble here. They want psalms to resolve into hope, to end with "but I will trust." Survivors resist that neatness. One woman said, "If you make me say it's going to get better, I'll stop talking." This matches research on emotional invalidation: survivors who are pressured into false positivity show increased shame and disengagement. Communities that allow lament to remain unresolved provide a different kind of sanctuary—one where honesty is more sacred than resolution.

In a small church, a pastor once invited congregants to write their unnamed prayers on slips of paper and nail them to a wooden cross. Some wrote pleas, some wrote curses, some wrote only scribbles. One survivor wrote nothing at all—just tore the paper and nailed the blank piece. "That was my psalm," she said. "Blankness." Theologically, this echoes apophatic traditions, where silence and absence speak louder than words. Clinically, it mirrors trauma's truth: sometimes experience resists narrative. Yet the act of naming even blankness in community can be healing.

Research on communal lament during national tragedies shows that public rituals—candlelight vigils, moments of silence, marches—reduce perceived isolation and foster post-traumatic growth. Survivors often describe these as the only spaces where their grief felt both seen and shared. One man whose brother died by suicide said, "At the vigil, when everyone cried together, I finally felt like I wasn't crazy. My cry was normal." His unnamed psalm found harmony in the cries of others.

There are also unnamed psalms in the body. A woman who had been mute during childhood abuse said that whenever she entered church as an adult, her hands trembled uncontrollably. At first, she thought this was sin. Later, her therapist told her: "Your body is praying what your voice cannot." Neuroscience confirms that trauma stored in the body often emerges as tremors when safety is near. Theologically, this reframes trembling as testimony: the body keeps the psalms when the voice cannot.

Not all unnamed psalms are cries. Some are refusals. A man with chronic depression said, "My psalm is staying in bed and not dying today. That's it. That's the prayer." Communities often miss this, insisting that prayer must be upward motion—kneeling, lifting hands. But the theology of incarnation says otherwise: God meets us in the body, wherever it lies. Clinical research on micro-movements of survival—getting out of bed, drinking water, breathing—confirms their significance in recovery.[9] To bless these acts as prayer is to sanctify survival itself.

The unnamed psalms are not failures of faith. They are faith at its rawest—the body demanding witness when doctrine feels hollow. Survivors who voice them join a lineage older than scripture itself, stretching through every tradition that has ever dared to name grief aloud. Their cries do not need to resolve. Their tears do not need translation. They are already holy.

Every generation of the wounded has its own hymnal of ache. Sometimes it is written in the slow breath of those who refused to give up. Sometimes it sounds like silence that refuses to disappear. In clinical language, we might call it *somatic discharge*, *nervous system recalibration*, or *affective release*. In sacred language, it is the same thing we've always called it—lament.

To hold space for the unnamed psalms is to proclaim that despair belongs in the sanctuary, that anger is not exile, that silence can be sacred, that screaming into the dark can itself be prayer.

When communities learn this, they stop silencing survival. They stop turning pain into shame. They stop demanding that joy arrive on schedule. They begin to hear God in the cries they once called blasphemy, in the shaking hands that reach without certainty, in the trembling voice that says, *I still want to live.*

Clinicians have long observed that naming the wound—the act of narrating pain aloud—reduces its hold on the body. Neuroscientists call it integration; mystics call it confession. Both recognize that healing begins when what was buried finds breath.

In therapy rooms and temple basements, in group circles and whispered confessions, survivors are rediscovering what ancient faiths never truly forgot: that lament is a communal act, not a private failure. When the heart cannot hold its own grief, another voice nearby says, *me too.* And something shifts—slowly, quietly, but unmistakably.

We have mistaken noise for aliveness, certainty for devotion. But perhaps holiness is what remains after both have dissolved. The unnamed psalm, whispered through tears, becomes the truest language of survival: not theology, but presence; not belief, but breath.

When survivors believe this—when they no longer fear that their lament disqualifies them—they discover that lament is not the absence of faith, but its evolution. It is faith stripped of performance, faith that no longer bargains with pain, faith that has learned to sit still inside the wound and still call it sacred.

There is no perfection here. Only presence.
There is no resolution. Only rhythm.
There is no triumphant chorus. Only breath continuing where silence once lived.

This, too, is praise.

The praise of survival.
The psalm without a name.

Liturgical Echo:

Inhale: We are still here.
Exhale: We are still holy.

✦ INTERLUDE IV *MICRO INTERLUDE: BREATH IN THE JAW*

Unclench.

Release the tongue from the roof of the mouth.

Let the exhale tremble.

The jaw is one of the body's oldest shields. It remembers arguments we never finished, grief we never spoke, prayers we swallowed because language was too dangerous. When it loosens, the body begins to believe it is safe again.

I used to grind my teeth during prayer. It wasn't anger—it was containment. The sound of enamel pressing against enamel was the only way I knew to keep from crying.

Now I understand: the body prays even when the mouth doesn't.
The hinge of the jaw, the curve of the spine, the quiet rhythm of the diaphragm—each becomes a sanctuary of movement. As the jaw releases, the shoulders drop. The nervous system exhales. The soul, too, learns to unclench.

Count four beats in, six beats out.
Let the breath fall all the way to the base of the spine.

Imagine the inhale as trust returning, the exhale as surrender.

Do not rush.

Healing never hurries. It listens. It waits for the body to believe the world again.

In this stillness, the smallest gestures are sacred: the softening of the jaw, the steady breath, the moment you realize you are no longer bracing against life.

CHAPTER TWENTY: THE LIGHT THAT DIDN'T LEAVE

"What remains after the breaking is not perfection.
It's the light that stayed long enough to prove we were never alone."

The first time the fog began to lift, it startled me.
Not because I felt joy—joy was still distant—but because the absence of pain felt suspicious. I remember sitting on the edge of my bed, blinds half-open, watching late-afternoon sunlight drag itself across the wall. For months, I had measured time by darkness: morning shadows, evening collapse, endless nights where breath itself sounded mechanical. That day, the light reached the corner of the room and didn't retract. It lingered, unbothered by whether I noticed.

I didn't smile. I just watched. The stillness felt foreign, almost indecent. I was so accustomed to managing collapse that calm registered as danger. My hands twitched for something to fix. My body, trained for emergency, didn't know what to do with survival.

Healing rarely announces itself. It arrives disguised as boredom.

You wake up one morning and realize the thoughts that used to scream are now murmuring. You check for despair the way a recovering patient checks for fever—cautious, half-expecting relapse. And when none appears, you wonder if you're betraying the version of yourself who fought so hard to stay alive.

That's the paradox of recovery: it asks you to release the intensity that once proved your existence. The crisis made you visible; stability makes you ordinary. I didn't know how to be ordinary.

Weeks later, I met with my therapist in her small office above a pharmacy. She asked what felt different. I hesitated. "It's like I can see light again, but I don't trust it." She nodded. "That's normal. After long darkness, the eyes ache before they adjust."

She told me about the biology of adaptation—how the pupils constrict, and how the brain recalibrates to new levels of brightness. "It's not the light that hurts," she said. "It's the return of vision."

Her words landed like a benediction I didn't know I needed. It made sense that hope could sting. The body, too, needs time to believe in safety.

On the walk home, I stopped by a small chapel near the bus station. The door was open; the interior smelled of wax and old wood. A single candle burned on the altar, its flame steady despite the draft. I sat in the last pew, hands resting on my knees, and realized I was waiting for permission—to breathe easily, to exist without crisis, to stop rehearsing catastrophe. The candle flickered once, then steadied. I exhaled. That was enough liturgy for the day.

In the months that followed, I learned to recognize light in smaller increments.

It showed up in the mundane: the hum of the refrigerator at midnight, the first sip of coffee, the unexpected text from a friend who remembered an inside joke. None of these moments demanded gratitude; they simply offered presence. I started thinking of them as lowercase miracles—ordinary mercies that accumulated quietly until they formed something resembling peace.

There were setbacks, too. Nights when exhaustion returned without warning, when the weight on my chest made breathing an act of defiance. But even then, the light never vanished completely. It dimmed, refracted, hid behind clouds of fear—but it didn't leave.

I began to suspect that grace was less about transformation and more about persistence. The divine, if it existed, wasn't the force that rescued me from the dark but the one that sat beside me until I remembered how to move.

Sometimes I still forget this. I still look for revelation in spectacle, waiting for the sky to split open with meaning. Yet more often than not, the message arrives as maintenance: take your medication, drink water, text someone back, open the blinds. These gestures don't feel holy, but they keep the light within reach.

One evening I visited the hospital chapel again—the same one where the grief group had once met. A different team was leading a mindfulness class now: half clinical, half contemplative. The chairs were arranged in a loose circle; a bowl of small candles sat in the center. Participants were invited to light one if they wanted, or simply watch the flame of another.

I didn't light mine. I just observed. The instructor spoke softly about how light behaves—how it disperses, reflects, and travels long after its source burns out. "Even when a star dies," she said, "its light continues for years. What we see is the echo of persistence."

Her words caught me off guard. I thought of the people I'd lost—friends, patients, mentors—and how their gestures still illuminated my days in subtle ways: a phrase I repeat, a kindness I mimic, a boundary I finally learned to keep. Light travels farther than its origin. Survival does, too.

When the session ended, I lingered behind. Most of the candles had melted to small puddles of wax. The smell of smoke clung to my sweater. I remembered the line I'd written months earlier—*the light that didn't leave*—and realized it wasn't a metaphor. It was a description of the human body's refusal to stop generating warmth, even in sorrow. Every heartbeat, every neuron firing, every act of care is combustion in miniature. We are made of endurance disguised as biology.

At home, I kept a small ritual.
Each night, before turning off the lamp, I'd place my hand over the bulb's fading glow. The warmth lasted only seconds, but I liked feeling how the heat lingered after the source dimmed. It reminded me that endings aren't clean—they taper, leaving afterglow. Recovery felt the same: a sequence of warm residues.

Sometimes I'd imagine what the world might look like if we treated that afterglow as sacred. If we stopped measuring healing by brightness and started honoring persistence—the faint shimmer that remains when everything else has burned out.

In conversation with others still navigating their own darkness, I began using the language of physics rather than faith. I'd say, "Light doesn't disappear; it diffuses." People seemed to understand that better than sermons. Maybe theology and science were always just metaphors competing for attention. The truth is simpler: whatever keeps you alive is holy enough.

There's a phrase from an old prayer that I've rewritten for myself: *Even the night shall be light about me.* I used to interpret it as divine rescue. Now I hear it as observation. Night itself carries illumination; darkness is not absence, only density. The work of recovery is learning to see within it—to notice that even here, even now, something still glows.

The candle in the chapel, the light on my wall, the warmth of a hand offered without condition—each one is evidence that departure and presence can coexist. The sacred doesn't erase shadow; it reveals what's still visible through it.

I once asked my therapist what healing looks like when it's complete. She smiled and said, "Completion is a myth. Healing just changes shape." Then she paused. "But you'll know it's working when you stop fearing the return of darkness."

I think of that often.

When the old ache resurfaces, I don't panic. I open a window. I let light and air recalibrate the room. I tell myself, quietly, *The dark is not punishment. It's just another spectrum of visibility.*

And somewhere in that simple acceptance, I feel the presence again—not dramatic, not blinding, just steady. A hum under the skin. The light that never left, waiting for me to stop running long enough to notice.

At first it's almost imperceptible, a vibration rather than a vision.
The pulse at my wrist steadies, the breath evens out, the room sharpens in outline. The presence doesn't announce itself; it waits for my attention.
It feels less like being visited and more like remembering—remembering that the body itself has been carrying this frequency the whole time.

When I was younger, I imagined divine encounter as rupture: thunderclap revelations, tears, surrender. I used to crave those eruptions because they felt certain. But this presence is quieter. It's cellular. It belongs to the same rhythm as digestion, heartbeat, circadian return. I realize now that holiness might have been physiology all along—the body rediscovering its own equilibrium after years of imbalance.

I test the hum by moving through ordinary life.

On the bus, jostled between strangers, I feel it steady in my chest.
At the grocery store, beneath the tinny music and the buzz of freezer doors, it persists.
At work, between tasks, it reminds me to unclench my jaw.
The light doesn't demand worship; it demands participation.
It asks that I stay awake to ordinary moments until they reveal their mercy.

Some days I still forget. Fatigue returns, the gray static of mind that dulls everything. But even then, something subtle in the body remembers how to recalibrate. I'll catch myself rubbing the space between my eyes, releasing tension, or taking a breath so deep it startles me. The hum responds, faint but loyal, like a heartbeat through a wall.

I start to map these sensations the way a cartographer maps a coastline—knowing tides will shift but the land beneath endures. The presence becomes less an event and more a geography: a landscape of endurance that extends beyond belief.

There are moments when I share this with others—friends still caught in their own darkness, patients in waiting rooms, strangers in coffee shops who confess too much and then apologize. I tell them the truth that once saved me: the light is not gone; it's only hidden by survival's smoke. You don't have to chase it. You just have to stop running from yourself long enough for your eyes to adjust.

Sometimes they look at me skeptically. Sometimes they cry. Sometimes they simply nod. I never offer it as advice—more as evidence. Healing doesn't need to persuade; it needs to be witnessed.

Weeks pass. The seasons shift. One evening I take a walk after rain. The streetlamps glisten against wet pavement, each reflection a duplicate sun. The air smells like petrichor and exhaust. I pause at an intersection and realize how familiar this light has become—not the spectacular kind that breaks clouds open, but the scattered one that lives in puddles, window glass, faces.

I think of all the times I mistook shadow for absence.
Light doesn't disappear when blocked; it repositions. It moves sideways, around obstacles, through translucent edges. Even grief obeys that physics. It doesn't vanish; it refracts. Every loss alters the direction of our seeing, but never extinguishes it.

I remember the therapist's phrase: *You'll know healing is working when you stop fearing the return of darkness.* I finally understand. Darkness isn't proof of failure. It's proof of continuation—the body still cycling through its seasons, the spirit still metabolizing what the mind can't yet name.
The hum beneath the skin is the sound of that metabolism, the constant rearrangement of what stays and what leaves.

Back home, I turn off every artificial light and sit near the window.
The city glows faintly outside, a constellation of small persistence. A neighbor's lamp. A car headlight sweeping the wall. The distant pulse of a plane. All of it stitched together into an unspoken assurance: illumination is communal. We survive by proximity to other flames.

I think about those who kept me tethered—therapists, friends, the group in the basement church, the ones who texted at the right hour without knowing why. Their presence built a kind of constellation across time zones and silences. Each gesture reflected the others until I could find myself again by their combined light.

This, I realize, is what redemption looks like now:
not rescue, but reflection.

Not a single blazing source, but the echo of many steady witnesses who refused to vanish.

When I write about recovery these days, I try not to call it victory. The word feels wrong, too final. What we gain is not conquest but continuity—the ongoing capacity to see and be seen, to light one another by ordinary means.

The hum deepens when I remember this.

It becomes almost musical: a low resonance between chest and throat, a private psalm without language. I sometimes hum aloud, just to feel the vibration bloom outward, to confirm that the light inside me is compatible with air.

Some evenings I take the candle from the shelf and relight it, not as ritual, but as recognition. I let the flame burn until wax pools and the wick bends toward the glow. I study how the light wavers but never retreats, how every flicker contains both endurance and exhaustion. That's how I recognize myself now—half flame, half fuel, alive in tension.

And as the candle burns lower, I notice the shadows shifting on the wall. They don't threaten anymore. They look like companions, shaped by the same light they once obscured. The room breathes with me—steady, quiet, equal parts glow and shade.

When I finally blow out the flame, the darkness that returns is not empty. It's full of afterimage. I can still see the imprint of brightness on my eyelids, a soft echo of radiance that lingers. It reminds me that visibility is optional; presence isn't. The light continues inside, stored in tissue and memory, waiting for its next chance to surface.

I go to bed thinking of that—how survival is not the absence of night, but the decision to rest inside it without fear. The hum follows me into sleep. It is small, human, persistent, and holy.

And when morning comes, I won't call it a miracle.
I'll call it the return of what never left.
The same light, the same pulse, the same steady whisper under the skin:
You are still here. Keep breathing.

Reflection

There is a kind of faith that outlives doctrine.
It begins in the body's smallest signals—pulse, breath, warmth—and expands until it feels like recognition.
The light never leaves; it waits.
And our only task is to remember how to open our eyes without flinching,
to meet it again and again,
until seeing becomes a way of staying.

✦ ECHO FRAGMENT – AFTER LIGHT, WE RESTED IN SILENCE

After light, we rested in silence.

Recovery never announced itself. It simply stopped resisting. The edges of struggle softened. The breath came without permission.

I used to believe healing would feel like triumph—radiant, certain, loud. But it arrived instead as quiet continuance: the ability to hold both pain and peace without rushing to resolve either. The light that once blinded now settled into something livable.

When the war inside me quieted, I realized that peace was never the absence of noise but the presence of gentleness. I began to notice the small mercies—how the body leaned toward warmth, how the lungs expanded without command, how morning kept arriving even when I did not ask it to.

There was no parade, no revelation. Only stillness learning how to stay. And beneath it, something ancient—a rhythm that outlasts language. Breath.

That sound has always been the first language of return.

In that silence, I finally understood what faith sounds like when it no longer performs. It hums. It hums through the body like light through glass, neither demanding nor defending, just existing.

To rest is not to give up. It is to trust the body enough to stop fighting itself.

To rest is to believe that healing can be gentle and still count as survival.

To rest is to worship in the smallest possible way.

So, after light, we rested in silence—

and silence, at last, was enough.

PART FIVE
THE RETURNED SELF

CHAPTER TWENTY-ONE: THE SPIRALPATH FORWARD

Healing does not move in straight lines. Survivors who try to measure progress like rungs on a ladder often feel crushed when they slip. But when healing is seen as a spiral, relapse and return take on new meaning. The spiral path does not erase the past. It curves back around it, each loop carrying fragments of memory, each return arriving slightly altered, slightly stronger. Survivors do not begin again from the beginning. They return bearing echoes, building layers.

One survivor of long-term depression described it this way: "Every winter I fall back into the same hole. But I don't fall as deep as I used to. And when I climb out, I recognize the walls. I know where the footholds are." Clinical research on relapse prevention echoes her story: recurrence of symptoms is common, but prior experience builds resilience, teaching survivors what tools to reach for. The spiral is not failure—it is accumulated wisdom in motion.

A man in recovery from alcohol dependence told me, "People say I slipped. But I didn't slip all the way back. I drank again, yes, but I didn't lose the years I had. They're still in me." His words embody what psychology calls cognitive reappraisal—reframing relapse as part of the journey rather than its negation. Theologically, his insight mirrors the Jewish tradition of teshuvah: return is never annulled by failure; every return, even repeated, is holy. The spiral does not cancel the past. It carries it forward, transformed.

The spiral path can feel disorienting. Survivors often say, "I thought I was done with this," when symptoms resurface. But recovery theory insists that symptom recurrence is not proof of collapse, but part of the pattern. The nervous system, shaped by trauma, does not heal through erasure.

It heals through repetition with safety—looping back to old pain, this time anchored in presence. This is why therapy often feels cyclical, why prayer sometimes revisits the same plea, why faith traditions repeat rituals weekly, daily, hourly. Spiral time is healing time.

One woman in grief described how she kept returning to her partner's belongings months after his death. "I would open the drawer, hold his shirt, cry, close it, and then do it again the next week. At first I thought I was failing to move on. But then I realized I was building a rhythm. Each time hurt less. Each time I breathed more." Her story illustrates what grief psychologists call oscillation—movement between loss-oriented and restoration-oriented coping. Theology would call it lament and doxology in alternation. The spiral path is not weakness. It is the only way humans metabolize unbearable love.

Communities, however, often expect linearity. Survivors hear phrases like, "Haven't you gotten over that yet?" or "Didn't we already pray for this?" These demands enforce shame. A trauma survivor who relapsed into panic attacks after years of apparent stability said, "I stopped telling anyone. They thought I was cured. I wasn't. I was looping." Theological communities that honor cycles—Sabbath every week, Ramadan every year, Easter every spring—already model spiral faith. But too often, they fail to apply the same rhythm to human pain.

Research in behavioral health confirms the spiral. The transtheoretical model of change describes recovery as stages revisited again and again—precontemplation, preparation, action, maintenance, relapse, return. Each cycle builds capacity. Survivors often speak this in their own words: "I failed less badly this time." "I stayed alive through it." "I reached out earlier." These small shifts are not linear milestones—they are spiral motions forward.

The spiral path is embodied. Survivors describe how their bodies remember trauma, circling back to tight chests, clenched jaws, restless hands. But with each loop, they add new practices: breathing, grounding, naming. A man with PTSD said, "The panic still comes. But now I know how to put my feet on the floor, how to tell myself I'm here." The nervous system learns not through elimination but through repetition with variation. The spiral is the nervous system's song.

One of the most powerful portraits came from a woman in therapy who brought in her journal filled with repeated sentences: I want to die. I want to live. I want to die. I want to live. Page after page. Her therapist said gently, "That is your spiral." She cried—not from despair, but from recognition. Healing was not a clean shift from one sentence to the other. It was circling between them until, eventually, the second outweighed the first. The spiral path is patient. It allows contradiction without collapse.

Theologically, the spiral is at the core of resurrection faith. Christians proclaim a risen Christ but still gather yearly to remember the cross. Jews return every year to the Exodus story, reliving both slavery and freedom. Muslims circle the Kaaba in pilgrimage, embodying the spiral in their footsteps. Buddhists speak of samsara—cycles of suffering that, with awareness, become steps toward liberation. Across traditions, the spiral appears not as accident but as design: human beings heal by circling.

A middle-aged man, long sober from opioids, described sitting in his car outside a pharmacy. "I hadn't thought about using in years," he said, "and then suddenly the craving was there like it never left." He drove away trembling, ashamed. "I thought I had failed all over again." His therapist reframed it: "Your body remembered. But you didn't buy. That's progress, not collapse." In recovery literature, this is called lapse versus relapse: the distinction between an urge and a return to old behavior. For him, that reframe shifted everything. "I realized the spiral had turned. I was in the same place but not the same me." Theologically, this insight resembles the Jewish concept of teshuvah: every return, even repeated, is unique; no spiral loop is wasted.

Another survivor spoke of grief returning every year on the anniversary of her child's death. "I would wake up weeping before I even opened my eyes," she said. For years, she saw this as punishment, as evidence of unfinished mourning. Then a rabbi told her, "Each year you circle the mountain again, but you are higher up." That image liberated her. She realized her grief was not regression—it was the spiral carrying her deeper into memory, but also further into resilience. Research on anniversary reactions confirms her experience: symptom spikes are normal and can coexist with long-term growth. What she thought of as failure was, in fact, evidence of enduring love. The spiral is not a closed loop—it ascends.

A young woman with chronic anxiety described the spiral in bodily terms. "It's like walking a labyrinth," she said. "I think I'm getting lost because I keep turning. But when I reach the center, I realize every turn was part of the path." Labyrinth walking, once a medieval Christian practice, is now used in trauma therapy as embodied meditation. Studies show it lowers heart rate and cortisol, regulating the nervous system through rhythmic pacing. For her, the practice embodied what her therapist had told her: "Healing is not straight. It is winding. And that's okay."

Spiral recovery is rarely acknowledged in communities shaped by linear models of success. A man whose depression resurfaced after ten years told his church small group. "They acted like I'd lied about being better the first time," he said. "They wanted a testimony, not a spiral." His shame grew until he stopped attending. Research in pastoral care shows that communities emphasizing final healing over ongoing process increase stigma and drive survivors away.[4] Yet those same traditions celebrate cyclical sacred time—weekly Sabbaths, annual fasts, repeated prayers. The hypocrisy wounds deeply: ritual is allowed to spiral, but human pain is not.

One survivor reframed the spiral through music. "I play the same song over and over when I'm anxious," she said. "It calms me because it repeats. But every time I hear it, something is different. My breathing. My thoughts. My tears." Neuroscience confirms her insight: repetition of familiar stimuli with slight variations stabilizes neural networks, training the brain toward resilience.[5] Theologically, chant and psalmody serve the same purpose: circling words until they carve grooves of trust. The spiral is not monotony. It is formation.

There are spirals of silence as well. A veteran described decades of refusing to talk about combat. Then, in therapy, he told one story. "It didn't fix me," he said. "But a year later, I told another. Each time I circle back, I can speak a little more." Trauma research calls this titration—releasing fragments of pain in manageable doses.[6] Theology calls it confession, though here the word means not guilt but truth-telling. Each loop into silence and back out is the spiral path forward, carrying both terror and release.

The spiral is visible in collective life, too. Communities grieve in rhythms. After a natural disaster, survivors rebuild, falter, rebuild again. Sociologists studying disaster recovery note that cycles of collapse and restoration repeat, but each round leaves new infrastructure, stronger bonds, deeper memory.[7] Theologically, this mirrors the exile-return cycles of scripture: Israel wandering, returning, wandering again, yet always carrying new covenant. Collective spirals teach us what individual spirals often obscure: circling is not regression. It is survival.

A striking portrait came from a woman with bipolar disorder. She drew her life not as peaks and valleys but as a spiral sketch. "It loops," she said, "but the loops get wider. I have more room to breathe." Her psychiatrist encouraged the drawing, showing how visualizing progress as a spiral reduced her self-blame. Research supports this: reframing illness trajectories visually reduces hopelessness and improves adherence to treatment.[8] Theologically, spirals appear in art across traditions—labyrinths, mandalas, whorls in wood and stone—symbols of the sacred written into creation itself. Her sketch was scripture in pencil.

The spiral also names the relationship between faith and doubt. Survivors often say, "I lost my faith," then later, "I found it again, but it feels different." This oscillation is not linear deconstruction but spiral reformation. Theologian Paul Tillich described faith as "ultimate concern," which often returns after apparent collapse in new forms. Clinical psychology parallels this in post-traumatic growth: meaning lost, rebuilt, lost again, rebuilt differently. Survivors embody it: "I don't pray the way I used to. But I still pray." The spiral does not return faith unchanged—it transforms it.

The spiral path forward refuses tidy narratives. Survivors loop through grief, relapse, silence, rage, faith, and despair, but each return carries memory and growth. Clinical research confirms that recurrence is not regression—it is recognition that the body learns by repetition. Theology sanctifies that repetition as sacred rhythm. Survivors testify that the spiral, however exhausting, is how they live.

The spiral is not proof of failure. It is proof of persistence. To walk it is to admit that healing is not straight, not final, not simple. It is to trust that every turn carries wisdom, that every return is not the same return, that forward can be curved. When survivors learn to see their path as spiral, not line, they begin to recognize what they already are: not failures circling back, but pilgrims circling deeper.

Each rotation refines the lesson. What once felt like relapse becomes rehearsal for resilience. A panic once unbearable becomes an echo the body now knows how to outlast. The curve bends toward integration: insight and exhaustion braided into endurance. Clinicians call it neuroplasticity; mystics call it grace. Both mean the same thing—change that does not erase the scar but teaches it how to breathe.

To spiral is to move with mercy through recurrence. It honors the biology of memory and the theology of return. It blesses the long work of being human—the pauses, the regressions, the fragile recoveries that keep repeating until the nervous system learns that safety is allowed to last.

If the line breaks, the spiral keeps going.
If the step falters, the circle widens to catch it.
And somewhere within that looping motion, survival becomes art.

CHAPTER TWENTY-TWO: THE THERAPIST AND THE TEMPLE

"Every sanctuary needs a threshold keeper,
and every therapist keeps a small altar behind the clipboard."

One therapist once described her office as *a confessional without hierarchy.*

She said, "My job isn't to interpret God. It's to help you notice the places where your breath hides."

It struck me that sacred work has always been shared work. Healing has never belonged solely to priests or doctors—it is communal architecture, built across centuries by those who refused to let one discipline own mercy.

The Room That Breathes

The building didn't look like a temple. It was a converted warehouse on the edge of the city—half-painted, half-forgotten. The parking lot cracked under weeds. Inside, the counseling collective had turned storage rooms into therapy spaces with thrifted chairs, chipped mugs, and mismatched lamps. The air smelled faintly of sandalwood, printer ink, and citrus cleaner. The scent alone told a story: something between the sacred and the administrative.

When I arrived, **Dr. Mira Patel** was on her knees, pressing tape to the edge of a rug that refused to stay down.
"Trip hazard," she said, smiling up at me. "Even sacred spaces need safety checks."

That line stayed with me long after the session. Even sacred spaces need safety checks. The statement felt like both confession and creed—an ethic that could have saved generations of people harmed by spiritual spaces that neglected their bodies in the name of their souls.

The Altar Behind the Clipboard

We sat opposite each other. Between us, a low wooden table held a candle, a small bowl of stones, and a folded card with the word *stay* written in blue ink. Dr. Patel gestured to the bowl.

"Each stone came from a client who struggled to remain alive," she said. "They leave one behind when they feel ready. Each one is different—rough, smooth, polished, cracked. Survival has texture."

I traced the candle's light flickering against the bowl, its shadows moving like breath. Outside, traffic rumbled along the main road; inside, silence gathered like a pulse.

She began, not with questions, but with rhythm: "Inhale through the nose, count four. Exhale through the mouth, count six."

The candle swayed in time with our breathing. The room seemed to exhale with us.

After a few minutes, she asked, "What does faith look like for you now?"

I hesitated. "Less like a structure, more like a frequency. Sometimes I tune in; sometimes I don't."

She nodded. "And the static?"

"That's most of it."

We both laughed, and that laughter—light, unguarded, momentary—felt like the most honest prayer I had offered in years.

The Temple of Incremental Grace

Dr. Patel explained that trauma therapy often relies on *titration*—approaching pain in increments so the body learns that it can survive contact. "Religion used to do that," she said. "Ritual was the original titration. Fasting, chanting, confession—all controlled exposures to mystery until it felt safe enough to touch."

Her words rearranged my understanding of worship. I saw the parallels everywhere: ritual as behavioral exposure, prayer as cognitive reframing, sacrament as embodied regulation. I realized that both faith and therapy are systems of controlled encounter—with pain, with mystery, with selfhood.

The candle burned lower. I watched a thin stream of smoke rise and vanish, and it reminded me of incense from my childhood church—the same smell of surrender, the same visible release of what cannot be said aloud.

On one wall hung a watercolor spiral drawn in gold lines.
"A former client painted it," she said. "He said it helped him imagine progress as circling inward, not climbing upward."

"That's theology," I said.
She smiled. "It's neurology too. The brain heals in loops."

Her matter-of-fact tone sanctified science without diluting mystery.
The conversation turned to her practice philosophy: *Every session is a rehearsal for safety.* She told me she thinks of her work less as treatment and more as liturgy—structured space for repetition, return, and release.

"Most people come here thinking healing is a mountain," she said. "I tell them it's a spiral staircase. It looks like you're going in circles, but you're rising with every turn."

Shared Language, Shared Devotion

When she learned that I write about theology and mental health, she nodded knowingly. "You're trying to build the bridge," she said.
"I keep trying to translate them," I admitted, "but sometimes it feels like they speak mutually suspicious dialects."
"Maybe stop translating," she said. "Let them share a sentence."

The line landed like an echo from another life. I thought of all the conversations between chaplains and clinicians that never happened, all the suicides that might have been prevented if someone had let the sacred and the scientific speak together instead of against each other.

The Corridor of Verbs

When I left, I walked down the long hallway of the collective.
Each door bore not a title but a verb: *Listen. Breathe. Restore. Witness.*

The corridor itself felt like prayer—structured repetition, intention in motion. A window at the far end poured sunlight across the floor in long rectangular pools. It wasn't cathedral light. It was hospital light—unromantic, dust-specked, ordinary. And yet it had the same effect: illumination without spectacle.

The Theology of Containment

That evening, I met Reverend Martin for tea—the same chaplain I'd met months before during the integrated-care pilot. I told him about Dr. Patel, about the rug and the candle and the stones.

He listened, eyes kind. "You've just described the theology of containment," he said.
"What do you mean?"
"Every act of care builds a vessel," he replied. "The vessel doesn't save anyone. It just keeps the light from spilling out before it can be noticed."

I thought of the rug she taped down so no one would trip. The bowl of stones that carried memory. The candle flame, steady and fragile. The watercolor spiral, circling toward stillness.
Vessels—all of them.

Reverend Martin sipped his tea. "Maybe therapists are the new priests of lament, and temples are the old clinics of the soul."
I smiled. "Then perhaps the patient is the new theologian—the one still willing to wrestle with pain until it speaks."

Outside, rain softened the city's noise into a steady hum. Inside, steam rose between us, curling like incense. Neither of us spoke. The silence between chaplain and writer, between the sacred and the clinical, was not absence—it was shared reverence.

Reflection

The temple was never only a building, and the therapist was never only a guide.
Both are threshold keepers—guardians of return. They remind us that holiness is not distance from pain but attention given to it.

Safety itself can be sacrament.

Every quiet room where someone exhales without fear is already a house of worship.

Every steady hand, every glass of water placed within reach, every moment a professional says, *"You can stay,"*—these are psalms.

And if God still walks among us, perhaps it is not in sanctuaries or clinics, but in the space between them—in the small, breathable rooms where people learn to trust life again.

Every candle that burns through session's end, every rug pressed flat against the floor, every therapist who carries a patient's story home in memory but not in burden—they are the modern monastics of mercy.

In the end, there may be no real difference between a therapist's office and a temple, only two rooms lit by the same devotion:
to listen, to hold, to keep the soul from falling apart before morning comes.

Echo Fragment – *After Containment, We Stayed*

After the fire and the trembling, we did not rebuild—we held.
After the sessions, the sermons, the sleepless nights,

we did not ascend—we circled.

We stayed.

Every taped rug became altar.
Every breath counted was prayer.
Every vessel that did not shatter
was gospel enough to begin again.

CHAPTER TWENTY-THREE: NO LONGER SPLITTING MYSELF

Survivors often describe life before healing as divided. One part of them belonged to the therapist's office, where they could speak of diagnoses and symptoms, but not prayer. Another part belonged to the temple, where they could cry out to God, but not mention panic attacks or medication bottles. Many lived in halves, stitching together fractured selves to meet the expectations of each world.

One survivor described it bluntly: "I had a church face and a clinic face. Neither one was my real face." In therapy she erased her faith, fearing dismissal. In church she erased her depression, fearing judgment. "The splitting nearly killed me," she said. "I thought maybe God wanted me divided." Research confirms that compartmentalization is linked with poorer treatment outcomes and heightened shame. Theologically, splitting echoes the language of exile—parts of the self sent away, banished, unseen.

A young man recalled stopping his antidepressants every Sunday morning, just so he wouldn't carry the pill bottle in his pocket to church. "I thought it was unholy," he said. By Monday he would start again, spiraling through withdrawal and secrecy. Only when his pastor preached openly about taking medication for his own anxiety did he stop splitting. "I felt like God finally allowed my brain to be whole," he said. Clinical studies affirm this: open disclosure by leaders reduces stigma and improves adherence. Faith that names medication as care removes the fracture between prayer and pill.

Others describe the opposite: therapists who treated prayer as pathology. A woman recounted, "When I said I pray every night, he wrote down 'obsessive ritual.' I stopped telling him anything spiritual after that." Her silence grew heavy until she sought a different therapist—one who asked, "How does prayer help you feel?" She replied, "It slows my breathing." In that moment, her therapist reframed prayer as nervous system regulation rather than symptom. The fracture mended. Research on spiritually adaptive therapy shows that when clinicians integrate religious practice into treatment, clients experience reduced shame and stronger outcomes.

No longer splitting means refusing to amputate parts of the self to survive in different rooms. Survivors who find integration speak of a relief that feels both clinical and spiritual. A man in grief group said, "For the first time, I could cry about my brother in therapy and then light a candle for him in church, and it was the same grief, the same me." Integration restored not just his healing, but his identity.

Communal practices can help weave these halves together. In some congregations, mental health support groups meet directly after worship. Survivors describe walking from the sanctuary into a circle of chairs and realizing they did not have to change masks. "I was still me," one said. "Praying in one room, talking about medication in the next. No split." These hybrid models reflect research on continuity of care, which shows that collaboration between sacred and clinical communities decreases dropout and increases long-term engagement.

Embodiment tells the same story. Survivors describe how splitting lives in the body: clenched jaw in church, shallow breath in therapy, headaches in both. One survivor said, "Every Sunday I came home with migraines. I realized it was because I was holding half of myself hostage the whole time." When she began speaking openly about her diagnosis in her Bible study, the migraines lessened. Neuroscience confirms this: concealment activates stress pathways, while disclosure in safe contexts reduces physiological burden. Theologically, truth-telling is sacrament—confession not as guilt, but as wholeness.

There are still risks. Integration is not welcomed everywhere. Survivors recount rejection from faith communities when they spoke of therapy, and dismissal from therapists when they spoke of prayer. "It takes courage to be whole," one said. Yet for many, that courage becomes the turning point. "The day I told my therapist I pray, and told my pastor I take meds—that was the day I stopped splitting."

A young seminarian described his first panic attack in the middle of leading worship. His vision blurred, his chest tightened, and he stumbled mid-prayer. Later, elders told him it was a spiritual attack, and he believed them—until he collapsed again in class and a doctor explained it was panic disorder. "For years I thought I had two selves," he said. "One that was attacked by demons and one that was broken by biology." Therapy gave him medication and breathing exercises; the temple gave him psalms and prayer. "I thought I had to choose," he said. "But when I began praying with my therapist's grounding script in my head, I realized both sides could meet. I didn't need to split."

His story illuminates what research on attribution styles shows: survivors who interpret symptoms solely as moral or spiritual failure experience heightened shame and poorer outcomes, while those who integrate spiritual and medical explanations show greater resilience. Theology must learn to echo what the clinic already knows: suffering is not sin, and healing is not betrayal.

Another survivor recalled her first communion after disclosing her bipolar diagnosis. "I stood in line shaking," she said. "I thought, if they knew I take lithium, they'd think I wasn't holy enough." But when the pastor placed the bread in her hands, he whispered, "This is for your whole self." She wept. "For the first time, I thought maybe I didn't have to split my faith from my brain chemistry." Clinical frameworks confirm that symbolic rituals can reinforce integration, reconfiguring fractured identities into a sense of whole self. For her, bread and medicine became parallel sacraments.

Communal casework shows how integration is often collective. In one urban church, a ministry formed where therapists and clergy co-led workshops on depression and prayer. Survivors spoke of it as life-giving: "I didn't have to code-switch. I didn't have to decide which language to use." The research backs this up: integrative care models, especially in underserved communities, increase treatment adherence and decrease stigma. Theologically, these workshops embodied ekklesia—church not as split space, but as gathering for whole persons.

Embodied analysis adds depth. Survivors often describe how splitting is felt in the body—tight shoulders in church, shallow breath in therapy, exhaustion in both. A trauma survivor said, "I clenched through sermons because I couldn't bring my depression into the sanctuary. I clenched through sessions because I couldn't bring God into the office." She lived clenched for decades until a therapist invited her to pray aloud at the end of a session. "My shoulders dropped for the first time in years," she said. Neuroscience explains this: concealment activates chronic stress pathways, while disclosure in safe contexts decreases cortisol and relaxes muscle tension. Theologically, her unclenching was confession—truth-telling that set her body free.

A veteran of military service recounted how he carried his faith and his flashbacks in separate boxes. "In chapel I was a Christian. In therapy I was a soldier. But I was never both." The turning point came when his chaplain and psychologist began collaborating, holding joint sessions. "When my therapist said 'trauma,' and my chaplain said 'lament,' I finally felt like the words matched." This pairing echoes clinical research on interdisciplinary trauma treatment, which shows that outcomes improve when psychological language and spiritual language coexist rather than compete. Survivors experience it as relief: the end of exile between selves.

The spiral toward integration is rarely easy. A woman with obsessive-compulsive disorder said her therapist initially pathologized her rituals of prayer. "He told me to stop praying altogether," she said. "I thought I had to kill my faith to heal my brain." Her condition worsened until she found another clinician who reframed her prayers: "Your faith is not the problem. It's how panic has hijacked it. Let's free the prayer from the compulsion." For her, this was salvation. "I didn't have to kill my faith. I had to unbind it." This approach echoes both trauma-informed care and theological discernment: prayer is meant to liberate, not imprison. The fracture healed when prayer was blessed, not banned.

Communities can create fractures too. Survivors tell of churches that welcomed their testimonies of healing but turned cold when relapse came. "When I had a panic attack after six months of 'victory,' they looked at me like I lied," one man said. His shame deepened until he withdrew. By contrast, another congregation publicly prayed for those who relapsed, treating return not as failure but as rhythm. "They called me brave for coming back," a woman said. Her story affirms what relapse prevention research insists: normalization of relapse as part of healing reduces despair and supports long-term recovery. Theologically, this echoes resurrection itself—not once, but daily.

There are smaller portraits too. A teenager with depression described slipping his antidepressant into his pocket like contraband before youth group meetings. "I thought I had to hide the thing keeping me alive," he said. But years later, he was invited to speak at that same youth group, openly naming his medication. "The kids didn't laugh. They clapped. I thought, maybe I never had to hide at all." His story demonstrates how testimony, when it includes the fullness of medical and spiritual care, dismantles stigma and models wholeness for others.

No longer splitting myself is not just personal—it is communal, clinical, and theological. Integration is not a solo achievement; it is a collective liturgy. Survivors cannot carry it alone. They need therapists who bless prayer, pastors who bless medicine, and communities that bless relapse as rhythm rather than failure. They need rituals that sanctify the whole body—the medicated mind, the trembling spirit, the aching flesh.

Because integration cannot happen where any part of the self is still considered unholy. The nervous system heals best where shame no longer lives. The psyche repairs itself where contradiction is allowed to breathe. Wholeness is not the absence of fracture; it is the refusal to keep pretending we are separate.

When these supports align—clinical, spiritual, communal—survivors stop code-switching between selves. They stop apologizing for complexity.

They live one life, one story, one healing. Clinical research calls this *integration of affect and identity*; theology calls it *sanctification of the whole person.* Both speak of the same mystery: that the divided self longs to be remembered, literally re-membered—gathered back into belonging.

To no longer split is to stand without mask in both temple and therapist's office, without hiding medication or silencing prayer. It is to tell the psychiatrist about the visions that still visit, and to tell the pastor about the pills that keep you here. It is to bring the whole self to every room that promises care.

Integration, then, is not perfection—it is honesty made flesh. It is living without translation, without disguise, without fracture between the sacred and the clinical. It is surviving as one continuous being: body, mind, memory, and spirit reconciled.

And that, in the spiral of healing, is sacred ground.
Where medicine meets mercy.
Where therapy and theology stop competing and start conversing.
Where the human heart—stitched together by science and Spirit—finally feels like home.

Liturgical Echo:

Inhale: One self.
Exhale: Still whole.

CHAPTER TWENTY-FOUR: RECOVERY WITHOUT SHAME

"The hardest part of healing was realizing there was nothing left to hide."

The first time I said out loud that I was in recovery, my voice broke halfway through the sentence.

It wasn't confession or victory—it was disclosure.
We were in a circle of metal folding chairs at a small community center, the kind with flickering lights and scuffed linoleum. Someone had asked us to introduce ourselves by first name and "something you're working on." The phrase sounded simple enough, but my throat tightened.

When my turn came, I said, "I'm—uh—still learning how to stay," and then added, almost as apology, "I'm in recovery."
The words hung there like steam. No one flinched. No one cheered. The woman beside me simply nodded, as if I'd said *coffee, two sugars.* That nod was the beginning of everything.

In Buddhism, compassion—*karuṇā*—extends first toward oneself.
To heal without shame is to practice compassion as a form of truth-telling: not "I am better," but "I am allowed to begin again."

For years I had carried recovery like contraband, tucked behind professional composure and spiritual vocabulary. I could speak fluently about resilience, about hope, about grace, but not about the slow, unglamorous work of getting well. Therapy notes, medication, relapse—all the invisible scaffolding that kept me functioning—felt like evidence of personal failure. I had inherited a faith that equated struggle with sin and a culture that equated need with weakness. Between the two, shame found plenty of oxygen.

Shame is efficient. It doesn't have to shout; it just rearranges posture. Shoulders curl, breath shortens, eyes drop. The body remembers humiliation faster than the mind can reason with it. Even after I knew better—after I'd studied the science of trauma and the theology of mercy—my muscles still folded at the first sign of exposure.

It wasn't intellect that freed me; it was company.
During group sessions, I began noticing how people's breathing changed when they told the truth. Tight at first, then looser. Shame contracted; honesty expanded. The room's air seemed to reorganize around whatever courage entered it. That physical shift—lungs reclaiming space—was my first working definition of grace.

One evening, after group, I stayed behind to help stack chairs. The facilitator, a soft-spoken man named Javier, handed me a rag to wipe the coffee ring off the table. "You looked lighter tonight," he said.
I shrugged. "Maybe. I still hate talking about relapse."
He nodded. "Most people do. We confuse recurrence with regression."
"What's the difference?"
"Regression erases progress. Recurrence proves you're still in motion."

He smiled, setting the last chair on the stack. "If the body can recover from pneumonia more than once, why shouldn't the mind?"

I laughed, a short exhale that felt like permission. For the first time, recovery didn't sound like punishment; it sounded like proof of resilience.

Weeks later, I met with Dr. Patel again, the same therapist from *The Therapist and the Temple.* She asked what had shifted since our last session.

"I'm less afraid of backsliding," I said. "Still embarrassed sometimes, but not devastated."

She leaned forward. “Embarrassment is social. Shame is existential. Which are you feeling?”

“Mostly social,” I admitted. “I still worry what people think when I say I’m in therapy.”

“Then practice telling the truth to people who have earned it,” she said.

“Not everyone needs your story, but someone does. Shame starves when witnessed.”

That night, I called a close friend and told her about the panic attacks that still visited like old debts. She listened quietly, then said, “I thought I was the only one.” I realized how many of us live inside parallel silences, ashamed of the same symptoms. Recovery, I was learning, isn’t personal triumph; it’s collective permission.

In church one Sunday, the pastor preached about the woman caught in adultery, emphasizing forgiveness. I found myself thinking less about the miracle and more about her posture—how she must have stood, half-bent, waiting for the first stone. I imagined her spine slowly straightening as the crowd dispersed. That was recovery: not the absence of accusation, but the slow reclamation of verticality.

Later, in therapy, I told Dr. Patel this image. She smiled. “Exactly. Healing is postural. When shame collapses the body, recovery begins by lifting the head, not by fixing the past.”

That image followed me everywhere. Each time I caught myself hunching, I practiced unfolding—shoulders back, jaw unclenched, breath lengthened. Not performative confidence, just physical honesty. The body, it turns out, tells the truth long before words do.

I began teaching this in small workshops—faith groups, recovery meetings, classrooms. I'd open with a simple exercise: inhale, exhale, say your name without a title. Then say one thing you're learning to forgive yourself for. The silence that followed was always thick, almost holy. People cried. Some laughed nervously. Everyone breathed. It wasn't doctrine; it was anatomy remembering safety.

In one session, a man in his sixties said, "I've been sober twelve years and still can't say I'm proud. It feels like vanity."

I asked, "What if pride is just gratitude standing upright?"

He sat back, eyes wide, and whispered, "Then maybe I can try."

Moments like that convinced me shame is not a moral issue but a relational one. It dissolves not through repentance but through resonance. Someone else's steady presence becomes the mirror that restores scale to our self-perception. Theologians call it grace; psychologists call it co-regulation. Both mean: you are still worthy of connection.

There are still days when shame sneaks in through subtler doors. The inner critic speaks in professional tones: *You should be further along. You should be cured by now.* I've learned to answer gently: *Maybe progress isn't forward; maybe it's deeper.* Then I breathe until the voice quiets.

Some mornings I light the same candle from my desk and watch the wax pool. The flame leans, steadies, leans again—a perfect metaphor for maintenance. The goal is not to burn without wavering; it's to keep from extinguishing under the weight of the air.

One afternoon, I returned to the group I'd started with months earlier. The room looked smaller, though maybe I had simply expanded. New faces filled the chairs. When introductions began, I noticed how their voices trembled, the same way mine once had. When it was my turn, I said, "My name is—" and paused. "I'm learning to live without shame."

The room exhaled with me.

Afterward, a young woman approached. "I thought recovery meant being done," she said. "You make it sound like staying in process is okay."
"It's more than okay," I said. "It's honest."

She nodded, shoulders lowering, the beginning of a new posture.

Something in the room shifted after that—subtle, but undeniable.
It was as if the air itself had registered the release. The fluorescent lights hummed softer. People began breathing in sync without realizing it, that gentle rhythm that only happens when shame loosens its grip on collective space.

We stayed like that for a while, not talking, just existing in the kind of silence that isn't absence but presence.

I remember thinking that if faith had a sound, it would probably resemble this: not music, not preaching, just bodies remembering how to breathe in the same tempo again.

When the session ended, no one hurried to leave.
Someone began stacking chairs, another collected the coffee cups, a third swept the crumbs from the counter. It felt almost liturgical—the slow restoration of order after disclosure, the sacred mundane.

I realized, watching them, that this was what a modern congregation might look like: not united by doctrine but by consent to stay.

On my way out, the young woman who had spoken earlier caught up to me at the door. "You made it sound like forgiveness doesn't have to be earned," she said.

"It doesn't," I replied. "It just has to be received."

She tilted her head. "Then why is it so hard?"

"Because it feels like doing nothing," I said. "And most of us were raised to think worth must be proven."

She nodded again, slowly this time, the movement deliberate—like she was memorizing the feel of acceptance in her muscles. Then she smiled, faint but sure. "I'll practice that," she said, and walked away.

That was months ago, but I think about her often.
I think about how every act of release becomes part of someone else's inheritance, how the way one person exhales can grant permission for another to do the same. Recovery is contagious when practiced honestly; it travels through nervous systems like light refracting through glass.

In therapy the next week, I told Dr. Patel about the session. She listened, then said, "Notice how you described it—not as success, but as atmosphere. That's what healing is. It's not achievement; it's climate."

I wrote that sentence down: *Healing is climate.*
It explained what faith communities and clinicians alike often forget—that recovery isn't a verdict, it's a weather pattern.

Some days clear, some days fog.
You don't control it; you prepare for it.
You learn to trust that even when the sky closes in, the sun is still behind it.

Dr. Patel smiled when I told her this. "You're learning the discipline of gentleness," she said. "It's the hardest one to sustain."

Gentleness used to terrify me.
I mistook it for weakness. In a world that rewards productivity, softness felt unsafe. But in recovery, gentleness is power redefined: it's the ability to meet your own fragility without punishment.

I began to test this in small ways—taking breaks without justification, saying *I can't* instead of performing capability, refusing to apologize for fatigue. Each act of mercy toward myself felt disorienting, then liberating.

Theology gave language for this long before psychology did.

In Hebrew, *rachamim*—mercy—shares its root with *rechem*, meaning womb. To practice mercy, then, is to become a safe space for what's still forming.

That etymology changed everything for me. Recovery wasn't self-indulgence; it was gestation. I was learning to cradle my own becoming instead of demanding it hurry up and arrive.

Months passed. Seasons turned. The edges of my old shame softened into memory.

I noticed I laughed more freely, without rehearsing whether joy was permissible. I sang again—not in church, but while doing dishes. I reached out to friends I'd withdrawn from, not to explain my silence but to rejoin the rhythm of presence.

At a small gathering one evening, a friend said she'd been too embarrassed to return to therapy after a relapse.

"Start where you are," I told her. "You don't need to apologize for having a nervous system."

She laughed through tears. "Is that in the Bible?"

"Not yet," I said. "But it should be."

Laughter filled the room—honest, collective, grounding. That's when I realized what recovery without shame truly sounds like: not solemn or triumphant, but deeply human. Laughter that doesn't erase pain, but integrates it.

Later that night, alone at home, I replayed the moment and felt something settle.

The old reflex to cringe—*Did I overshare? Did I sound weak?*—didn't arrive. Instead, there was space. Spaciousness where guilt used to live.

It reminded me of a line from an old psalm: *You have set my feet in a broad place.* I'd always imagined that line as escape; now it felt like embodiment. Broadness wasn't elsewhere—it was inside me. My body had stopped shrinking to accommodate fear.

I sat at my desk and lit the candle again. Its light trembled against the windowpane, catching my reflection—older, steadier, still flawed but unashamed. I whispered to my reflection the words I once needed someone else to say: *You're allowed to heal in public.*

That sentence became a kind of prayer. I began repeating it before lectures, before interviews, before family gatherings—the spaces where performance once replaced authenticity. Each time I said it, the room seemed to expand a little more.

Recovery, I've learned, is cumulative. It builds not through milestones but through micro-integrations:

a jaw unclenched,
a breath released,
a boundary held.

Each small mercy rewrites the body's theology, replacing condemnation with curiosity.

One day, while teaching a seminar on trauma and spirituality, a student asked, "So what's the end goal? When are we fully healed?"
The room fell quiet.

I thought of all the years I'd spent chasing completion. Then I smiled and said, "The goal is to stop asking that question."

She frowned slightly.

"Because healing," I continued, "isn't a project you finish. It's a relationship you maintain. And like any relationship, it requires attention, forgiveness, and rest."

She nodded slowly. "So we don't graduate from it."

"No," I said. "We live in it."

The next morning, I walked through my neighborhood before sunrise. The air was damp, the streets half-lit. A jogger passed, nodded hello, and I nodded back—a brief exchange, meaningless to most, but to me it felt sacred. It was the kind of moment shame once blocked—the simple ease of being seen without self-consciousness.

As I reached the corner café, light began to bloom along the horizon, thin and deliberate. I thought of all the people waking up to their own mornings—some tired, some afraid, some beginning again. We were all participating in the same invisible covenant: to keep returning.

That realization felt like prayer, too. Not the supplicating kind, but the living kind—the kind that thanks the air by breathing it.

Reflection

Shame thrives on secrecy.
It dissolves in community, in laughter, in breath shared without apology.
Recovery without shame is not perfection—it's permission.

Permission to relapse and return,
to speak the truth without performance,
to stand without armor and still belong.

To recover without shame is to become your own sanctuary—

the body as temple, the mind as witness,
the breath as daily absolution.

And when we learn to live that way,
we discover the quiet miracle waiting beneath every scar:
the self was never unworthy of healing—
only waiting to believe it.

CHAPTER TWENTY-FIVE: BREATH THAT STILL SPEAKS

Breath has always been the last witness. Survivors say that before they could pray again, before they could sing again, before they could even speak their names without shame, they could breathe. Sometimes shallow, sometimes ragged, sometimes held so tightly in their chest it felt like suffocation. But breath remained. "When everything else was gone," one survivor said, "I could still hear my lungs moving. That meant I was still alive." Research confirms what survivors intuitively know: the body's breath is not only a biological rhythm but a regulator of nervous system states, capable of soothing trauma and anchoring survival. Theologically, breath is origin and persistence—God breathing into dust, prophets carried by the Spirit, disciples filled with wind at Pentecost.

A woman who had survived years of domestic violence described learning to breathe again in therapy. "I would hold my breath whenever a door slammed," she said. "My chest would freeze like I was back in the house." Her therapist taught her to exhale deliberately. "At first it felt stupid," she admitted. "But one day, I exhaled and realized I wasn't in danger anymore. My body didn't know it until my breath told it." Polyvagal theory explains this: exhalation activates the parasympathetic nervous system, signaling safety to the body. For her, the exhale was not just biology, it was liturgy. Each breath out was a prayer of release.

Another survivor, a choir singer, spoke of losing her ability to sing during depression. "I couldn't find air deep enough to carry a note," she said. For months she sat in rehearsals, mouthing words. Then one day, a note escaped—fragile, trembling, but hers. "It was like my lungs remembered before my heart did," she said. Singing, research shows, increases vagal tone and reduces symptoms of anxiety and depression. For her, it was also theology. "I didn't have to believe the lyrics yet," she said. "The breath carried them for me."

Communal practices reveal how breath becomes collective testimony. In some churches, the congregation sighs or hums together in prayer. Survivors describe those moments as salvation. "When I couldn't breathe for myself, I borrowed the breath of the room," one said. Neuroscience supports this: breathing in synchrony with others regulates heart rhythms and fosters social connection. Theologically, it resembles the Spirit moving through the body of believers—breath not as individual possession, but as shared life.

A veteran with PTSD spoke of hyperventilating during flashbacks. "My body thought I was still in war," he said. He learned grounding techniques in therapy, placing his hand on his chest and counting breaths. "At first, it was survival," he said. "Then it became prayer. Inhale: I'm here. Exhale: I'm safe." Trauma research confirms that rhythmic breathing reduces hyperarousal and anchors presence. He discovered what mystics have long known: every inhale is a reception, every exhale is surrender.

There are traditions where breath itself is worship. Survivors who practice dhikr describe repeating the name of God until it merges with inhalation and exhalation. Others describe Buddhist metta, extending compassion through each breath. In synagogues, the shofar blast mirrors the body's cry for air. Even in secular therapy rooms, clinicians guide breath as grounding. Survivors testify: "My prayer life began again when I realized my breath was already praying." The convergence is striking—clinical science and sacred practice both naming breath as the hinge of survival.

Embodied reflections show how shame fractures breath. Survivors describe holding their breath in sanctuaries, terrified of sobbing aloud. One woman said, "Every time I tried to inhale, my body told me I didn't deserve air." Her healing began when a chaplain whispered, "Even breath is grace." That sentence loosened her ribs. Research calls this reframing—when language interrupts shame's grip and transforms experience. Theology calls it gospel: good news in the chest cavity.

Breath also carries memory. A man grieving his father's death said he could still hear the old man's sighs during prayer. "I thought I lost him, but then one day, I caught myself breathing like him." Grief studies note that survivors often embody rhythms of the lost, carrying their breath patterns, gestures, or cadences. For him, it was not haunting—it was inheritance. "His breath still speaks in me," he said.

To say recovery is "breath that still speaks" is not metaphor only. It is clinical fact and theological confession. Survivors live because lungs expand and contract. They heal because breath regulates body and anchors soul. Communities sustain one another when breath moves in unison—humming, chanting, sighing, singing.

When words fail, when faith feels absent, when shame suffocates, breath remains. And every inhale is proof of survival. Every exhale is prayer. Breath speaks even when the survivor cannot. And in that speech, shame loosens, trauma yields, and life continues.

A man who survived a suicide attempt spoke of waking in the hospital with a ventilator tube down his throat. "I hated the sound of the machine at first," he said. "It made me feel weak, like I couldn't even breathe on my own." But weeks later, when he heard that same sound in his dreams, it had shifted. "It was the sound of life continuing," he said. "It told me I was still here." Researchers studying post-attempt recovery describe the breath as a potent anchor for meaning-making; survivors who reframe the act of breathing as testimony report greater resilience and reduced risk of further attempts.[1] For him, the ventilator was no longer shame—it was liturgy in plastic and air.

Another survivor described panic attacks that stole her breath in church. "I'd sit in the pew, and suddenly I couldn't inhale. I thought I was being punished." She began leaving services, ashamed. Later, in therapy, she learned to count her breaths in fours: inhale, hold, exhale, rest. The next Sunday she returned, and when panic seized her chest, she began counting silently. "It was the first time I survived a panic attack in church," she said. "The sermon was a blur, but my breath was still speaking." Research on paced breathing demonstrates its efficacy in reducing panic symptoms and restoring agency during attacks. Theology offers parallel witness: the psalmist does not say, I understood everything, but, Let everything that has breath praise the Lord. Even gasps and counted inhales become worship.

A young father battling depression recalled how his daughter would crawl onto his chest at night. "She would fall asleep listening to me breathe," he said. "Even when I wanted to die, I couldn't stop breathing because she trusted the sound of my lungs." This portrait illustrates what psychologists call relational anchoring: the way one body's rhythm sustains another. For him, his daughter's weight on his chest kept his own chest rising. Theologically, it echoes Genesis again: God breathes life into humanity, and humanity breathes life into each other.

Communities have long known the power of shared breath. In one Buddhist sangha, survivors of trauma gather weekly to practice metta meditation. They sit in silence, synchronizing inhales and exhales, extending compassion first to themselves, then outward. A participant said, "For years my breath was my enemy. Here, it became my friend." Neuroscience confirms that synchronized breathing enhances empathy and increases oxytocin levels. For her, it was more than science: "It felt like forgiveness filling my chest."

Christian communities too have embodied breath as liturgy. In a Pentecostal church, survivors described sighs and moans during prayer as more healing than words. "I couldn't pray in sentences," one woman said. "But my groans carried me." Research on vocalized breathing shows it reduces cortisol and anchors nervous system regulation. Theology had long anticipated this: Paul writes that the Spirit intercedes with "groans too deep for words." Her breath, broken and groaning, was gospel.

There are stories where breath holds memory of trauma but becomes re-scripted. A Holocaust survivor described the suffocating air of the camps. "Every inhale felt stolen." Decades later, in therapy, she learned to breathe deeply for the first time. "I thought I was breathing all my life," she said. "But only now do I know what breath is." Her testimony underscores what trauma clinicians say: survivors often live with constricted breathing patterns that signal danger even in safety. Relearning to breathe is not just therapy—it is reclaiming existence. For her, every exhale was defiance.

Children carry breath differently. A boy with generalized anxiety learned "bubble breathing" in therapy—inhale through the nose, exhale as if blowing a bubble. He began practicing it at night with his mother. "We filled the room with invisible bubbles," she said. "For the first time, he fell asleep without nightmares." Clinical studies confirm the effectiveness of playful breath exercises in reducing childhood anxiety. Theology may not name bubble breathing, but it does name children as prophets of the kingdom. Their lungs remind us that breath is both medicine and miracle.

Shame often suffocates survivors. A man with schizophrenia whispered in group therapy, "I shouldn't be alive. My breath is wasted." Another member responded, "Every breath you take tells me you are still fighting." The words shifted something in him. "I started listening to my breathing at night. I told myself: this means I am still worth it." Research shows that group affirmation reframes symptoms and dismantles shame, improving self-concept. Theologically, his fellow survivor became prophet, proclaiming breath as sacred testimony.

Communities across traditions are reclaiming breath as ritual. In some churches, services now begin with guided breathing: "Inhale peace. Exhale fear." In mosques, imams invite congregants to notice their breath during recitation. In synagogues, rabbis teach mindfulness of breath as prayer. Survivors say these practices allow them to carry sanctuary into their bodies. "When I breathe, I don't leave worship behind," one said. "It goes with me." Clinical integration research affirms this: embedding breath practices into spiritual life increases resilience and reduces relapse.

Breath remains when everything else fractures. Survivors testify that words can fail, rituals can crumble, faith can feel absent, but lungs persist in their rising and falling. Breath holds memory, carries shame, and yet speaks hope. It synchronizes communities, regulates trauma, and sanctifies bodies.

Recovery without breath is impossible. Recovery with breath is already unfolding. To breathe is to resist despair, to testify without words, to proclaim survival with every inhale and exhale. Survivors say, "My breath is my prayer." And indeed, when language fails and theology falters, breath still speaks. Yet breath is not only survival's residue—it can be cultivated, practiced, expanded into ritual. Survivors remind us that recovery is not found in rare epiphanies but in daily rhythms: one breath slowed, one exhale released, one inhale received as grace. This is where solutions emerge, not abstract but lived.

A trauma clinician recalled teaching diaphragmatic breathing to survivors of sexual assault. "At first, they rolled their eyes," she said. "It felt too simple for the depth of their pain." But weeks later, one client returned, saying, "I used it when the flashback came. It didn't erase the memory, but it gave me enough air to stay." The therapist called it the one-breath margin: the space that allows survival when collapse threatens. Clinical literature affirms that structured breath practices lower cortisol, increase heart-rate variability, and reduce trauma reactivity. The solution is not grand—it is learning to reclaim breath as the smallest, holiest act of self-defense.

Faith communities can embody these practices too. In one synagogue, a rabbi began each Yom Kippur service with silence, inviting congregants to "listen to the breath God placed in you." Survivors described this as revolutionary: "It was the first time my synagogue named breath as prayer, not just words." Integrating breath practices into ritual does more than comfort—it dismantles shame by placing embodied survival at the center of sacred life. Theology here aligns with science: what calms the vagus nerve also sanctifies the body.

In hospitals, chaplains have begun using breath-centered rituals with patients on psychiatric wards. One chaplain described sitting with a woman in deep depression who had stopped speaking. Together they inhaled slowly, exhaled slowly, repeating until tears came. The chaplain said, "Her breath became her psalm." Research on chaplaincy confirms that embodied rituals like breathing reduce distress and foster spiritual resilience. The solution is not to force words from survivors but to honor the language already moving in their lungs.

Communal solutions matter as much as individual ones. In a support group for veterans, sessions began with collective breathing exercises. Some mocked it at first, calling it "hippie stuff." But over time, survivors began to anticipate it. One said, "It was the only time my body felt safe all week." Synchronizing breath created belonging where shame had built walls. Research on group interventions shows that shared breath fosters cohesion and reduces isolation, especially among trauma survivors. Theology would name it differently: breath becoming communion.

Solutions also require dismantling theologies that suffocate. Too many survivors have been told their panic is sin, their shallow breath a sign of weak faith. Recovery requires pastors, imams, rabbis, and priests who will bless breath as sacred survival rather than condemn it as faithlessness. Theological education must integrate trauma physiology alongside scripture, so that leaders learn to interpret sighs as prayers rather than shortcomings. Pastoral theology scholars argue that training clergy to recognize the embodied dimensions of trauma transforms congregations from spaces of shame to sanctuaries of breath.

At the level of policy, mental health systems can expand access to breath-based interventions—mindfulness programs, trauma-sensitive yoga, breathing groups—especially in marginalized communities where therapy is scarce. Research shows such low-cost, embodied practices improve outcomes even when access to medication or psychotherapy is limited. Solutions here are not supplemental—they are survival infrastructures, simple as air, profound as liturgy.

And at the personal level, survivors speak of daily rituals: lighting a candle and breathing in its glow; placing a hand over the heart and inhaling until the pulse steadies; whispering "I am here" on the inhale and "I am held" on the exhale. These are not treatments to replace therapy or medication, but practices to anchor both. One survivor said, "My prayer used to be words I didn't believe. Now it's just breathing in and out until my body believes it is safe."

Breath still speaks.
But for survivors to hear it, communities must amplify it—not only through ritual, but through systemic care.

Therapists must teach it not as a coping trick but as sacred ground, where the nervous system and the spirit meet. Faith leaders must bless it as prayer—the same holy rhythm once mistaken for weakness. Families must honor it as resilience, the quiet proof that survival is still underway. Policymakers must fund it as medicine, recognizing that healing requires infrastructure as much as intention. And survivors must be allowed to practice it without shame, without surveillance, without having to justify why breathing itself is a sacred act of persistence.

Recovery does not begin in a program or a pulpit. It begins in the inhale that says *I am still here,* and the exhale that answers *and I am not done yet.* The work of institutions is to make that breath possible—to create spaces where people can exhale without fear. Because a breath held too long becomes a wound; a breath released freely becomes communion.

Solutions for recovery are not far off. They are as close as lungs filling, as steady as a chest rising and falling.

Every breath is both diagnosis and cure—both evidence of fragility and proof of endurance. To breathe without shame is to participate in a universal liturgy older than any creed.

Clinical science describes it as parasympathetic regulation, the recalibration of a system that once lived in survival mode. Theology has known it by other names: *ruach, pneuma, prana, spiritus.* Each word translating the same miracle—the invisible made audible through breath.

And when survivors finally breathe without fear, they rediscover what every wisdom tradition has whispered for centuries:
that Spirit and air, body and soul, are not divided;
that breath is not only the sign of life but its continual renewal;

that each inhale is an arrival, and each exhale is a letting go.

Breath is the first language of the sacred.

And to reclaim it—to breathe without apology—is to return home to both self and God.

Inhale: I am alive.
Exhale: I am enough.
Inhale: I am still becoming.
Exhale: And I am not alone.

INTERLUDE: THE QUIET WORK OF A HEALED LIFE

"Healing does not announce itself; it hums."

Healing doesn't announce itself. It arrives like dawn—slow, reluctant, sometimes unnoticed until we look up and realize the light has changed.

Before that light, though, there's the long night—the one where we think we'll never make it out. Healing, when it finally comes, doesn't erase that darkness; it simply sits beside it until it softens.

The truth is, healing doesn't look like transformation from pain to peace. It looks like the quiet work of living with both. It looks like folding laundry again without crying. Like remembering to eat before the hunger hurts. Like answering a message instead of disappearing.

It looks like the ordinary.

We learn that healing is not a single act but a slow apprenticeship in presence. Some days it's a full breath. Some days it's just getting out of bed. Sometimes we call that progress; other times it's simply maintenance.

There are mornings when we wake without dread—and we panic, mistaking calm for absence. Our nervous system still expects threat. We touch the stillness and wait for it to break. Healing, then, becomes an exercise in trust: believing that peace isn't a trap, that quiet can be safe.

Once, we thought healing would mean feeling nothing at all. Instead, we find ourselves feeling *everything*—joy mixed with grief, hope tangled with fatigue. The work now is learning not to pathologize what feels tender.

We are not symptoms to be solved.
We are lives learning to breathe again.

So, we practice gentle consistency: eat, rest, stretch, take the medication, pray, show up. None of it is dramatic. Most of it is invisible. Healing often hides in habits no one else will applaud.

Some days we regress, and shame starts whispering again—*Shouldn't you be past this by now?* But healing refuses that timeline. It asks for honesty instead of performance. It invites us to admit that recovery is cyclical, not linear; that wholeness includes relapse, fatigue, and pause.

Healing changes our relationships too. We start noticing who can meet us in quiet instead of crisis. We outgrow the need to be saved and discover the grace of being witnessed.

It's not that we no longer need help; it's that we've learned to ask for it differently. With clarity instead of apology. With gratitude instead of guilt.

Some friendships fade, others return in gentler form. New ones arrive and feel like rest instead of rescue. Healing rearranges the architecture of belonging—we build smaller, steadier spaces that can hold us as we are.

Spiritually, healing shifts our language. We stop demanding miracles and start recognizing maintenance as holy. We stop praying for removal and start praying for endurance. The divine becomes less about intervention and more about accompaniment—less thunder, more breath.

We start to see how theology and therapy whisper the same truth: that we were never meant to heal alone.

There's no final reveal, no crescendo of deliverance. Healing is the gradual softening of the nervous system's grip—the quiet moment when we realize that peace is possible even here, even now.

We still tremble sometimes. We still check the exits. But the trembling no longer decides the day.

And somewhere in that simple acceptance, we find presence again—not dramatic, not blinding, just steady. A hum beneath the skin. The light that never left, waiting for us to stop running long enough to notice.

Ritual: A Letter from the Healed Self

Dear one who is still waiting,
We did not get better in a single moment. We practiced small kindnesses until they stitched themselves into muscle memory. We learned to breathe through the ache instead of against it.

Healing didn't make us unbreakable—it made us porous enough to let light through.

We are not finished. We are still learning ease. Still fumbling toward rest. But look how far tenderness has carried us.

When you forget that softness is strength, place your hand on your chest. Feel it rise. Feel it fall. That is proof.

You are already living the healed life, even if it trembles.

With gentleness,
—The self that stayed.

Healing isn't loud anymore. It hums quietly in the ordinary—breath, dishes, laughter, rest. Maybe that's all the liturgy we ever needed: small rituals of attention. What follows are the ones that keep us steady when silence becomes home again

CHAPTER TWENTY-SIX: THE LITURGIES WE NEEDED

"When the old prayers failed to hold us,
we made new ones out of breath, touch, and staying."

We were never meant to live without ritual.
Even in our most secular hours, the body still looks for pattern: morning coffee, evening walks, the quiet ceremony of washing dishes before bed. Every repetition is a kind of reassurance—proof that we're still here, that the day had structure, that we belong to time again.

I used to believe liturgy belonged only to churches. But when the old words stopped fitting, I began to notice how the world kept inventing its own: commuters holding doors open for one another, a nurse adjusting a patient's blanket before leaving the room, the barista who remembers a name even when we forget ourselves. These gestures were sermons in disguise—small, exacting acts of attention.

After years of clinical work and grief groups, I started collecting these improvised rituals the way some people collect hymns. They became a portable theology, a living archive of how we make meaning when language falters.

1. The Liturgy of Arrival

It began in the waiting room.

Every Thursday evening, we gathered in that same circle of metal chairs. No incense, no music—just fluorescent light and the rustle of paper cups. Someone always arrived early to plug in the coffee pot. That small sound of percolation became our call to prayer.

There was no formal opening, but the ritual was unmistakable: we nodded at one another, acknowledging survival. The facilitator would smile and say, "Take a breath. You made it."

That was the liturgy we needed most—the one that didn't require belief, only presence. Each inhalation was a verse, each exhalation a psalm. The theology was simple: *You are still here.*

I began to use that phrase outside the group, whispering it to myself in moments of panic, writing it on sticky notes for clients, embedding it in lectures and prayers. It felt like gospel stripped to its essence.

2. The Liturgy of Maintenance

For a long time, I treated self-care as a task list. Eat. Sleep. Meditate. Repeat. It wasn't until I understood these actions as ceremony that they began to matter.
The first glass of water in the morning became an act of consecration.
The evening walk—pilgrimage.
Medication—communion of chemistry and grace.

Maintenance, I realized, is devotion disguised as routine.
It's not the ecstatic kind of faith, but the durable one—the faith that washes the same dish every night and believes it still matters.

In the hospital, I saw nurses practicing this liturgy constantly: checking vitals, fluffing pillows, adjusting drips. Their prayers had names like *charting* and *rounds,* but their movements were pure mercy. Holiness, it turned out, had callouses.

3. The Liturgy of the Ordinary Table

A few months after my last major relapse, I invited friends to dinner for the first time in years. The table wasn't fancy—mismatched plates, half-burned candles—but it felt like resurrection.

No one prayed aloud. Still, reverence filled the room. We passed dishes slowly, as if aware of what it meant to feed and be fed again.

Halfway through, someone laughed so hard that wine spilled across the table. No one rushed to clean it. We just watched it pool between the plates—a red reminder that joy can stain as deeply as grief.

I caught myself smiling without thinking about it, my body remembering celebration without choreography. That was the liturgy of return: ordinary fellowship sanctified by survival.

4. The Liturgy of Honest Words

Language had once been my hiding place—scripture quotes, clinical jargon, metaphors polished to distraction. Recovery demanded a different vocabulary: smaller, truer, less afraid of silence.

Now my prayers sound like this:
"I'm tired."
"I don't know."
"Help."
"Thank you."

The simplicity of those phrases feels radical in a world that prizes eloquence. Honesty has its own cadence. Every truth spoken aloud recalibrates the nervous system toward safety. In that way, confession and regulation are twins—the body catching up to what the mouth dares to say.

5. The Liturgy of Staying

The hardest ritual to learn was staying.
Not praying. Not performing. Just staying.

Staying through the awkward pauses in conversation, through relapse, through silence that felt like rejection.

In the clinic, I watched a chaplain sit beside a patient who hadn't spoken in days. She said nothing, only adjusted her breathing to match his. After a while his lips moved, barely audible: "You stayed."

That's the whole creed, isn't it?
The sacredness of presence, the gospel of proximity. No sermon, no cure, just endurance as a form of love.

6. The Liturgy of Release

Eventually I learned that every ritual must end. Even staying has its rhythm of letting go.
There's a point in every session, every visit, every season when closure announces itself. The trick is to honor the ending without dramatizing it—to recognize that leaving can also be holy.

I've come to see release as its own sacrament:
blowing out the candle, closing the notebook, turning off the light.
Each gesture says, *Enough for today.*
And in a world addicted to progress, that sentence might be the most countercultural prayer we have.

7. The Liturgy of Beginning Again

What comes after release is not emptiness but renewal.
Recovery is cyclical; grace recurs. Every morning the world rehearses resurrection: light spilling through blinds, lungs filling with air, coffee brewing its quiet benediction.

We keep beginning, not because we failed, but because continuation is the shape of being alive.

Once, after a lecture, a student asked me how to "stay healed." I told her the truth: "You don't. You start over every day."
She looked confused. "That sounds exhausting."
"It is," I said. "But it's also freedom."

Beginning again means the story never closes on despair. It keeps writing itself toward light.

8. The Liturgy of Witness

Every community needs witnesses—those who hold the memory of others' survival when they forget it themselves.
I've been that witness and I've needed that witness.
Sometimes it's as simple as a text: *Thinking of you.* Sometimes it's a glance across a room that says, *I still see you.*

Witnessing transforms pain from private torment into shared meaning. It's how the human nervous system learns to trust safety again—through eyes that do not look away.

That's why every recovery group, every therapy session, every shared meal becomes an act of public theology. Presence itself is our profession of faith.

9. The Liturgy of Gratitude That Doesn't Pretend

Gratitude once felt performative, a forced optimism to mask despair. Now it feels quieter. It lives in my shoulders when they drop, in my breath when it slows, in the simple fact that I can name where I hurt.

I no longer thank God *for* the pain, but I thank life *through* it.
Gratitude without pretense is a form of integrity—it refuses to lie about suffering yet insists on noticing what remains.

Some nights, that gratitude is wordless. I just sit near the open window, listening to the city's low hum, the pulse of ongoingness. That sound is prayer enough.

10. The Liturgy of Wholeness

Eventually, all these fragments—arrival, maintenance, honesty, staying, release—begin to overlap.
They form a rhythm more than a rule, a way of moving through the world that turns ordinary acts into sacraments.

Wholeness doesn't mean unbroken. It means all the pieces are allowed to belong.

I see it now in the mirror: the face lined with laughter and loss, the hands that still tremble but also heal, the breath that continues its steady litany. This body, once my enemy, has become my temple. Every scar is architecture. Every inhale, a hymn.

That's the secret I wish someone had told me earlier:
We didn't need new beliefs; we needed new liturgies—rituals elastic enough to hold what the old prayers could not.

The world is still teaching them to us:
the teacher who pauses class to let students breathe,
the therapist who lights a candle before sessions,
the parent who whispers, "You're safe," at bedtime,
the friend who texts, "Still here," after months of silence.
Each is a small gospel of endurance, a script for belonging in a century that keeps forgetting how.

We don't always need more faith. We need faith translated into motion.
The rituals are already happening; our task is to notice.

Notice the way morning begins before we do.
The kettle warming water, the streetlights dimming as the sky shifts color.
Notice how you reach for your phone not just for information, but to confirm that the world still exists—that someone, somewhere, has already posted proof of life.
Notice how breath meets body before the mind even wakes.
Each of these moments is liturgy in disguise.

We keep looking for holiness in spectacle, when it's been whispering under our routines all along.

I've begun to think the divine prefers subtle choreography: the mundane repetition of kindness that no one sees, the small mercies we perform without credit.

Maybe heaven is the aggregate of unnoticed gestures—the nurse's hand steadying a vein, the teacher who stays after class, the stranger who holds the elevator for someone still running.

In the early years of recovery, I believed healing required dramatic proof—tears, testimonies, a visible transformation others could applaud. But now I see the quieter evidence: the unpaid bill finally mailed, the appointment kept, the apology offered, the friend texted back.

These are resurrections measured in inches, not miles

They don't announce themselves as miracles, but the nervous system knows better.

Each completion restores a small unit of trust in the body, reminding it that follow-through is still possible.

That's the secret the ancient liturgies understood: faith is repetition sanctified by intention.

Rituals train the body to keep showing up even when belief lags behind. You don't have to feel ready to light a candle; you light it, and readiness follows.

You don't have to believe the words of a prayer; you speak them, and belief grows in the echo.

The gesture precedes the revelation.

One afternoon, I found myself watching a mother and child in a park.

The boy tripped and scraped his knee. The mother didn't panic. She knelt, brushed away dirt, blew softly on the wound, whispered something too low to hear.

It was instinctive—a ritual older than language.

I thought: this is theology rendered through touch.

Every act of care is a sermon in flesh and breath.

Rituals evolve because need does.

Where once we built cathedrals, now we build kitchens and clinics.

Where once incense rose to signal divinity, now steam rises from soup cooked for a friend who's grieving.

The setting changes; the intention doesn't.

We're still trying to say: *You matter. You belong. You're safe to start again.*

Some of the most profound rituals I've witnessed weren't designed at all.

They happened between colleagues in hallways, between lovers reconciling after an argument, between parents learning to say *I'm sorry* to their children.

Ritual happens every time someone refuses to abandon tenderness.

A man in one of my workshops once said, "I don't pray anymore. I just talk to the air and hope someone's listening."

I told him, "That's prayer—stripped of pretense, still reaching."

He smiled. "Then I guess I never stopped."

We laughed, and in that laughter something holy passed between us. Not doctrine, not certainty—just mutual recognition.

That's the anatomy of liturgy: attention transforming ordinary air into sanctuary.

There's a practice I've developed in recent years.

When I sense despair returning, I name three ordinary mercies aloud.

Today: a clean sink. A text from my sister. A cup of tea still warm.

Naming them doesn't erase pain, but it interrupts despair's monologue long enough for light to reenter the conversation.

Each naming is a rung on the ladder back to equilibrium.

Gratitude, when practiced this way, is less about thanks and more about recalibration—a nervous system rebalancing through recognition.

Sometimes I teach this to clients.

We call it the *breath inventory.*

One deep inhale, one exhale, then three things that tether you to the moment.

It sounds simple. It is.

But every great ritual is built on simplicity repeated with intention.

I think often about how early communities survived exile and dislocation. When temples were destroyed, they made prayer portable—turning memory itself into sacred space.

We do the same today, though our exiles look different.

We build sanctuaries out of playlists, group chats, shared recipes, weekly check-ins.

Faith, at its core, is continuity under duress—the insistence that connection will find a new form.

That is why our most enduring rituals fit in the body: the bow, the breath, the tear, the touch.

They travel easily through history and still make sense to anyone who has ever needed to feel safe.

In one of our hospital workshops, a patient once asked me, "What if I don't believe in God?"
I told her, "Then believe in continuity."
She tilted her head. "You mean hope?"

"Not exactly," I said. "Hope is a wish for change. Continuity is the willingness to keep showing up, even if nothing changes today."
She smiled faintly. "That I can do."
When she died a few months later, her sister found a note taped to her mirror: *Keep showing up.*

That, too, became a liturgy—paper and ink as testament, handwriting as relic.

Liturgy, I've realized, is not just repetition; it's remembrance.
It's how the body keeps faith when memory falters.
I think of trauma survivors whose bodies flinch before the mind recalls why, yet who still reach for safety despite not feeling safe. That reach itself is ritual—the body rehearsing trust until the soul catches up.

Every prayer ever written began that way: an organism reaching toward what it could not yet name.

And maybe that's what our new liturgies are doing now—helping us remember how to reach again.

Not upward, but outward. Not for certainty, but for contact.

We live in a century of noise. Algorithms harvest attention, screens flatten intimacy, the nervous system never fully rests. In such a world, ritual is rebellion.

Lighting a candle before sleep, setting the phone face down, breathing once before answering an email—these are acts of resistance.

They say: I refuse to live only at the speed of urgency. I choose rhythm.

That rhythm is where the sacred still hides.

Every pause, every deliberate breath, is a sanctuary reclaiming its walls.

Sometimes, when I finish a session or close my laptop late at night, I sit

quietly with my hands resting on my knees.
No music, no mantra, just awareness.
I notice how the pulse in my wrists syncs with the ticking clock, how breath slows of its own accord.
I tell myself, *This, too, counts.*
No incense, no choir, no witness—just a human being acknowledging existence without shame.
If there is a God, I suspect that's all God ever asked of us: to pay attention long enough to remember we are alive.

I think back to the earliest pages of this book—how everything began with silence, survival, and breath.
Every chapter since has been its own small liturgy of noticing: noticing pain, noticing help, noticing the body's refusal to surrender.

Writing has become my altar, each word a candle lit against forgetting.

When readers tell me they see themselves in these stories, I hear it as call-and-response. The echo completes the ritual. What begins in isolation ends in communion.

In the end, the liturgies we needed were never about religion.
They were about rhythm, remembrance, and return.

We needed ceremonies that could outlast certainty, rituals wide enough for grief, spacious enough for doubt, gentle enough for the body's slow re-entry into trust.

We needed prayers that could be whispered mid-panic, blessings that could be texted, sacraments that could survive the hospital, the waiting room, the long commute home.

And we found them. Not all at once, but in fragments—
in the breath that steadied,
the hand that stayed,
the light that didn't leave.

Maybe that's the truest liturgy of all:
the ongoing choreography of attention,
performed in kitchens and clinics,
where every gesture of care says, without ceremony or applause,
You are still here. You are still held.

Reflection

Ritual is the body's way of remembering meaning.
When faith breaks, ritual repairs it one motion at a time.
We are not waiting for sacredness to return—it never left.
Our task is simpler, harder, and infinitely holier:
to keep noticing the ordinary,
until it becomes extraordinary again.

CHAPTER TWENTY-SEVEN: AN ALTAR FOR THE ANXIOUS

"Anxiety is not faithlessness.

It is the body keeping vigil for what it has not yet learned to trust."

It begins, as most evenings do, with the hum.
The refrigerator, the street outside, my own pulse in my throat — a symphony of small alarms. There are nights when anxiety feels less like emotion and more like architecture: a scaffolding of vigilance built to keep me upright.

Once, I would have called this restlessness sin, or failure, or lack of faith. Now I know better. Anxiety is the body praying without words, the nervous system's way of saying *I want to live, but I don't yet feel safe.*

So I light a candle.

It's the only ritual that still makes sense when the mind begins to spiral. The flame steadies me, though it doesn't calm the panic completely. I don't ask it to. I just let it exist — a focal point for my attention, a small sanctuary flickering on the edge of overwhelm.

This is my altar: a desk covered in ordinary things.
A stack of books. A chipped mug. The prescription bottle I used to hide.
None of it holy, except that it's mine.
An altar, I've learned, doesn't need to be beautiful. It just needs to hold what feels unbearable without flinching.

For years, anxiety meant failure of control.
Now it feels more like devotion. The mind replays every possibility, not because it wants to suffer, but because it wants to prepare, to protect.
There's a strange kindness in that impulse, even if it hurts.
I used to fight it. Now I listen.

When my heart races, I place a hand on my chest and whisper, "You think we're in danger, don't you?"

It sounds absurd, but it works.
The body answers with a slower beat, surprised that someone finally asked what it needed instead of ordering it to behave.

Therapy has taught me to name sensations before they name me.
Fear. Pressure. Tightness. Tremor.
Sometimes I trace them like constellations — a map of all the places I am still learning to trust.
Each point of tension is a petition: *Be patient with me. I'm trying.*

And in that acknowledgment, something like worship begins.

I think often about the phrase *peace that passes understanding.*
For a long time I assumed it meant serenity beyond logic.
But maybe it means peace that doesn't need to make sense — the kind that coexists with racing thoughts and still manages to hold them gently.

Peace doesn't erase panic. It just sits beside it.
Like a therapist waiting for breath to return.
Like a friend who doesn't hang up when you say you can't talk right now but don't want to be alone.
Like the light that stays on in the next room, proof that presence still exists even when you can't enter it yet.

That, I think, is what faith feels like now: proximity without demand.

I built my first real altar during the height of my panic attacks.
It wasn't planned. I just started gathering what helped me breathe: a smooth stone, a small wooden cross, a photograph of the ocean, the lavender oil my therapist recommended. Each object held a fragment of calm. Together they formed a geography of safety.

Every night, I'd sit before it and let my thoughts scatter. Sometimes I prayed. Sometimes I cursed. Sometimes I said nothing at all. The altar didn't mind. It wasn't measuring devotion. It was offering containment.

Over time, that small practice became my theology: God as containment,

not correction.
A presence big enough to absorb the chaos without condemning it.

Anxiety still visits.
Sometimes in the grocery store, sometimes in traffic, sometimes during prayer.
But the difference now is that I greet it like an old relative — exhausting, yes, but familiar.
I make space. I breathe slower. I name what is true: *I am safe enough in this moment.*
The words don't banish fear, but they frame it.
Boundaries are also sacred architecture.

I think of all the anxious bodies I've sat beside — friends, clients in waiting rooms, strangers trembling in public places — and how each one taught me something about holiness.
We've been told that God lives in peace, but what if God also lives in panic?
What if holiness isn't the absence of fear, but the willingness to stay with it until it softens into trust?

There's a small chapel downtown where I sometimes sit when I can't find language. It's usually empty, except for the caretaker polishing the railings. The pews creak like knees. The air smells of wood and wax.
I light a candle and watch its reflection ripple in the metal bowl of holy water. The motion steadies my breathing. Each flicker reminds me that stability is not stillness — it's movement that knows its limits.

I watch people enter: a woman with a stroller, a man in hospital scrubs, a teenager in headphones. None of us speak, yet we form a temporary congregation of pulse and presence. Everyone brings their own reasons; everyone leaves a little lighter. That's the secret of anxiety's liturgy—it's communal even when silent.

I remember the first time a panic attack subsided without shame.
I was in bed, hands gripping the sheets, body shaking, convinced I would

die.
But somewhere beneath the storm, another voice emerged—steady, quiet, maternal.
Stay here, it said. *This will pass.*
And it did.

The fear didn't disappear; it dissolved into exhaustion.
I fell asleep with tears on my face, half-believing that something sacred had just happened.

I still think it had.
Not a miracle of rescue, but of endurance.
I had learned to let panic finish its sentence without interrupting it.

In the years since, I've begun to see anxious people as the prophets of our time.
We are the ones who sense imbalance before it becomes catastrophe.
We are the ones whose bodies insist that something is wrong, even when systems pretend otherwise.

Our trembling is information. Our vigilance, inconvenient truth.

If the world had listened to its anxious ones sooner—those who warned of injustice, climate, loneliness—we might have healed faster.
But prophets are rarely honored in their own nervous systems.

So we build altars.
Not to worship fear, but to befriend it.
To remind ourselves that hypervigilance was once survival, and that even now it deserves compassion before correction.

Some nights I imagine every anxious soul on earth lighting a candle at the same hour.
Each flame small, trembling, imperfect.
From above, the world would look covered in constellations — tiny points of endurance refusing to go out.
That, I think, is the true shape of faith: billions of flickers saying in unison, *Still here.*

Anxiety is not the opposite of peace.
It is peace's bodyguard — the proof that something still cares enough to warn us when we've gone too long without rest.

An altar for the anxious does not demand silence.
It invites honesty.
It teaches the trembling hand to stay steady long enough to light its own candle.

And in that trembling, a new kind of prayer emerges:
not for calm,
but for company —
for the grace to keep breathing
until peace remembers our name.

Because it does remember.
Not always immediately, not always gently, but eventually peace finds its way back—like sunlight negotiating its return through clouded glass. Sometimes it comes disguised as fatigue, sometimes as quiet hunger, sometimes as a sudden realization that you've been breathing evenly for several minutes and didn't notice when that began.

Peace is rarely dramatic.
It arrives with the humility of maintenance.
A glass of water within reach.
A body no longer flinching at its own pulse.
The air no longer tilting toward panic.

I used to think recovery meant silence in the mind, an absence of anxiety altogether.
Now I understand it as *conversation resumed.*
Peace doesn't cancel the noise; it reenters it.
It sits beside the hum, listens, and hums back—slightly lower, steady enough to retune the room.

That's what healing feels like now: the sound of resonance returning after years of discord.

Not triumph. Not cure. Just balance, rediscovered in fragments.

Some mornings I still wake with my heart already racing.
I've stopped calling that failure.
It's just the body rehearsing its old lines, testing for danger out of habit.
I don't shame it for that anymore.
Instead, I stretch my arms above my head, let the first inhale expand my ribs, and whisper, *You're safe enough now.*

That phrase is my new prayer.
Not *safe forever.* Just *safe enough now.*
Enough for breakfast. Enough for this hour.
Enough for the next step in the day.
It's a liturgy of increments—faith measured in small doses of breath.

There was a time when I needed faith to be absolute.
I needed guarantees.
But living inside anxiety teaches you to love the partial, the imperfect, the nearly steady.
Because that's what life actually is: a series of almosts sustained by grace.
The anxious heart is not broken—it's attuned.
It feels too much because it refuses to forget that everything matters.

And maybe that's its holiness: a nervous system still awake to tenderness in a world that numbs so easily.

So, I've stopped praying for calm.
I pray for capacity.
To stay with the ache without drowning in it.
To hold fear by the hand and still look for beauty.
To find peace, not by escaping sensation, but by expanding to include it.

On the bus the other day, I sat behind two teenagers whispering about a test they'd failed. One said, "I couldn't breathe during it," and the other answered, "Same."

They laughed.
Something in their laughter felt redemptive—a reminder that even panic, when shared, loses its sharpest edge.
I thought of how communal anxiety is the soil of compassion: it's what teaches us empathy faster than theology ever could.

Maybe that's the altar I've been building all along—not of objects, but of attention.
A portable altar carried inside the body.
No candles required, only pulse.
No scripture, only repetition: *still here, still breathing.*

Each anxious breath a small offering,
each heartbeat a bell,
each trembling moment proof that life continues its patient work inside us, whether or not we feel ready to participate.

I've started thinking of my body as a small cathedral—
one where panic and peace take turns lighting the candles.
The nave is my chest, the pulpit my lungs, the choir my bloodstream singing oxygen's hymn.
Some nights, anxiety still preaches too loudly, but the architecture holds.
The walls have been reinforced by years of staying.

When I finally fall asleep, I imagine the body itself kneeling,
grateful for another day spent keeping vigil.
And somewhere between heartbeat and dream,
I can almost hear the whispered benediction:

You stayed. That was enough.

Peace is not a prize for the untroubled.
It is a rhythm that returns when we've learned how to listen.
It remembers our name because we were never truly forgotten.

Every breath is the body calling the spirit back home.
Every exhale writes the same message into the air:

I am still here. I am still held.

That is the final altar—the one carried everywhere,
where anxiety itself becomes devotion,
and trembling becomes prayer.

Reflection

Anxiety prays even when we don't.
It calls the body back from distraction,
reminds us how fragile, how fierce, how faithful our breathing can be.

The altar for the anxious was never in a temple or clinic;
it was always the heart learning, again and again,
that survival is sacred.

And so we bless the tremor,
we bless the heartbeat,
we bless the holy work of staying—
until peace, faithful as ever,
remembers our name and answers back.

CHAPTER TWENTY-EIGHT: REWRITING THE BENEDICTION

"We were told to say 'Amen' when it was over.

No one taught us how to say it when we were still becoming."

For most of my life, benedictions meant closure.
Hands raised. Lights dimmed.
A room emptied of its congregation.
Every blessing was a curtain call — gratitude for what had passed, anticipation for what might come next.

But healing is not linear, and neither is grace.
You can't bless an ending that never really ends.
You can only pause inside its unfolding.

So I've begun to rewrite the benediction.
Not to change the words, but to change the posture.
To speak it not from the pulpit of conclusion, but from the threshold of continuation.

The first time I tried to write a new blessing, nothing came.
The old vocabulary still carried too much authority — *Go in peace. Depart in faith.*
They sounded too certain, too final.
I didn't feel peace. I hadn't departed. I was still here, still halfway between collapse and return.

So I started smaller.
I began blessing things that never made it into formal prayers.

Bless the messy apartment, the unmade bed, the unanswered texts.
Bless the breath that trembles but keeps arriving.

Bless the body for staying even when the mind couldn't.
Bless the voice that broke mid-sentence and the friend who didn't flinch when it did.

Bless the half-remembered verse, the unfinished journal entry, the apology still forming.
Bless what remains unfinished, unspoken, ongoing.

This, I realized, was how real benediction begins — not as closure, but as companionship.

I once thought blessings had to come from authority — a priest, a parent, a professional who knew what to say.
But the most healing benedictions I've ever received came from ordinary mouths.

A nurse who whispered, "Take your time."
A friend who said, "Text me when you can, even if you don't know what to say."
A stranger at a bus stop who noticed my shaking hands and offered gum without comment.

Each was a liturgy of unscripted grace.
Each carried the same theological truth: that holiness happens whenever compassion speaks first.

Now, when I imagine blessing someone, I picture this:
No pulpit, no robe, no spotlight.
Just a hand on a shoulder, the kind of touch that says, *I see you. You don't have to be fine to be loved.*
That's the only sermon I trust anymore.

Because a benediction is not permission to leave — it's permission to continue.
It says, *You can go now,* but also, *You can come back anytime.*

One afternoon, during therapy, my counselor asked what the word "Amen" means to me now.
I told her it used to mean finality — the seal on a prayer, the last breath before the lights came on.
Now it means *so be it,* but softer.
It means *I'm still here for whatever comes next.*
It means survival without performance.

She smiled. "Then you've rewritten it already."

When I think about the last five years — the breakdowns, the breathwork, the slow unlearning of shame — I see how every small return was its own benediction.
Every relapse forgiven. Every appointment kept. Every morning that began with panic but ended with stillness.
None of them dramatic, but all of them sacred.

Maybe that's what healing has been teaching me: that the real benedictions are written in behavior, not ink.
They live in the body's willingness to try again.

If I were to bless you now, I wouldn't start with scripture.
I'd start with breath.

Inhale: what you carried.
Exhale: what you no longer need to hold.

I'd tell you that endurance counts as devotion, that tears are a form of baptism, that anxiety is just vigilance misplaced.

I'd tell you that every time you choose to stay, you rewrite the benediction again.

Because staying is the new Amen.
Not the closing word, but the continuing one.

Some nights I reread the ancient blessings — Aaron's priestly words, the psalms of ascent, the doxologies that end in shining light and everlasting peace. I love them still, but differently now.
They're not instructions anymore. They're echoes.
They remind me that people across centuries have all been trying to say the same thing: *Don't give up yet.*

Even the oldest liturgies began as improvisations of hope.
Someone, somewhere, once had to be the first to speak light into a frightened room.
We inherit those voices and add our own — a lineage of trembling benedictions whispered through time.

I think of all the names this book could have ended with: grace, peace, release.
But the truest ending is not an ending at all.
It's a continuation — a collective inhale that carries us into what's next.
We have said the words *Hold me while I break.*
Now the invitation widens:
Hold me while I heal.

Not a demand. Not a doctrine. Just a prayer that makes room for process.
So here's the blessing I finally found — the one that doesn't pretend to close the wound, only to hold it gently while it closes itself:

May the breath you take next remind you that you are already participating in the sacred.
May your body learn to rest without apology.
May you find, in your own timing, a peace that remembers your name.
May you know that this, right here, still counts as faith.

And when the world asks for your Amen,

you may whisper it softly,
or not at all —
knowing that your staying
has already said enough.

After years of speaking blessings that didn't belong to me, I'm learning how to speak my own—haltingly, experimentally, without guarantee that the words will land.

Some evenings I walk to the park near my apartment and sit on the bench where the light lasts longest. The trees stretch their shadows across the grass, and I whisper small benedictions into the wind. They're not for anyone specific; they're practice. A way to remind my mouth that tenderness can be spoken aloud without requiring audience or approval.

"Bless the body that still wakes up afraid," I say.
"Bless the heart that can't yet forgive itself."
"Bless the one who keeps trying anyway."

Sometimes I repeat them. Sometimes I run out of language and let the silence finish the sentence. The silence always knows more than I do.

The Body as a Script for Blessing

I've started to think of the body as the oldest liturgical text.
When we bow our heads in exhaustion, that's reverence.
When we unclench our fists, that's confession.
When we breathe all the way down into the stomach and exhale slowly, that's Amen.

No doctrine required—only awareness.
Every physical act is a potential benediction waiting to be noticed.

In therapy we call it regulation.

In theology, incarnation.
Both name the same miracle: meaning returning to matter.
The sacred was never lost; it was hiding inside our anatomy, waiting for permission to speak through us again.

So now, when I say a blessing, I move.
I stretch my fingers. I roll my shoulders. I let the body write what the mind can't yet phrase.
It's a slower grammar, but a truer one.

The Communion of the Ordinary

One afternoon at a café, the barista slid my drink across the counter and said, "Take care of yourself."
He meant it casually, but something in his tone reached me.
It sounded like a line from a liturgy older than language.

Take care of yourself.
Not because you've earned it, but because you're here.
Not as reward, but as recognition.

I thought about how many secular benedictions pass between us every day—on sidewalks, in emails, in checkout lines—tiny transmissions of care disguised as etiquette.
Maybe the sacred is not diminishing in our century; maybe it's decentralizing.
Maybe every "be safe," "sleep well," "text when you get home" is the modern church service continuing without the steeple.

We bless one another constantly, usually without realizing it.
And maybe that's the purest form of prayer—one that doesn't need acknowledgment to count.

The Benediction of Imperfection

There are still days when I forget everything I've written here.
Days when I rush through the ritual, lose patience, curse at the mirror.
I've stopped trying to banish those moments; they're part of the liturgy too.

The ancient priests used to repeat the entire service if they stumbled over a single word.
I used to admire that precision.
Now I find holiness in the stumble itself—the proof that the sacred tolerates imperfection.

So when I falter mid-blessing, I start over, not from shame but from rhythm.
The mistake becomes another verse.
That's how recovery works: repetition transfigured into renewal.

Language After Silence

A few months ago, I attended a small interfaith gathering.
At the end, the facilitator asked each of us to share one word we would carry into the week.
Around the circle came: *gratitude, patience, surrender, love.*
When it was my turn, I said, "again."

It wasn't poetic; it was honest.
Again is the most faithful word I know.
Again is what resurrection sounds like in real time.

Afterward, a woman I'd never met came over and whispered, "Thank you. That's my word too."
We hugged, two strangers agreeing that continuation is sacred enough.
I realized then that benediction doesn't have to end with a blessing spoken *to* others.
It can be a word spoken *with* them.

A shared breath disguised as language.

The Architecture of Continuation

There's a chapel near my neighborhood built entirely from recycled materials—broken glass, salvaged brick, wood pulled from old barns. When the afternoon sun hits it, the walls shimmer with fragments of color. No two pieces match, yet together they hold.

Every time I see it, I think: that's what my faith looks like now.
A patchwork of salvaged prayers.
A structure built from what survived the collapse.

Inside, the altar is plain concrete. People leave handwritten notes on it—pleas, confessions, thanks, drawings by children. The caretaker never removes them; he lets the wind scatter them when it's time.
It's the most honest benediction I've ever seen: impermanent, porous, alive.

That chapel taught me something essential:
A blessing doesn't have to last forever to be real.
It only has to hold long enough for someone to breathe again.

Writing as Benediction

When I began this book, I thought I was writing my way *out* of pain.
Now I see that I was writing myself *back* into belonging.
Each chapter became a small benediction for a self that once felt unworthy of being addressed.

I am still in therapy.
I still forget to rest.
But every time I return to the page, I feel a little more human, a little more possible.

That's what benediction does—it restores possibility.

So I keep writing, not to prove healing, but to remember it.
Each sentence a new *so be it,* a quiet *again.*

The Blessing of the Reader

If this book has reached you, you have already entered the circle of its blessing.
You are part of the benediction now.
Every reader becomes a continuation of the voice that began these pages—another echo saying, *still here, still trying, still worth saving.*

Maybe that's how collective healing happens: through echoes that refuse extinction.
One person breathes a blessing they don't yet believe; another hears it and remembers their own.
And somewhere between those two breaths, the world mends by a fraction.

A Closing Without Ending

The night before I finished this manuscript, I sat on the floor surrounded by drafts and notes.
My body hummed with the same anxious electricity that once meant collapse.
But this time, it felt different—less like danger, more like aliveness.
I realized the hum had always been there, even in silence; I had just learned to hear it differently.

So I whispered into the quiet room:
"Bless the unfinished. Bless the ongoing. Bless the light that hasn't decided where to land."

And the air, ordinary as ever, seemed to pause just long enough to agree.

RITUAL – A LETTER FROM THE HEALED SELF

Find a quiet space. Sit where your breath feels unhurried.
Place a hand over your chest and take one deep inhale. Let the exhale fall all the way through you. Imagine tomorrow's version of yourself—steady, rested, alive.

Pick up your pen and begin:

Dear Me Who Stayed,

Tell yourself what it feels like to breathe without panic. Describe the quiet of a morning where survival is no longer the only task. Write about the way light moves across the room, about how the body—your body—feels like home again.

Remind yourself of the moments you thought you would not make it through and did.
Write in detail the strength it took to stay, even when hope felt mechanical. Let the healed voice be honest, not perfect. Let it speak tenderness into every wound that once named you broken.

You might say:
I know how hard it was to believe the pain would pass. I remember the sleepless nights and the shaking hands. But I also remember how you kept breathing. You kept showing up for the smallest tasks—the cup of water, the text to a friend, the walk around the block. Each act was a prayer disguised as routine. Each breath was a benediction.

Thank your former self for enduring what healing required.
Forgive the days you disappeared.
Bless the version of you that kept trying.

Close the letter however you need: with a promise, with a sigh, with an unfinished sentence.
When you are done, read it aloud as if offering a prayer for both the person you were and the one you are becoming.

End your letter with these words:

I forgive you for forgetting that you were never alone.

Seal the page.
Fold it once.
Keep it somewhere near your breath.

Reflection

Benediction is not a sentence; it's a cycle.
It moves through us, gathers what we've carried, and returns as breath.
Every attempt to begin again is another verse in its eternal refrain.

So let this be ours:

May the words you cannot yet speak still find their listener.
May the silences you endure become fertile with meaning.
May your body learn to bless itself for surviving the day.
May you know that grace is repetition, not reward.

And when you reach the edge of language,
when all you can manage is a whisper,
let that whisper count as prayer.

For every quiet *again*
is a rewritten *Amen.*

CHAPTER TWENTY-NINE: A GOSPEL OF SMALL RETURNINGS

Relapse is not foreign to faith. It is written into scripture's cadence, into the nervous system's rhythms, into every survivor's testimony. What religion has often called backsliding, what psychology names recurrence, survivors know as the spiral of coming and going, leaving and returning. "Every time I slipped, I thought it meant I was disqualified," one woman said. "But the truth was, every return was still holy." Clinical evidence confirms that relapse is part of most recovery trajectories—substance use, depression, anxiety, trauma alike. Theological reflection mirrors it: Israel wandered, Peter denied, Thomas doubted. Each time, return was still welcomed.

A man in recovery from alcohol addiction described how his congregation struggled to understand his relapses. "They prayed for total deliverance. When I drank again, they thought it was a lack of faith." He nearly left church altogether until a small group leader reframed it: "Every time you come back, that's victory." That shift—from shame to dignity—saved him. Research on addiction treatment shows that reframing relapse as part of recovery increases long-term sobriety. Theology echoes this in the parable of the prodigal son: return is celebrated, not penalized.

Another survivor, managing bipolar disorder, spoke of her repeated hospitalizations. "Every discharge felt like a false start," she said. "People in church stopped asking how I was. It was like they were tired of my story." In a therapy group, however, she discovered a different narrative: "They told me every hospitalization was another return to care, not a failure to stay well." That perspective aligned more with the gospel she longed for—mercy that never ended. Research on chronic illness affirms that repeated engagement with treatment is protective, even when symptoms recur. Theologically, it reflects lament psalms that end with hope again and again, not once for all.

Portraits of small returnings emerge in everyday acts. A woman with depression said, "Sometimes my return was just brushing my teeth after three days. Sometimes it was making it to morning prayer. Small, but it was return." She began blessing these moments as sacrament: a liturgy of the toothbrush, the prayer whispered half-asleep. Psychology recognizes this as behavioral activation—small steps that accumulate into recovery. Theology calls it faith as small as a mustard seed.

In another community, a pastor began ending services with: "Even if you return only by inches, it is still return." Survivors said it shifted their imagination. "I stopped believing I had to come back all at once. I believed God counted every step." Clinical research on motivational interviewing highlights the importance of affirming incremental progress. Theology affirms it too: the father runs to meet the prodigal "while he was still far off."

A young man with panic disorder told of missing months of church. "The first time I went back, I left halfway through. I thought it didn't count." But when a friend texted later, "It counts—you showed up," he began to cry. That single line became his gospel. "Showing up halfway was enough." Research on social support in anxiety confirms that partial participation increases tolerance and lowers avoidance over time. Theologically, it recalls the widow's mite—small, but holy.

Communal rituals can reframe relapse as return. In one church, a liturgy of "again" was created. After confession, the congregation prayed: "We return again. We return again. We return again." Survivors said it was like balm. "It gave me permission to keep coming back without apology." Theology recognizes this as teshuvah in Jewish tradition—return not once but continually. Clinical evidence shows that repetitive affirmations of return strengthen resilience against shame.

Another community designed a ritual for addiction recovery anniversaries. Instead of celebrating only milestones of abstinence, they honored "returns" of every size—returning to meetings, returning to therapy, returning to prayer. One man said, "It was the first time anyone clapped for me when I admitted relapse." Clinical literature affirms that nonjudgmental acknowledgment of relapse increases treatment re-engagement. Theologically, it resembles communal festivals of renewal, where the whole people return together year after year.

Embodied testimony reminds us that return is often quiet. A survivor of trauma said, "My return was lying on the floor breathing after a flashback instead of hurting myself. No one saw it, but it was sacred." Her therapist called it grounding. She called it grace. Research confirms that survivors who reframe grounding as spiritual practice show greater long-term resilience. Theology affirms that unseen acts are still sacrament: "Your Father who sees in secret will reward you."

A woman living with chronic depression remembered the shame she carried each time her symptoms resurfaced. "The community wanted my healing to be linear," she said. "I wanted that too. But my depression came in waves." Each time she returned to therapy or restarted medication, she felt like she had failed. Then a therapist told her, "Returning to care is not failure—it is resilience." She began writing that sentence on sticky notes and posting them around her house. "It became my gospel," she said. Clinical research confirms that normalizing recurrence reduces dropout from treatment and increases long-term wellness. Theology echoes this in the cycle of the liturgical year: Advent, Lent, Easter, Pentecost—returns that repeat, never once for all.

A young man navigating substance use relapse described how his family treated each slip as betrayal. "They said I had wasted their prayers," he recalled. He carried that shame until a recovery mentor told him, "Relapse is not the opposite of recovery—it is part of it." He began to frame each return to sobriety as liturgy: day one as prayer, day two as psalm, day three as sacrament. Over time, he stopped asking if he had failed and started blessing the act of returning again. Neuroscience research supports this reframing, showing that recovery involves repeated rewiring of neural pathways through cycles of practice, relapse, and return. Theology finds the same in Peter's denials and his repeated returns to Jesus—three failures, three restorations, three times told: feed my sheep.

Portraits of small returnings are often hidden in daily acts. A survivor of anxiety said her gospel of return was walking into the grocery store after months of avoiding public spaces. "I walked down one aisle, shaking, then left. It wasn't much, but it was return." Another survivor said his gospel of return was simply answering a phone call after weeks of isolation. "I heard my friend's voice and knew I was still part of the world." Psychology calls these exposure victories; survivors call them holiness.

In one congregation, a ritual of pebbles emerged. At the end of every service, congregants dropped a pebble in a bowl as a sign of showing up again. "It didn't matter how broken we felt," one survivor said. "The pebble meant we returned." Over time, the bowl filled with thousands of stones—evidence of countless small returns. Survivors said it was like a collective gospel: fragile, repetitive, and holy. Theologically, it resembled Israel's cairns of remembrance—stones stacked by rivers to testify that they had passed through. Clinical literature affirms that tangible markers of persistence increase resilience.

A woman with eating disorder recovery described how relapse often made her feel disqualified from faith. "I thought if I slipped, I had no right to pray." But a chaplain reminded her of daily bread: "Grace is renewed every morning, not stored for a lifetime." That became her mantra. Each meal she managed to eat was framed as daily bread, each relapse as an invitation to return the next day. Clinical findings on eating disorder recovery emphasize that recovery is often non-linear, requiring repeated returns to nourishment. Theology affirms it too: manna given each day, enough only for that day.

Other survivors rewrite ritual itself as return. A man who had left church for years due to panic disorder described his first time stepping back inside. "I sat in the last pew. I left before the service ended. But I touched the wood of the pew and thought: I am home again." He later described the moment as his gospel of return. Researchers call this incremental exposure; he called it resurrection. Theologically, it resembled the prodigal son's first step toward home, long before the feast.

In another community, relapse anniversaries were reframed. Instead of silence, they named the day a person returned to care, not the day they first fell. "We marked the date I re-entered treatment," one survivor said. "That date became holy." This reframing aligned with therapeutic emphasis on treatment engagement as progress, not failure. Theology mirrored it in exile and return: Israel remembered not only captivity but the day they came home.

Survivors also describe private liturgies of return. A woman wrote down every day she took her medication, not as compliance but as prayer. "I blessed the pill bottle before swallowing," she said. "It was my way of returning to life." For her, relapse was missing a dose; return was blessing the next one. This echoes research showing that ritualizing treatment improves adherence. Theology recognizes sacrament in ordinary objects—bread, wine, water, oil. For her, it was a small orange pill.

Communal casework illustrates institutional changes. A trauma-informed church stopped measuring belonging by attendance consistency. Instead, they celebrated each return, however brief. One pastor said, "When someone comes back after weeks away, we say: welcome home." Survivors said it changed everything. "I stopped hiding when I disappeared. I knew they would rejoice when I returned." Clinical evidence shows that reducing shame around absence increases re-engagement in care and community.[8] Theologically, it recalls the lost sheep—celebration over one return, not condemnation for wandering.

The gospel of small returnings is not a gospel of triumph. It is the gospel of fragments gathered, of footsteps retraced, of prayers repeated, of treatments restarted, of chairs returned to after long absences. It is a gospel that blesses relapse as rhythm, not rebellion—a gospel that knows progress is less a line than a spiral, widening and deepening with each turn.

It is the gospel of the toothbrush on the bathroom sink.
The pill bottle reopened after months of shame.
The therapist's waiting room revisited, even after silence stretched too long.

The sanctuary door pushed open, even for five hesitant minutes.

Each of these moments is a small resurrection, a sacrament of return.

Clinically, this gospel reframes recovery as cyclical and compassionate. It validates persistence over perfection. It names recurrence not as moral failure but as the nervous system's attempt to relearn safety. When clinicians hold this stance, shame loosens its grip. The survivor's story is no longer about relapse, but about resilience—a long apprenticeship in staying.

Theologically, this gospel proclaims that grace does not expire after one fall. It is not a one-time pardon but a renewable mercy—grace that revisits, repeats, and reforms itself around our humanity. The divine does not count collapses; it counts returns. Every exhale of surrender becomes an Amen.

Survivors testify:

"I thought every relapse meant the end. Now I know every return means the beginning."

And that is the gospel: not linear, not loud, but faithful. It is not the absence of breaking but the blessing of reassembly. It is the quiet discovery that holiness hides in the mundane: the morning meds, the laundry folded, the voicemail finally returned, the body that still breathes.

Every step back is a pilgrimage. Every tremor toward re-engagement is sacred ground. Each return, no matter how partial, is gospel.

When faith communities and clinicians bless these returns together—when they speak with one voice that healing is not in never falling but in always being welcomed home again—something remarkable happens. The walls between the clinic and the church, between the sacred and the psychological, begin to dissolve. What remains is presence, unsegmented and whole.

This is the saturation layer of healing:

the point where body, faith, and practice begin to speak the same language;
where the survivor no longer performs recovery but lives it;
where grace and neurobiology finally agree—both whispering, *you are allowed to start again.*

And when that whisper becomes a chorus—of therapists, friends, pastors, and survivors—healing stops being a theory. It becomes communion.

Liturgical Echo:
Inhale: Begin again.
Exhale: Welcome home.

EPILOGUE – HOLD ME WHILE I HEAL

"Healing was never an ending.
It was the quiet art of continuing—
of learning how to stay inside one's own skin without fleeing."

What we carried in, we now carry differently. The same wounds that once silenced us now speak in softer tones of wisdom.

The morning after I finished the last chapter, I woke before sunrise. The air was still heavy with sleep, that hour where the world is undecided between silence and motion. I sat on the edge of the bed and waited for breath to find its way back into rhythm.

It came slowly, as it always does: inhale, hold, exhale, repeat.
Each breath felt like a letter in an unfinished word.
Maybe this is what healing truly means—remembering how to spell one's own aliveness again.

For so long I mistook recovery for an ending. I thought there would be a day when the ache left completely, when anxiety retired, when grief finally paid its debts. But healing is not erasure. It's integration. It's what happens when pain stops demanding explanation and starts coexisting with peace.

Healing isn't what happens *after* the breaking.
It's what happens *within* it—when something inside us decides to hold the fragments long enough for light to leak through the seams.

The candle I keep on my desk is almost gone now, wick bent, glass rimmed with soot. I don't replace it right away. I let the space stay empty for a few days. The absence feels honest.

Healing, too, makes room for absence.

In the quiet, I trace the lines of wax hardened at the bottom of the jar and think about everything that has melted to make this light possible:
the sessions where silence did the talking,
the nights when panic didn't end but softened into fatigue,
the prayers I whispered into my own hands,
the names I said out loud so they wouldn't vanish.

Each one left residue.
And maybe residue is another word for memory—
a proof that what burned still illuminated something while it lasted.

If the first half of my life was a theology of endurance, the second half, I hope, will be a theology of ease.
Not passivity.
Ease as in *allowing*.
Allowing breath to come without evaluation.
Allowing joy to enter without permission slip.
Allowing sorrow to visit without calling it backsliding.

The therapist once said, "Your body will teach you what your doctrine never could."
She was right.
The body is the first scripture and the last altar.
It never lies.
It only waits to be listened to again.

Now, when I feel the old tightness in my chest, I don't rush to interpret it. I place a hand over it gently and say, "I'm still here."
It's both confession and creed.
The simplest theology I know.

Sometimes, when words fail me, I imagine God breathing beside me—not

as judge, not as cure, but as presence.
We sit in silence like two tired beings sharing air.
And in that quiet, I sense the most merciful truth of all: that holiness never required perfection, only participation.

That's all healing ever asked of me—to keep participating in life, even when I don't feel whole.
To keep breathing, not because I'm unbroken, but because I'm willing to begin again.

There is a memory I return to often.
A night years ago when everything felt unbearable—when the future narrowed to a single impossible breath. I remember sitting in my car, hands trembling, whispering a sentence I didn't believe: *I can't hold myself right now; someone, please hold me while I break.*

That plea became the title of this book.
But what I didn't know then was that the holding I needed would eventually come from within—from the patient, unglamorous process of learning to befriend the body that wanted to flee.

The same body that once terrified me has become the one holding me still.
That is grace.
Not rescue, but recognition.

I still light a candle some nights.
Not because I expect peace to descend, but because I like the company of a small, steady flame.
It reminds me that I can be both fragile and luminous.
That melting doesn't mean disappearing.
That even diminished light is still light.

When the wax pools, I whisper the same closing prayer every time:
Hold me while I heal.
Not to keep me from breaking,

but to remind me that breaking and healing
have always shared the same heartbeat.

The words settle into the air, then into me.
They aren't a demand, just a recognition of need.
A way of saying, *Stay a little longer. I'm almost at peace.*

Outside, the morning expands.
Windows glow in other apartments.
A neighbor's kettle whistles, a child laughs, a bus sighs at the curb.
The city stirs itself awake, unaware that it's participating in resurrection.

This, I think, is how every benediction continues: not through grand revelation, but through the daily decision to rejoin the world.
To pour the coffee.
To check the mail.
To take one steady breath and call it enough.

Healing is not an arrival.
It's a rhythm we keep returning to.
It's the body's way of saying, *You're still invited to exist.*

So, if these words have found you in the middle of your own unfinished season, know this:
You don't have to rush toward completion.
You don't have to apologize for the days that feel like relapse.
You don't have to wait until you are "better" to belong again.

Your healing is already happening.
Even now, in the pause between inhales, in the kindness you extend to yourself when no one sees it.
That is the work.
That is the worship.

When I close this final page, I want the silence that follows to feel less like an ending and more like breath held between verses.

Because none of this is over.
It just keeps unfolding—in the reader, in the body, in the slow pulse of the ordinary world.

We began with breaking.
We end with becoming.

And somewhere in between,
if only for a moment,
we learned to stay.

Final Reflection

May you find a gentleness that does not depend on circumstance.
May you be patient with the slow architecture of healing.
May you remember that every return—no matter how small—counts as resurrection.

And when you forget all of this,
may you begin again,
held by the quiet mercy
of the One, the breath, the body,
that never left.

You have breathed through confession, through collapse, through the quiet of return. The same breath that began this book ends it—only steadier now.

✦ INTERLUDE VI – *Transitional Benediction*

Light a candle. Sit still.
You've reached the end, but not the finish.

Every breath you've taken through these pages counts as prayer.
Every tear that blurred the words became a kind of liturgy.
Whisper this softly—
"I made it this far."

Let that sentence become a benediction.
Let it rest on your tongue like communion.
Let it remind you that survival, too, is sacred.

May you find a gentleness that does not depend on circumstance—
the kind that lingers even when certainty disappears.
May courage meet you not in the roar of clarity,
but in the quiet moment you choose to try again.
May peace learn the rhythm of your body,
breathing with you through the night and into morning.

If faith feels distant, let curiosity take its hand.
If love feels too heavy, let compassion carry the lighter end.
If hope feels impossible, let breath stand in for it until it returns.

And when you close this book, remember—
you are not closing the story.
You are carrying it.
It lives now in the rhythm of your own inhale and exhale,
in the prayer that begins whenever you begin again.

You are both reader and resurrection.
Both witness and continuation.
The world still needs the sound of your staying.

So, breathe once more before you go—
a breath for all that has been lost,
a breath for all that remains,
a breath for what you are still becoming.

Go in quiet strength.
Go in breath that remembers.
Go knowing this: you made it this far—and that is holy

✦ AUTHOR'S NOTE TO THE READER

When I began writing *Hold Me While I Break,* I didn't know where it would end. I only knew I wanted to tell the truth — that healing is rarely linear, that faith can coexist with doubt, and that therapy and prayer often speak the same language, only in different accents.

I wrote this book while still in therapy, still learning how to breathe through panic, still searching for words to match what the body already understood. Every page came from within the process, not beyond it. Nothing here is written from arrival. It is written mid-breath — from that trembling interval between collapse and clarity.

The voice that sometimes sounds like a therapist is not performance. It is memory — the echo of what I needed to hear when silence was loudest. It is the gentler voice I keep trying to cultivate toward myself.

If you found resonance here, it is not because I arrived anywhere certain. It is because we're standing in the same in-between — that middle space where endurance becomes grace and survival becomes sacred practice. This book was never meant to instruct; it was meant to accompany.

Thank you for letting me sit beside you through these pages. For allowing your own breath to mingle with mine. For joining a conversation that refuses neat endings — the dialogue between pain and persistence, between faith and the nervous system, between what breaks and what rebuilds us.

Wherever you are reading from — a hospital room, a sanctuary, a train, a sleepless night — I hope you carry this with you:

You do not have to be fixed to be worthy of belonging.
You do not have to be finished to be whole.

Healing isn't a prize for the patient; it's a rhythm we relearn, a practice of staying present inside what's still uncertain. It asks less for answers than for breath.

If these words helped you feel less alone, even for a page, then they have done their work.
The rest belongs to you now — the breath, the body, the becoming.

With gratitude and quiet faith,

— M. Anum-Addo

Acknowledgments

Books like this are never written alone.
They are built from conversations that lasted longer than courage, from the hands that steadied me when I forgot how to breathe, from the faith of people who saw light where I only saw exhaustion.

To the therapists who sat across from me in quiet rooms and taught me that silence could be safety—thank you. You gave me language when I thought I had none left. Every sentence in these pages carries traces of your patience.

To the friends who stayed through the seasons when I withdrew, who texted at the right hour without knowing why, who reminded me that presence counts even when words fail—you kept me tethered to the world.

To the readers and early listeners who believed this story could matter before it had a title—thank you for lending it your attention, your breath, and your empathy. You reminded me that honesty travels farther when it's shared.

To the faith communities that held space for my doubt, and to every person who taught me that prayer can look like therapy, and therapy can sound like prayer—your integration shaped this book's heartbeat.

And to my family—those who taught me endurance and tenderness in equal measure, who reminded me that love is not a rescue but a rhythm—thank you for being my first sanctuary.

Finally, to anyone reading this who is still somewhere in the middle of their own recovery: I see you. This book is as much yours as it is mine. You are part of the breath that made it possible.

With deep gratitude for every companion in the long work of staying,

— M. Anum-Addo

Afterword

When I first began these pages, I wrote out of desperation — to name what hurt before it consumed me.

Now, as the final line rests on the page, I understand that I was also writing toward you.

You, the reader sitting in a quiet room or a crowded train, turning a page because something in you still hopes words might steady the air.
You, who came here not for instruction, but for company.
You, who know what it means to break in private and still return to the world carrying kindness like a fragile light.

I can't tell you that healing will be quick or complete.
But I can tell you that it will find you — not once, but many times.
Sometimes through therapy, sometimes through prayer, sometimes through an ordinary moment so small it almost escapes your notice.

This book began with a plea: *Hold me while I break.*
It ends with a promise: *We will hold one another while we heal.*

Because that's all any of us can do—
keep breathing,
keep noticing,

keep offering the gentleness we once begged for.

And if you forget everything else, remember this:
you were never reading someone else's story.
You were remembering your own.

Reflections for Returning

These prompts are not assignments. They are invitations—to pause, to notice, to name what your body and spirit have carried.

1. When have I mistaken silence for absence?
2. What does my body know about prayer that my mind forgets?
3. How do I rest without apology?
4. What would it mean to forgive myself for surviving?
5. When have I confused control with safety?
6. Where does belonging live in my body?
7. What breath do I still owe myself?
8. Who do I trust to see me as healing, not broken?

Closing Note:

You are not asked to finish these. You are only asked to begin again, gently.

✦ READER'S BENEDICTION

Beloved journeyers—
you who have walked through both darkness and light,
may your breath find peace.

May the sacred breath that guided you through these pages
continue to ground you in hope.
May the Gods, the Ancestors, the Great Mystery—
or whatever name your spirit gives to the Holy—
walk beside you in quiet strength,
never louder than your heartbeat,
never farther than your next inhale.

May you feel the embrace of community in every step,
even when you walk alone.
May your body know rest deep enough to trust its own softness,
and may your spirit rise again when the world feels too heavy.
In hours of weariness, may you remember this truth:
you are stronger than you know,
more resilient than you imagined,
and infinitely more loved than you believed.

May the kindness you need be gathered
from the faces that wait for you in the world,
and from the tenderness that still lives within you.
When fear whispers lies,
may truth rise quietly in your chest like breath returning to form.
When doubt builds its walls,
may grace find the cracks and pour itself through.

Carry forward all that has kept you safe:
the prayers of friends, the lessons of pain, the light of forgiveness.
Carry forward the softness that dared to stay open

even after everything tried to close it.
Carry forward the stillness that taught you
that peace need not be loud to be real.

And when you falter—as all who live deeply will—
may your breath remind you that you are held:
by the earth beneath you,
by the sky above you,
by the Love that encircles all things and forgets no one.

Go now in peace.
Go with tenderness enough to meet the world as it is,
and courage enough to imagine it healed.
Carry with you the prayers we have spoken together,
the silences that became songs,
and the quiet conviction that you are not beyond redemption.

Find solace in the circle of belonging that holds you always.
Remember that your story, like breath, repeats—not to punish, but to renew.

You are not alone.
You are beloved.
You are whole.

Amen.

✦ POSTSCRIPT FROM THE AUTHOR

I have written from both sides of the conversation—sometimes as the therapist, sometimes as the patient—because in life I am still both.

Every scene you've read was imagined from the waiting room, not from behind a desk. I have sat on both sides of that door: the one who listens, and the one who trembles before speaking. The clinician's voice that appears in these chapters is a mirror, not a mask—a way of letting compassion speak to itself. Writing this way became my form of integration, a dialogue between the self that guides and the self that grieves.

The truth is, I am still learning how to heal without performing healing. I am still practicing what it means to recover without resolution—to sit across from my own questions and breathe through the silence they create. Some days, I manage it. Other days, I simply start again.

I am still in therapy. I still have nights when anxiety folds the edges of my breath. I still have mornings when faith flickers and the body forgets how to rest. But I have learned that honesty is its own kind of practice—that saying *I don't know yet* is not surrender, but prayer.

What I know now is that recovery is not a single arc but a conversation—between disciplines, between theologies, between parts of ourselves that once refused to meet. When I write about the sacred, I do not mean a certainty; I mean a tenderness that keeps showing up even when nothing feels sacred at all. When I write about the body, I do not mean perfection; I mean the long work of listening to what the body has been trying to say all along.

If these pages have met you somewhere between despair and endurance, then they have done what I hoped they would: offered presence, not perfection.

Because presence is what saves us—the therapist's stillness, the survivor's breath, the reader's willingness to stay a little longer with what hurts.

So let this be our quiet understanding:
we are both still learning how to stay.
And that, too, is holy.

ABOUT THE AUTHOR

M. Anum-Addo is a writer and policy professional exploring the intersections of faith, trauma, and belonging. His work bridges theology, psychology, and lived experience—examining how healing takes shape in the body and how language itself can become a form of care.

He has served in public policy and defense analysis while continuing to write about the sacred dimensions of survival and endurance. His essays and books invite readers to imagine faith and recovery not as opposing disciplines but as shared vocabulary—one that speaks gently to both the spirit and the nervous system.

Hold Me While I Break is his most personal work to date: a meditation on grace, resilience, and the quiet art of staying.

McCarthy "Mac" Anum-Addo writes at the crossroads of theology and trauma, exploring how breath, body, and belief can coexist after breakdown.

www.ingramcontent.com/pod-product-compliance
Lightning Source LLC
LaVergne TN
LVHW010643110826
845149LV00014B/2933